THE SHRINKING ISLAND

MICKEY SPILLANE

ROUGH
EDGES
PRESS

The Shrinking Island: Three Novels by Mickey Spillane
Paperback Edition
© Copyright 2022 Mickey Spillane

Rough Edges Press
An Imprint of Wolfpack Publishing
5130 S. Fort Apache Rd. 215-380
Las Vegas, NV 89148

roughedgespress.com

Paperback ISBN 978-1-68549-051-5
LCCN 2022930480

THE SHRINKING ISLAND

THE "JOSH AND LARRY" TRILOGY AT LAST

AN INTRODUCTION BY MAX ALLAN COLLINS

In a way, Mickey Spillane was hijacked by his own success.

In this, the 75th anniversary of his legendary private eye Mike Hammer's debut in *I, the Jury* (1947), Spillane remains understandably linked with the hard-boiled mystery genre, a master of the tough guy tale, the godfather of pulp fiction. But his first success as a fiction writer was in the four-color world of comics and what we now call super-heroes. As a young man, he scripted numerous comic-book features from the still well-known (*Sub-Mariner, Human Torch*) to the largely forgotten (*Dick Cole, Sgt. Spook*).

Hammer's beginnings were in comics, with *Mike Lancer* appearing in a *Green Hornet* issue (#10, 1942) and with *Mike Danger*, a failed post-war project created by Spillane that he reworked into Mike Hammer. Mickey never downplayed Hammer's funny-book roots and took great pride in – and looked back fondly on – his work in the comic-book field.

He was proudest of his text stories, which appeared (generally two pages of prose) as fillers to meet certain postal regulations of the day. That pride had a lot to do with the big money the texts brought in – $25 per, a fine prewar payday – but the important thing was the venue provided for the young writer to develop a facility with prose. He was writing for young readers, primarily, although plenty of adults read comic books in those days, and those mostly third-person tales formed the basis for a style he returned to relatively late in his career.

Mickey's enormous success with Mike Hammer – the first six Hammer mysteries are still the best-selling private eye novels of all time – kept him working at his particular brand of tough action (and sexy romance), which made him not only a household name but a controversial one. Yet throughout the 1950s and well into the '70s, he was teasing interviewers with plans for non-mystery novels about subjects ranging from fighter pilots to Roman legionnaires.

Those books never were written.

His comic book text stories had been adventure-oriented, and he considered the Mike Hammer thrillers to be more action adventure than pure mystery, although an element of Agatha Christie-style puzzle was almost always present. For various reasons, Spillane twice paused his novel writing despite his blockbuster success – no novels appeared between *Kiss Me, Deadly* in 1952 and *The Deep* in 1961, and again slowed to a crawl after *The Last Cop Out* in 1973.

The first of Spillane's three Josh and Larry adventure novels for younger readers appeared in 1979, *The Day the Sea Rolled Back*, collected here. It came about when an editor, responding to Mickey's claim that a professional writer should be able to write anything, dared him to write a "kid's book." The provocateur was not aware that the writer often responded to such challenges as when he bet one editor he could withhold the solution to a mystery until the last word (*Vengeance Is Mine!*) and another that he could put in a blatant error the editor could not spot (*One Lonely Night*).

Mickey won a thousand-dollar bet both times.

Whether the editor who inspired the writing of *The Day the Sea Rolled Back* was involved in a money bet with Spillane is unknown. But Spillane won, all right – the publicity for a notorious sex-and-violence writer doing a story for young readers got written up in scores of newspapers and magazines, and generated numerous radio and TV appearances for the writer. That he'd written books for younger readers became a constant subject of inquiry in subsequent interviews until the end of his life.

Mickey himself gave marketing as his reason for doing books for kids – "They grow up to be adults, you know," he wryly commented.

But a larger reason was the opportunity, in his later years, to move into a type of story his Hammer fame had precluded – the adventure yarn, but also nautical subject matter. He lived on the South Carolina coast for decades and was an avid boating and deep-sea fishing enthusiast, as well as an ardent conservationist. With his friend Paul Vernon, he co-helmed a fishing show in the late '80s and into the 1990s, and hosted sportfishing tournaments for charity.

Also, he was aware of Peter Benchley's great success with *Jaws*, and saw potential for a different kind of Spillane story in that vein (sharks turn up in *The Shrinking Island*). When Benchley wrote a *Jaws* follow-up called *The Deep* (1977), Mickey sent him a telegram referring to his own 1961 bestseller of that name: "Mine sold five million copies. Hope yours does as well."

Mickey was famous for writing quickly – he sometimes claimed *I, the Jury* had been written in nine fevered days. Other times that grew to nineteen days, but during his first four or five decades, he had an ability to dig in and write a novel in a matter of a few weeks or even, yes, days.

He liked the intensity of writing fast over long hours. During the decade between *I, the Jury* and (his) *The Deep*, Spillane wrote novellas for men's adventure magazines, which – while almost always having crime story aspects – often hinted at his bent for adventure as subject matter (many collected in the upcoming *Stand Up and Die!*). He considered the short novel his favorite form.

The Day the Sea Rolled Back dipped a toe into the nautical adventure waters. He had, after some years away from the church, become again involved with the Jeho-vah's Witnesses, and had himself mellowed from an angry young man into a content older one. Writing for adoles-cent readers allowed him to present his bent for adventure without the expected Spillane extreme sex and violence.

Not only did Spillane win his bet with that editor, but his novel won a Junior Literary Guild award. *The Day the Sea Rolled Back* was published in hardcover by his regular publisher, Dutton, and the paperback was issued by Bantam. Possibly Dutton viewed this as a one-off – a kind of stunt – and the second Josh and Larry novel, *The Ship That Never Was* (1982), was issued as a paperback orig-inal by Bantam. A third was announced but never appeared – *The Shrinking Island*, published for the first time anywhere here, and completing the Josh and Larry trilogy.

Also in the '80s, Spillane began his novel *Something's Down There*, which he conceived as an adult variation on the Josh and Larry series and as a competitor to *Jaws* and its many imitators. Also an influence was his friend Clive Cussler, whose work he admired. During this period, however, he became involved with the Miller Lite beer campaign, shooting award-winning and extremely popular commercials with the "Doll," Lee Meredith (of *The*

Producers fame). These commercials paid him well and built interest in his existing novels. During the eighteen years of making those "spots" and doing personal appearances, Mickey puttered with *Something's Down There* even as he fussed with the book that would become *Dead Street* (2007) and several Mike Hammer "final" novels, including *The Goliath Bone* and *King of the Weeds*.

Mickey would not exactly lose interest in a manuscript, but he would follow his enthusiasm into a fresh idea, which is why he left so many incomplete works behind (that he entrusted them to me in his last weeks is a bittersweet but incredible honor).

Among the completed manuscripts was *The Shrinking Island*, which brings the Josh and Larry trilogy to a memorable conclusion. For a writer so strongly associated with the first-person technique of the Mike Hammer (and other tough) mysteries, Spillane was a master at third-person narrative as well. Two of his later works, *The Last Cop Out* and *Something's Down There*, were adept third-person works.

Something's Down There, which was written over a period of twenty years or more, was a book of which Mickey was extremely fond. He loved the sea and the out-of-doors and relished crafting an adventurous world well away from Mike Hammer's Manhattan. He never stop devising Hammer stories, even though he only published thirteen Hammer novels in his lifetime, and was keenly interested in, and involved with, the Stacy Keach TV movies and three separate series, all produced by his friend Jay Bernstein.

Spillane considered Hammer his "bread and butter boy," but – like Conan Doyle – somewhat burdened by his famous detective. He felt there was only so much he could do with Mike – feared "over-characterizing" him. The Hammer novels in the 1950s were the cornerstone of

NAL Signet's success, but the editors there in the early 2000s told him they would not publish *Something's Down There* unless he rewrote it as a Hammer.

He turned them down and Simon & Schuster published it in 2003. The book was well-reviewed but sales were modest, while the last Hammer published in his lifetime, *Black Alley* (1996), had been the usual best-seller. His final novel, *The Last Stand* (2018) published posthumously, found him again writing of adventure with only a minor crime element.

With all three Josh and Larry short novels collected in one substantial volume, the Spillane love for adventure and the sea is finally front and center for his many readers – young and old, new and existing – to enjoy. It's a book with a clever twist hidden in its very title. It's a book that belies certain stupid attitudes about Spillane by way of its two young heroes, one of whom is a person of color, and displays a great respect for nature and mankind: "Buddy," a character here tells us, "we're people. All of us are people."

Who is the audience for these three short novels?

Anyone who likes a good adventure yarn. Kids of all ages. Those with a sense of wonder, as there's a dash of the magical on display in all three. Josh and Larry begin at age 12 and are 14 or so by the end of the saga. Mickey's belief in the future by way of new generations is clear.

As *The Shrinking Island* tells us, "They were young and they were boys, but they were growing and soon would be men, and the men would be formed by the boys they were."

M.A.C.
March 3, 2022

THE DAY THE SEA
ROLLED BACK

CHAPTER ONE

FROM THE TOP of the eastern crest of Peolle Island, Vincent Damar watched the noon sun bounce magically off the gentle waves of the Caribbean. Until now, it had always been a sight to fill him with pleasure. The uncanny brilliance of the clear green waters that had such a delicious salty smell when the spray hung in the breeze made him feel a touch of sadness for all those city-bound people he had left fourteen years before.

But now the pleasure was only partially there. It had been four months since the *Blue Tuna* had plunged to the bottom someplace out there in that vast sea, another victim of the sudden vicious line squalls that could rise unpredictably out of a clear sky and destroy anything not big enough to fight back.

Or was there something to the myth of the "Atlantic Triangle" whose southern corner enveloped this very area?

He let out an annoyed grunt and dismissed the idea. He had been on the side of science too long to pay attention to superstitions. It was science that had led him to this island in the first place, diverting his mind from his wife's death when Larry was born. In his research on the Spanish Plate Fleet of 1732, he had come across a remarkable document that pinpointed the sinking of the treasure-laden galleon *San Simon* somewhere off the reef that encompassed Peolle and Ara islands.

For a moment he grimaced sadly. Somewhere, in the ocean, could cover an awful lot of territory, he thought.

But he had sold the house on Long Island, picked up the 42-foot ex-Navy cutter, had it outfitted for salvage work, then took his son to the sparsely peopled atoll named Peolle and set out to astound the world of historical discovery with his new find.

Vincent shook his head in disgust. If he had been a fisherman, everything would have been fine. By now, he would have had a dozen friends scattered throughout the islands. But hint that you had a lead on a sunken treasure ship everyone knew was somewhere in the area, and gold-fever greed turned them into enemies who hated with a fierce anger.

For 140 years small clusters of coral-encrusted gold and silver coins had been washed ashore at various points, and nets had snared other isolated artifacts that definitely established the graveyard of that ancient ship to be somewhere between where Vincent was standing and the horizon thirty miles away. Unfortunately, the radius of that sweep made a gigantic semicircle that included several hundred square miles. He still couldn't figure how it had happened. His boat should have been more than enough to weather that squall. The engine was running smoothly, they had been sailing into the teeth of the wind with no difficulty, rolling somewhat but not dangerously, enjoying the adventure, then . . . the *Blue Tuna* just sank. It just plain sank as if something had taken a bite out of the bottom, and he and Larry were in the dingy with the storm all around them and rode it out for eight hours before the weather lifted. It was another two hours' row to Ara Island and even before he had tied to the dock, Vincent knew there wouldn't be any real sympathy handed out to them at all.

Oh, they'd fake it, all right. Old lady Betts at the grocery would click her tongue, and Jake Skiddo, who ran the pumps, would give that wink that could mean anything, but they'd have that secret look of enjoyment like everybody else on Ara because the treasure was still out there where they still had a chance at it.

Crazy, Vincent thought. If they had it, what would they do with it? Not a doggone one of them would ever leave the place they lived in now. They'd only take it and bury it someplace else, then spend the rest of their lives guarding it, and when they died it would still be a lost treasure.

The Jimson brothers had been the worst, though. They didn't even bother to disguise their gloating. Bud Jimson had been standing on the dock and had said, "You city fellers oughta know better than to put that green water to the test. Joie and me, we barely got back ourselves and we been sailing these waters nearly forty years."

A surge of anger turned Vincent's face red. Most of his life had been centered around boats off Long Island, but he didn't say anything. Instead, he looked at Bud Jimson with eyes that had gone hard and curious. He was remembering the swirling cloud masses that had broken for a moment, just long enough so that he was sure he had seen the dirt-splotched hull of the Jimson boat on the same heading he was on. "Yeah," Vincent said, "I know. I tried to raise you on the radio when we were going down."

Bud Jimson glowered at him. "We never heard any call," he said abruptly. "Anyway, why would you call me?"

"Because you were running a couple hundred yards off our starboard."

There was no way of telling whether Jimson's expression was real or feigned. "Impossible! We were. . ."

"Forget it," Vincent said.

He had wanted to get back to Peolle right away, but no one on Ara seemed to have any means of getting him there, even for hire. All the boats were lashed to the rickety dock, but according to their owners, all were in such need of repair that it would be days before they could be moved.

It didn't take long for the message to get through. The Jimson brothers had passed the word and nobody had the guts to buck them. They just lied, made excuses and cast anxious glances to where Bud and Joie were stowing gear away on the *Petrel*. Vincent and Larry were going to be stuck here on Ara until the mail boat came by in three days and the next stop after that would be Miami. By the time they got back to Peolle, the house they had built, their possessions, everything. . . would be gone.

He had been about to call it quits right then, but a voice with a strangely accented lilt called up from under the dock and said, "I say, Mr. Vincent, sar.. ."

The man was a Carib his own age he didn't recognize, but he remembered seeing his handmade sailing skiff out at sea many times. "Yes . . . hello."

I'm Tim . . . short for Timothy, sar. From the backside of Peolle. If you don't mind riding with me, I'll be happy to take you back to the island."

"Mind?" Before another word was spoken, both Vincent and Larry were in the skiff, watching Timothy shake out the single sail. When they rounded the dock, Vincent nodded toward the Jimson brothers, who were watching them from the stern of their boat. "ı think you just made some enemies, Tim."

From his spot at the rudder, Tim flashed a toothy grin. "Oh, no, sar. You have to hate to be an enemy. I do not hate them. My people were here before they came and they will be here after they go. They are just mean. I leave them alone. The sea will take care of them."

Vincent snapped himself out of his thoughts and looked down at the beach below where Larry and Tim's son, Josh, were crabbing. He whistled and, when they looked up, pointed toward the house. Larry waved back and indicated with outstretched fingers that they'd be there in five minutes.

Vincent took one last look eastward, wondering idly how such a clear green sea could conceal anything as large as the *Blue Tuna* , . . or, for that matter, the old *Nantucket Belle* herself.

And the Belle was what he had to explain to Larry before he left with Tim in the skiff to intercept the trade packet on its monthly run back to the Florida coast. Not that he expected any accidents, but in case one should occur, the secret of the *Nantucket Belle* would be in good hands, at least. Larry might be only a young boy, but the wisdom of maturity was already beginning to show.

When they had finished lunch, Tim and Josh went down to the cove with the stores for the skiff and Vincent unlocked the plastic fishing-tackle box on the table.

For a moment he hesitated and frowned. Larry gave him a funny grin and said, "Pop, will you quit worrying about leaving us here alone."

"Come on, you're still my little kid." Vincent laughed.

"When do I get to be your big kid?"

"Maybe when you're ninety. That sound okay?"

Larry's eyes laughed back. "Sure is tough to be some-body's kid."

"Pipe down or I'll send you back to school on the mainland."

"I'm piped, I'm piped. I'd rather have you for my teacher. Now, what's with the tackle box? You said you were going to the bank, not out fishing."

Vincent reached in and took out a folded yellow document encased in a transparent plastic envelope. He laid it down carefully, then put a typewritten sheet beside it.

Larry was plainly puzzled. "What is it, Pop?"

"It's a page from the log of the *Nantucket Belle,* sunk in these waters in 1872. She was an iron-hulled, paddle-wheeled, three-masted bark whose master was another student of the Spanish raids on the gold coming out of the mints of Mexico City and Vera Cruz."

An expression of recognition touched Larry's face. "You mean . . ."

"The *Belle* located the *San Simon* and recovered most of the treasure. The Spanish wreck was in thirty-one feet of water, perfectly visible as a wreck at that time even though most of the wood had been destroyed by teredo worms. They anchored over the spot, and teams working out of a diving bell removed what proved to be about ninety-five percent of her cargo of gold bullion and precious gems destined for the courts at Madrid and the church at Rome."

Larry finally nodded. "You know something, Pop?"

"What?"

"Now I know why everybody thought you were a bit nutty. The only natural place for one of those galleons to get hung up on the coral would be the extension of the reef off Ara Island. You weren't looking around anywhere near there."

"Oh, but that's where the *San Simon* is, all right. Her captain clearly marked his position in his log and it's still in the archives in Madrid."

"Then how come nobody can find it?" Larry asked.

"Let's see if you can remember some of the history I

taught you," his father said. "What year did the *San Simon* set sail back to Spain?"

"1732," Larry told him.

"When was the first Toledon earthquake reported?"

Larry thought a moment, then: "Ummm . . . 1740. Two merchant ships in the area that managed to survive brought the news back."

"You remember what was special about that earthquake?"

Larry shrugged. "Just that there was a new island formed . . . and part of Oomlo fell into the sea." He thought for a moment; then understanding came into his eyes. "The wreck was still there, but the checkpoints the captain sighted in on had changed."

"Exactly. And the master of the *Nantucket Belle* finally figured it out."

The story fascinated Larry and it showed in the subdued excitement on his face. "But. . . the Belle . . . Did a storm get her too?"

His father shook his head. "No, it wasn't necessary. Gold fever and a mutiny did it all instead. During the on-board battle the boilers blew and the Belle went down like a stone. The First Mate had one single sighting before he went over the side with the logbook, and that one reference point he indicated was our cliff on Peolle Island, right here."

Larry's face reflected his disappointment. "Just that *one* point?"

"Apparently that's all he had time for."

"But.. . you can't triangulate a position from only one point."

Vincent ruffled his son's hair. "I know. Why do you think we were carrying on that pattern search for all this time?"

"Pop. . ."

"Yes, son?"

"If all the other islanders thought you were on a wild goose chase, why would they get all upset about what you were doing?"

"Good question," Vincent said. "My guess is that somebody got on board the *Blue Tuna* one of the times we were getting supplies at Ara. They could have seen the copy I made of the page from the *Belle's* log. They never got a chance to read it all or make a copy, but they knew I had information they didn't have."

"And if you looked long and hard enough, you'd find the wreck."

"Unless somebody beat me to it." Vincent paused, then slipped the papers back in the tackle box. "You hang on to this. Keep it someplace safe and don't let anybody near it. If anything happens to me, at least you'll have a crack at all that money someday. There is a critical distance factor in that log that will give you a head start over anybody else."

"Come on, Pop, what's going to happen to you? Besides, who needs all that money?"

"Right now we could use a little bit of it. If I can't negotiate a loan, there won't be another boat, the property here goes back to the government, we go back to the mainland, where I'll probably teach school again and you'll be delivering papers for spending money."

"Really that bad, Pop?"

His father let out a small laugh. "Well, let's say you won't have to deliver papers."

"Pop ... I hope you get it. I know you like it here . . . about as much as I do."

"I know, son. Just don't sweat it. Something will turn up. It always does." He grinned at Larry's seriousness. "At least we've got something going for us."

"What's that?"

"Both of us like fish," he said. "And sleeping on the sand under a tree isn't too bad either," Larry added.

"Until it storms," his father reminded him.

CHAPTER TWO

THE DAY after his father left, Larry and Josh netted their day's haul of fish just before noon. They picked out an eight-pound snapper for their supper, kept a pair of conchs aside to be dropped in the tidal pool by the house for a later meal and emptied the net back into the sea. Having fish die on the beach for no purpose at all didn't make sense to either of them.

When they were cleaning the net, Larry looked up and spotted the boat a half-mile offshore. Josh followed his glance and said, "That is *Petrel,* the boat of the brothers Jimson."

"I wonder what he's doing around here."

"Well, he is not fishing, there is nothing to salvage out there, so I imagine he is looking over this place to see if anyone is at home."

A momentary glint of the sun bounced from the stern of the boat. "He's got glasses on us," Larry said.

"Then he sees us, so he will not come in."

"He'd better not!"

"What would you do, Larry, if he did?"

"Come on, Josh, you know what I'd do. I'd get you on

the bicycle mount to grind the generator, get the power up and call the Coast Guard on the emergency channel."

"But the Coast Guard Station is a long way off."

"Not by helicopter, it isn't," Larry told him.

"Well, ı don't think you'll have to call. Look."

Offshore, the *Petrel* was making a 180-degree turn and when she was headed north again, she gradually faded into the distance.

Josh was grinning as he rolled up the net. "See, you scared him off."

"Yeah, sure," Larry chuckled. He threw the loops over the end of the net to secure the roll, then glanced up at the sky. "What time do you think it is, Josh?"

"Maybe about one o'clock, eh?"

Larry made a wry face. "I didn't think we were here long, but look at that sky."

"Funny color."

It was peculiar. A yellow-orange haze that didn't seem to come from anywhere and gave everything a faint pinkish glow.

"Think it's a storm coming in?"

Josh raised his head, sniffing the air with eyes half closed. It was something that only the Caribs seemed to master and they were never wrong. "No . . . there is no storm."

A gentle breeze touched the back of Larry's neck, coming out of the east For some reason goose bumps raised the bleached hairs on his forearms. "You feel that?"

Josh nodded. "The wind shouldn't be from that quarter."

"I don't like it," Larry said. "Let's see what's on the marine radio. If any freak storm is headed this way, we'd better be ready for it."

But there was no storm warning on any of the Channels. The weather reports from both marine and aviation centers were for warm and clear days through the next week at least.

Outside, the yellowish look deepened and the wind dropped a few degrees in temperature. But there was no unusual wave action at sea and the birds flew until just before sunset. Larry and Josh ate their supper, figured the strange atmospheric condition was probably due to an off-course dust storm from the mainland, then hung their hammocks from the trees outside the house and went to sleep.

There was no logical explanation for what had happened during the night. No scientist saw it, no sophisticated machines recorded it, no great populated areas were affected by it.

It just happened.

And it was seen.

Larry and Josh could very well have been the first to see it.

Sometime during the night the sea had rolled back and left the bottom a great barren place splotched with giant coral heads, Stretches of dark purple vegetation and strange rolling configurations that still glistened wetly in the early light of dawn.

The smell was different, too. The normal salt tang was sharper now, enhanced with a wet, weedy aroma from the vast acres of marine growth that were lying flat against their sandy beds. Above it all, even now, the boys' senses could detect that minute organic smell of dead things that hadn't escaped and had already begun decaying in the first sunlight.

The awe of the incredible sight sent a chill up their backs, and Josh's voice was almost inaudible. "Larry . . . what happened?"

"I don't know."

"The sea ... the water—it isn't there anymore."

"Whatever it is. . . we saw it coming last night. Remember the odd color in the sky .. . and the wind from the wrong direction?"

Josh nodded. "You think . . . it could be . . . well, a tide, a very low tide?"

"If it is, this one goes all the way to the horizon." Larry turned, squinting toward the north. He could see the very tip of uninhabited Ramu Island, and although there didn't seem to be any water there either, there was no way of determining just how far the condition extended.

"Larry . . . what would your father, with all his schooling, say at a time like this?"

For a small moment Larry suddenly felt as though he were fifty years old. Then he shrugged and said, "Well, what goes up has to come down, so what goes out has to come back sooner or later."

"Your father is a very smart man."

"That's what I *think* he'd say," Larry explained.

Josh was grinning, a glint in his eye. "Would he say . . . that such a time should not be wasted?"

Now Larry was feeling a tug of adventure. The initial uneasiness couldn't last long with youth and he knew he was smiling at his friend. "Is that what *your* father would say, Josh?"

"That's what my father would say, even though he is not a man of much education."

"We'll never get another chance, will we?"

"I don't think so."

"Then," Larry said, "let's go see what the sea has left behind."

They ran to the beach, slowing as they neared the point that formerly had been the low watermark, then stepped out gently, testing the consistency of the sea floor. It didn't take them long to discover that it wasn't much softer than the surface behind them. Some areas were sandy, others of more solid coquina, and where the sea grass grew, it was simply spongy but firm. Within fifteen minutes they were able to choose the sections that gave the best footing and stay away from those that were still wet enough for them to sink down to their knees.

Three hundred yards out they came to a spot they both knew well, the fluke of an old, rusted anchor from some ancient ship. A wide growth of weed almost covered it, running in a long S pattern between four huge coral heads. Until now it had been a favorite fishing place, and the holes that housed the groupers that lived there were gaping wide open, still wet but empty of occupants.

"Everything's gone," Larry said. "You see anything?"

"Just some crabs buried in the sand back there. No fish except one dead one."

They stood there a minute, surveying the emptiness around them. Finally Josh said, "Are you thinking the same thing I am?"

"About how far to go out?"

"Yes. And how quickly we can get back if the sea decides to return."

Larry chewed on his lip a moment, giving thought to the situation, trying to recall all the many details he had scoured from books in his father's library. "You know, Josh . . . the sea leaving like that. . . it was a quiet thing, like a continual tidal flow, so it's probable that it will come back the same way. At any rate, if we keep a close eye on the horizon, we'll see an immediate reflection when there's any change. That ought to give us plenty of time to get back to dry land."

"Or we swim a lot," Josh put in. "By the way, what are we going to do out there?"

"Look for an old iron wreck. It was called the *Nantucket Belle*."

Six miles north two nervous men were trying to

recover from the shock of finding themselves anchored to dry sand an hour's run from their dock. Joie Jimson's face was white with fear of the unexplained, and as superstitious as he was, his voice was still stuck in his chest. Bud was tougher. He had no idea of what had happened either. They had anchored offshore for the night, hammocks swung from hooks in the stern. They never felt the water leave or the boat settle crookedly on the bottom, because the hammocks kept them in a stable position. Now he was sore at Joie for shaking like a scared old woman just when certain new possibilities were opened to them by the good graces of nature.

He still had to admit to himself that looking at what had been the bottom of the sea was an unnerving experience. It wasn't as he had imagined at all. There were hills and valleys that weren't at all discernible from the surface, depressions that could conceal the wreck of a boat or even the remains of a ship from anyone standing on the sea's floor.

Overhead the birds were collecting but, instead of diving, were settling onto the wet sand to snatch live, wriggling things from their seabed nests. Bud Jimson had dived enough on these bottoms to know the consistency of the sand, so he had no qualms about going over the side to test the solidity of his footing.

Joie finally found his voice and said, "Doggone it, Bud, you crazy?"

"Knock it off, will you. I know what I'm doing."

"Doing? The only thing to do is get us outa here!"

"Think you can do it better up there on deck?"

Joie took a startled look around him and licked his lips.

"Now, go get the fire ax and get yourself down here."

"What do ya want the ax for?"

"To make you ask stupid questions, dummy. Just do what I told you."

When Joie had tossed the ax down, it took all his nerve to clamber over the tilted railing and slide down the side of the hill to the sand. He was clumsy about it and the barnacles ripped his pants and carved a few furrows into his hide.

Bud watched him with disgust. "Why didn't you come down the other side?"

Joie shrugged, looking foolish. "I dunno."

"Look for a boat."

"What boat?"

"The *Blue Tuna,* that's the boat!"

"But it sunk. . ."

For a moment Bud Jimson was about to lay his heavy hand right across his brother's jaw, but that wouldn't have made him any smarter either. "I know it's sunk, but do you want everybody to know *why* it's sunk? You think we're the only ones that'll be out there. Come on. Just as soon as they get their nerve up, everybody from the island will be scavenging for anything they can find."

"Yeah, but there's no fish . . ."

"Oh, you nitwit," Bud said. "The wrecks, the wrecks! You know how many wrecks are around here that we never knew about?"

It finally dawned on Joie what his brother was speaking about and a tight greedy look edged into his grin and he nodded quickly.

Bud looked back toward Ara, then checked the sun's position overhead. He pointed in a southeasterly direction and said, "This way, come on. And don't step in any of those soft places."

Had they a mind to, Larry and Josh could have made a fortune saving the lead sinkers they yanked out of the sand by their leader lines. So far on their trail they had left four fishing poles with reels too corroded to be useful anymore, two cheap watches and a 35-horsepower motor that had been underwater a year or so. They had skirted a dozen wet sinkholes they knew would be like quicksand, then had come to a flat, moist depression that stretched a hundred yards on either side of their course.

Josh said, "What do you think?"

"Let's try it slowly. I'll go ahead and you be ready to grab me if it gets soft."

"Okay."

Treading gently, the boys eased forward. Larry was concerned with the area immediately about his feet and didn't look up until he heard a loud hiss behind him. He stopped suddenly and turned around. "What is it?"

Josh was staring straight ahead, his finger coming up to point at the sand. "Look."

Larry followed the direction of the finger, then involuntarily took a step backward, his breath catching in his throat. Very gradually, a huge section of the sand in front of them was rising, an area as big as a tractor trailer heaving upward until suddenly there was a gap in the sand as something brown and horny with great scale-markings barely began to show. Only inches of it were visible for a 30-foot length, but it was hemispherically shaped with a serrated ridge running lengthways down its middle.

Without realizing it, both boys were holding each other tightly. Until now, this walk on the seabed had been a fun thing, but now stark reality was facing them. "You know what that looks like, Josh?"

Softly, Josh said, "Almost like the back of a turtle. They do that in the ponds on the island."

"If that's a turtle, and we're only seeing part of him, do you know how big it is?"

"We will know better when he lifts his head up. Then we will see."

They looked at each other, startled. "Then he will see

us, too," Larry told him.

"I would not like to be here then."

"Maybe it's not a turtle," Larry suggested.

"A *something else* would be even worse. Let's not wait to find out," Josh said.

In their haste to get away from the area, they nearly stumbled and fell several times, but when they reached the solid bottom again they turned and stared back at the great wet depression. Whatever had risen out of it had gone back again and it seemed like just another placid spot at the bottom where the sea used to be.

"Who would believe us if we told them?" Josh asked. "I can hardly believe it even though I saw it." He paused for a moment, thinking, then, how there were strange beasts out here, huge beasts they saw only after the great hurricanes. Sometimes they would attack the boats and once they destroyed a village above the beach. "I always thought they were just silly stories to scare children."

"Now you know," Larry said.

"I liked it better when I thought it was just a story."

Larry's face squinted in a frown again. "My dad always said there's no way of telling what's at the bottom of the sea. Things there never have any reason to come up and it's only by accident we ever get to suspect their existence at all."

This time Josh's tone was very somber. "Larry . . . we should be very careful, no?"

"Very careful. . . yes," Larry said. "In fact, the next time I'm fishing and something awfully heavy that shouldn't be in these waters hits my line, I think I'll cut loose instead of trying to reel it in." He nodded toward the northern end of the wet spot and they headed that way, angling around it, then taking the gradual dip down, pointing toward the rise that seemed to spread over several acres, covered with the dark purplish weed that was beginning to emit an odd odor from standing bared to the sunlight.

It wasn't until they had reached the edge of the mound that Josh put his hand on Larry's arm. "Look," he said, separating the grasses. "Ballast rock!"

A few yards farther on they got a better look at it. The rock ran up the slope a good fifty feet and even some of the worn and eaten timbers were visible protruding from stones. Whatever ship it had been had ground itself to destruction on this abrupt peak in the sea's floor.

Larry pulled several of the rocks out of the pile and studied them. Each one weighed about fifteen pounds, rough, angle-edged rocks with tops layered with coral encrustments. He tried a few more, then nodded. "A British ship, most likely. They used any old rocks for ballast. The Spanish were a little more particular. They didn't want to cut their hands passing these things on board, so they selected only smooth stones."

"Pirate vessel?"

"Merchantman, most likely. There would have been a pile of cannon around if it were a pirate ship."

"Wouldn't merchant ships carry guns?"

"Not if they could help it. . .or could get protection from the fleet. The more guns, the less cargo, and they were out for trade goods. If we looked, we'd probably find a few small brass cannon, the anchor and some old relics."

"Would it be worth poking around later?"

"I doubt it," Larry said. "The only good thing would be those brass cannon and they're probably under tons of sand." He looked back, checking his position from Peolle Island. "We're a mile and a half off-shore now. Let's see if we can make it to Skittle's Rocks."

"But Skittles is another mile out. I thought we were. . ."

"We were over Skittle's when the *Blue Tuna* went

down," Larry told him. "Someplace in the same area was the *Nantucket Belle*."

They chose to climb over the slope of the ridge rather than take the long way around in the softer sand. They scrabbled for footholds in the irregular crevasses of the ballast rock, then got past them and hauled themselves to the top by grabbing hold of the thumb-thick sea grasses. When they reached the peak they squatted there and caught their breath, searching the vast dry area in front of them.

It was a distinct vantage point, that was sure. For the first time they were able to make out shapes that from the water's surface had meant nothing. A quarter-mile away was Pierre Combolt's old two-masted hulk that had been torn from the dock at Ara last year and had been thought disappeared forever. Now here it was, upside down on the bottom, the green paint of the hull blending perfectly with the grasses around it, dotted with clusters of barnacles that disguised it. From above, it was unidentifiable; from a side angle view, it was evident what it was, even down to the pair of broken masts that jutted out to the side.

"How would it turn over like that?" Josh asked.

"Dad said hurricane waves in waters this shallow can do almost anything. Once that wreck got set in the sand, it was there to stay."

Josh nodded and swept his arm out in an arc in front of him. "Do you see that trench there?"

Larry saw it, all right. He followed the line of it with his eyes, a mile-long gap in the ocean bed that ended in a large circular area on either end. "It looks like a long, skinny dumbbell."

"It's filled with water," Josh said.

"I don't remember that being there. We've sailed over that area plenty of times and our depth finders never showed it."

"You know," Josh said, "it could be like the rain. When the water runs off downhill it makes new channels and new holes. Maybe when the sea went back the water running around these hills dug itself that trench."

"Well, we can always swim it. . . and we'd better not wait too long. A few more hours and we'll have to turn back."

Carefully, they picked their approach path to the gorge in the sand, staying on the lanes that gave them the most solid footing. Behind them their footprints were blazing a natural path for them to follow on their return, which made them feel a little easier about what they were doing.

When they reached the edge of the channel they stood back from the soft, sloping sand and saw it for what it was. "You were right, Josh. This whole section is soft as mush, and the water carved out its own skinny lake. If it hadn't happened, we never would have known how to cross it. The place must have been like quicksand."

"The banks still look pretty soft," Josh said.

"Well, we can dive in from this side and scramble up over there. I'm a little bigger than you, so supposing I go first, then give you a hand up on the other side."

"Fine," Josh told him. "You better get a good run to hit the water. Looks like it's not very deep."

Larry couldn't back off very far. He planned his dive, took three fast steps forward and pushed off and hit the water in a shallow belly flopper. A few strokes took him across and he dug into the sand with his hands and knees, clawing hard to get to a place that would support him. When he made it, he turned around and waved to Josh. "Your turn ... let's go!"

Josh grinned and followed Larry's lead. He hit the surface and splashed his way across, laughing at the experience.

But Larry wasn't laughing. He was yelling at the top of his voice for Josh to hurry, his face pinched with terror. He had caught the movement out of the corner of his eye just in time . . . the two dull gray angular triangles sweeping around the gentle bend of the sea's new canal, the dorsal fin and tail of a shark that was reacting to the splashings in the water and was putting on a sudden burst of speed to reach his prey before he could escape. Josh had lived on the edge of the sea all his life. He recognized the urgency in Larry's voice and his laugh froze in his throat and he put everything he had into the last few strokes and the last time he turned his head for a breath of air he saw the surging of the water from the back of the monstrous fish that came at him like a missile. He saw the tail make a final sweep, the mouth open, but Larry had him by the arm and with that wild strength given to people in moments of life and death emergencies, Larry snatched him up the sand and they rolled onto the top together.

For a few minutes they couldn't move. Their hearts were still pounding furiously and when they finally calmed down, Josh said, "That was a tiger shark."

"I know." Larry nodded.

"How big, you think?"

"Too big. He could have swallowed both of us."

"Why would he be there, Larry?"

"Who knows what a shark is going to do? I imagine he found that trench when the water was going out and got himself stuck there. Nothing else seems to be moving in that water, so he just keeps cruising around. We must have sounded like a good lunch to him."

"That was close," Josh said. "The shark, he can move very fast."

"I wouldn't want to go through that again," Larry said.

He got a strange look from his friend. "We may have to," Josh reminded him. "We have to go back."

CHAPTER THREE

THE JIMSON BROTHERS were competent seamen, but in this new environment they were totally out of place. So far they had covered a half-mile from their grounded boat, but they were wet and sandy from numerous falls into the sinkholes and had just begun to select the better isles of travel from hard experience.

"I hope you know what you're doing," Joie said.

"Shut up and save your breath." Bud looked at his pocket compass a moment, snapped it shut and put it back in his pocket. "We're not far from Skittle's Rocks now . . . maybe an hour."

Joie heaved a deep breath and looked behind him. Ara Island was a dim smudge on the horizon. But between them and the island there were a few dots of motion that hadn't been there before. "We'd better get moving then. Company's behind us."

Bud said something under his breath, his face dark with annoyance. "Everybody and his brother is gonna be out here treasure hunting today."

"So why do we have to mess around with the *Blue*

Tuna? Okay, so you don't want anybody to know how it sunk ..."

Holding back his anger and explaining as if his brother were a child, Bud said, "Everybody's looking for the *San Simon,* right?"

Joie thought a moment, then nodded.

"Now, Vincent Damar, he never bothered looking where everybody thought the *Simon* went down, did he?"

"Nope . . . that's why we thought he was dumb."

"He was smarter than everybody, you blockhead. He studied up on that wreck. He found out that somebody else salvaged it first and that the salvage boat got sunk too. It's probably around Skittle's Rocks, because that's where Vincent Damar was doing all his searching."

"Then let's go there and forget about the *Blue Tuna,*" Joie whined.

"Oh, you flounder head. If anybody reaches the *Tuna* and finds that tank in there with our name on it, we'll be looking out from behind bars for the next ten years. You had to be dumb enough to use one of our own tanks to sink somebody else's boat. Brother!"

"Come on, Bud. Who knew this was gonna happen? It was just supposed to sink and that was the end of it."

"Ever hear of diving gear, stupid? Suppose the wreck was located and they decided to use SCUBA and look it over."

"Yeah, I guess you're right, Bud."

"Okay. Now pick up that fire ax and let's go."

They stepped down from the mound carefully, their feet wetly slapping the sand. The bottom was changing now. The sand was darker, the grass in smaller clumps and the gradual drop-off very discernible. Both of them knew that had the sea been in, they would have been fifty feet below the surface. Even though they were dry now, it was an unnerving thought. What made it worse was that they had no direct line of sight ahead, the curves of the bottom leaving only a small area visible in front of them. The worst part was, they didn't know when there might be a sudden inrush of the sea itself. It had gone out quickly and quietly. If it returned the same way, it could sweep them right along with it. Bud considered all of this but didn't want to mention it to his brother. He was afraid Joie might panic if he realized the possible consequences.

Overhead, the sun was a bright, burning disc making heat waves rise from all directions. As the sand heated and the water evaporated, a haze of wispy steam seemed to hang over the bottom like a gentle ground fog on land. All around their feet small things trapped in a warming sand bed began heaving themselves toward a cool environment, making the bottom crawl as though it were alive. Joie made a disgusted sound in his throat and closed the distance between himself and his brother.

Directly before them was another of those strange-shaped hills, larger on the east side, falling off sharply, and it wasn't until they got around it that Bud held out his hand and stopped abruptly. There, jutting out of the sand, were huge, water-rotted timber stubs aligned in such order that they both knew they were looking at the partial skeleton of a centuries-old wreck. Ten feet farther on, the confirmation was complete. A great chain lay coiled in the rock-strewn rubble, almost hidden by the grass and coral, that ended at a mighty anchor nearly buried under the debris.

Both the Jimson brothers could read the ballast rocks. It was a Spanish ship, all right, but whether or not it was a gold-laden galleon, one of the plate ships carrying silver, or an empty vessel enroute to the Mexican coast, they couldn't tell. The pair of cannon visible on the side of the mound wasn't indicative of anything either, but the sight of them made Joie's hands shake with anticipation.

"Bud. . . ya know what we got here? We got ourselves a wreck. . . a real Spanish wreck. It ain't even on the charts. Nobody even knew about it before!"

"We're not looking for that," Bud yelled at him.

"Maybe you ain't, but if you think . . ." Joie took a swing with the fire ax at a lump of coral and powdered it into a shower of pieces that came apart and left a lump of pure tar standing black against the sand.

Bud forced himself to be patient. He took out his compass, climbed up on the wreck and managed to find Ara in the distance. He scribbled on a pad, then took another fix on Ramu Island, which was still visible, estimating the distances, noting the directions and writing them all down. "What're you supposed to be doing?" Joie hollered up at him.

"Making it easy for us to find the place when we come back, stupid."

"It's easy now! What are we gonna do when the water's back?"

With total exasperation, Bud said, "Dive, you nut. We're the only ones who know it's here. Right now we haven't got time to waste. Later we'll have plenty. Now, do you savvy that or do you want me to draw you a picture?"

Joie grunted and shrugged. "Guess you must think I'm pretty dumb, huh, Bud?"

"Now why would I think that?" Bud said. He took another look at the wreck that had lain there hidden for so many years. No wonder you could sail over them for a lifetime without ever knowing they were there. It was only by sheer luck that they were ever uncovered at all. They might have gone down a mile away, and following storms could have rolled the hulks this far in. If they did, treasure could be scattered all over the seabed. But at least they had a starting place. Bud patted the paper in his pocket.

As long as he had the map, he thought, this wreck was only the beginning.

Larry and Josh stood at the base of "The Old Lady," the largest of the nine natural rock outcroppings that thrust themselves up from the sea floor to take the bottoms out of countless hulls whose navigators never knew they were there. All around the sand were parts of both wooden and iron ships that had lost the battle of survival to those jagged peaks . . . planks with rusted spikes, yard-square pieces of torn iron plating, chunks of machinery and parts of rotted cargo.

The peaks of Skittle's Rocks were just high enough to tear the guts out of a ship like a deadly knife wound, letting her live long enough to clear the rocks and die a mile or more away. Larry remembered his father studying a chart one night, speculating on how far a ship could last after an impalement, sketching in a rough circle he intended investigating when his present project was completed.

And right now Larry could appreciate the possibilities in this quest for gold. How many millions of dollars in bullion from the bowels of Mexico was scattered over the area within view from the cliff at Peolle Island? The archives at Madrid, Spain, told one story of the immense treasure, but the other—that of what was being stolen by the ship's captains and crew and not accounted for—was another. His father had told him it could have been as much as half again the listed amount.

Larry was silent a long moment, deep in thought. If they could only stumble over one Single bar of bullion, or a congealed mass of silver coins, the kind in McKee's museum ... his father wouldn't have to beg the banks for a loan or mortgage his future at all. They could renew the lease on their part of the island, they could get another boat... all they had to do was find the tiniest fraction of the wealth strewn so close to their own home.

Josh snapped him out of it when he said, "From the top of the rock you could see everything, Larry. There is no higher point."

"Yeah, you're right. Let's try it."

"Be careful of the coral. A cut from it can give a bad infection."

"Right, Josh. You want to take the side on my left?"

"Let's go," Josh said.

They climbed slowly and carefully, picking their hand and footholds deliberately. Twice Larry paused, to work rusted pieces of metal and a foot-long iron spike out of the coral that covered them, mementoes of deathly kisses between nature and man in years past. Beside him, Josh was reaching for the final plateau and when they both heaved themselves up on the crown of "The Old Lady," they knew they were doing something no one had done before.

Now their visibility was almost unrestricted. They could see the ever increasing angular drop-off of the bottom that dipped another fifty feet a quarter-mile away before leveling. They knew that another mile out the great drop began that went down to the immense depths where strange creatures lived in total darkness.

But where was the sea? The heat waves and drifting fog obscured nearly everything past the quarter-mile range, and there was no telling what was happening out beyond. Josh had his hand shading his eyes, peering into the north, staring at something intently. After a minute he said, "Larry . . . whose boat was just painted a very bright red?"

"Why . . . that's the Jimsons'."

"Look." He pointed so that Larry could follow his

direction. "Just a small spot of red, right near the horizon. See it?"

Larry nodded. "Yeah, yeah. I see what you mean. But it could be something on the bottom ..."

"Not that color red," Josh interrupted. "It's still new and shiny. See the way the sun bounces from it."

"They must be stranded out there."

Josh shook his head. "Wait." He shaded his eyes again, cutting out as much glare as he could. Then he realized what had bothered him. There was a pair of dark dots out there, slowly moving in their direction. "Look, they're not stranded. They're coming this way."

After a moment Larry spotted them too. They stayed in sight a full minute, then a rise of sand cut them from view. "Let's get down," he said.

"What do you think they're after?"

"The same thing we are," Larry told him.

Together they turned and started back down the way they had come, but then something stopped Larry. For a brief instant he was able to see between the Skittle's Rocks and what he saw made his hands clutch the coral tightly.

"What is it?" Josh asked.

"I think ... I spotted the Blue *Tuna*," Larry told him.

"You sure?"

"I couldn't miss the shape of that hull. It hasn't been down long enough to break up and is lying there just as nice as you please."

"How long will it take to get there?" Josh asked.

"About fifteen minutes, I'd say."

"Well, if those *are* the Jimson brothers over there, it'll take them at least an hour to reach here . . . which should give us enough time to do what you think we have to."

Without another word, they finished their climb to the bottom, then, using the sun as a guide, headed for where Larry saw the wreck of their boat. From the rock it didn't seem like a difficult trip at all, but once again, the "terrain" was a series of depressions and weird hillocks they had to circumnavigate to reach their destination.

They rounded what they thought was their last outcropping of coral and thought they'd be on the flat, but what had appeared that way from a position above, wasn't that way at all. It was a long, conical ridge that tapered to slim ends, completely sand-covered with narrow paths of grass running over it to subvert its shape completely.

Both boys gave a shrug of annoyance and trudged alongside the ridge, staying away from the yard-wide rivulet of water that still bordered it. They were on the shady side and there was activity in that still water. There were some creatures that didn't go out when the sea left and twice they saw the glint of eyes and the slow movement of teeth-lined mouths and pulsating gills.

A coral bulge protruded from the center of the mound and Larry picked up an empty conch shell and threw it at the protuberance. It connected with a dull smash and the pieces scattered across the bottom.

But there was more than that. A crack appeared in the coral, widened and, with a sharp snap, split away from the rest of the mass and smashed itself against the sand below.

There was wide-eyed wonder in their faces when they saw the metal that was beneath the coral. There was another muted crack and a huge slab simply slid off like melting snow from a rooftop. Josh gasped, "Larry . . . !"

And Larry knew what it was. He would have been able to tell from the shape of the mound and the center protection if he had studied it carefully, but with the coral falling off of its own weight, exposing the unmistakable structure beneath, there was no doubt at all.

"That's a submarine," he said.

"A . . . submarine?"

"What you're looking at is a conning tower. The sub's lying rolled over on its side."

"But Larry. . . there is no submarine here. My father, he would know about these things. He was here all during the war ..."

"Not that war," Larry told him.

"What do you mean?"

"Look at the length of it. It's only a little thing compared to the newer subs. And look at the thickness of that coral growth." He paused for a moment, edged up to the exposed metal and ran his eyes across the surface. Along the rim of metal he saw a stamping. He couldn't read it, but the language was identifiable. "That's a World War I German submarine, Josh."

"Here?"

"Oh, it's not impossible. Others have been discovered in pretty shallow waters before."

"How could they get in here, Larry? This is no place for a ... a submarine! Why ..."

Larry interrupted him. "They didn't intend to come here. Don't forget, that war was a long time ago and the machinery was almost primitive. You know what a Kingston valve is?"

Josh shook his head.

"Well, it's a valve that lets the water come in to submerge the boat and lets compressed air blow the water out so the sub can surface. Sometimes those valves got stuck when the boat was underwater, and that was the end of the journey for the crew. It might have taken months, or even years, but when the air leaked past the Kingston valve, the boat almost floated again and tide and wave action washed it ashore ... or at least into these waters."

"And . . . you think . . . there are still. . . people in there?"

"Long dead if they are."

"Larry, listen to me ..."

"Come on, Josh, we're not going to go in there. In the first place, we can't."

Josh looked suspicious. "What's the second place?"

A serious look crossed Larry's face. He realized the importance of what was here and the place it could take in history. "My father could report a find like this and I bet the government would be glad to help recover the boat."

"But isn't it. . . well, sort of like a big coffin?"

Larry gave it a moment's thought. "True, but look what they did with the *Arizona* at Pearl Harbor. In a way, this is a memorial too, and it is a piece of history. Anyway, I'll let Dad decide."

Josh nodded and glanced at the area around them. "You know, Larry, I'm not scared. *Really* scared, I mean, but I'll sure be glad to get back on the real beach."

"That makes two of us, but we have things to do first." They walked to the end of the tapered ridge and from the partially covered bulge they knew they were at the stern. Under that smaller mound would be the single propeller and rudder.

"Think we can find her again, Josh?"

"Sure. It's right in line with the last two peaks of Skittle's Rocks. Maybe six hundred yards off. It'll be easy to find now that some of the coral's off that place."

"The conning tower," Larry told him.

Josh took another look at the strange shape. From where he stood the outline was clear and he felt a cold chill when his mind tried to picture the interior of that steel casket. He turned around, glanced past Larry, then said softly, "There's the *Tuna,* my friend."

Bud and Joie Jimson hadn't elected to go around the obstacles they came across. Somehow, they seemed to think they could make better time with a straight course, but it didn't take them long to find out how exhausting it was to scramble up damp, sandy hills, the grit filling their shoes and scraping away at the skin of their feet. Both of them had coral scratches on their arms, and the spines from a sea urchin had pierced Joie's canvas shoes and gouged holes in his heel. Walking on the toes of one foot was wearing him down fast.

They lay on the crest of a sand pile, the stink of the drying seaweed coming up around them now, and Joie said, "Man, let's stay here awhile. I can't go much farther."

"You'd better, little brother, or I'll leave you here alone."

Joie licked his dry lips and swallowed hard. "You wouldn't!"

"Try me and find out. Right now I'm so sick of your complaining I could feed you to the crabs."

"Bud. . ."

"Knock it off." He turned over and lay on his stomach. "You look where I'm pointing, Joie, and maybe you'll see something."

"Where?"

"Follow my finger, dummy."

"You mean that dark thing way over there?"

"That dark thing's the *Blue Tuna.*" He frowned, annoyed. "Can't you ever tell one boat from another? Look, the hull lines. You can still see the mast and there's not a speck of weed on her yet. She hasn't even been down long enough to collect a barnacle, but if anybody gets to her ahead of us, you know what we'll collect."

Joie didn't bother glowering back at his brother. He simply shrugged and said, "Then you better move a little faster, Bud."

"What're ya talkin' about?"

With a nod in the direction of the *Blue Tuna,* Joie said, "There're a couple more dark things out there and they move like people." Bud felt the sand grate between his teeth and he yanked his brother to his feet and gave him a shove down the other side of the hillock. He even jerked the fire ax from his hand to be sure it wouldn't be dropped and his fingers were wrapped around the handle as if he wanted to smash something with it.

Right then Joie was sorry he had said a word. In Bud's mad anger they'd both be pushed at a killing pace across the treacherous sand and he was already practically exhausted.

CHAPTER FOUR

IT WAS AN EERIE FEELING, Walking around the boat like this. The Blue *Tuna* was lying on its port side, her pennant still attached to the masthead. Almost as if she were sleeping, Larry thought. The fishing rods were still in their brackets, and chrome and brass fittings still had a sheen to them under the sun, although the salt had begun its destructive work on most of her.

He walked around the stern, his hand touching the transom lovingly, then dropping to the big brass propeller. He leaned on it, felt it move slightly, but even now corrosion was making inroads against the fine metal.

Josh had gone toward the bow and was waiting for him beside the gaping hole in the bottom of the hull when he got there. Larry looked at the gap in the wooden planking. He and Josh could have gone through that opening at the same time. Whatever had done that had delivered a death blow so quickly it had almost engulfed the crew.

He reached up and felt the edges of the exposed planks. There was something about their color and shape that annoyed him. They weren't jagged or fresh-looking around the rim, but black and smooth, and when his fingers touched them. pieces crumbled into his palm. The wood was pulpy soft for a good six inches back from the edges, almost as if it had been eaten and digested.

"It looks like it was burned," Josh suggested.

"That's no burn," Larry said. "What could burn it?"

"Spilled gas in the bilge, a spark ..."

"Gasoline would float on *top* of the bilge water."

"Did you *have* any bilge water?"

Larry shook his head. "Very little. The *Tuna* was a pretty dry boat and Dad kept her in good condition. Besides, if it had been a fire, we would have had a whiff of smoke. There was none of that."

"Ah," Josh pointed out, "but you were in a storm. The hatches were closed; the wind was in your faces."

"No, we would have had some indication. All we knew was *wham* ... and the bottom fell out Suddenly we were knee deep in water and going over the side." He nodded at the hole. "You know how many gallons of water could come in there in ten seconds."

"I don't like to think about it," Josh said.

"Me either, but I sure want to know why it happened."

"You're going in, aren't you?"

"This isn't an old sub."

"Okay." Josh grinned. I'll go in with you."

They went back to the port side, hoisted themselves in, reaching for handholds to help them up the inclined deck. It was still damp, coated with a slimy natural carpet of sea algae. Gradually, they inched their way to the mahogany doors that led below and with a sharp kick, Larry broke the small brass lock and the doors flew inward.

Light streamed through the starboard portholes, gleaming off the water that still filled the hull like a half-emptied cereal bowl. Another larger shaft of light came in through the uneven hole in the bottom, splashing over the engines that were still crusted with grease. A pair of life jackets bobbed on the surface, surrounded by unopened coffee cans, part of a wooden catwalk and his dad's float-able tackle box.

Beneath Larry's feet, three steel bottles of compressed air were wedged under the steps and he kicked them loose, watching them roll in the oil-slicked water. He moved gently, working his way closer to the gap in the bottom. There was something peculiar about that hole and it took him a full minute to figure it out. The thing extended from the raised keel up between the ribs and stopped on an almost even horizontal line. But when he looked at the sides of the ribs and keel around the hole, they had the same charred effect too.

No, it wasn't an outside force that had ripped the boat apart, and it certainly wasn't a fire. He knew *what* had done it, but didn't quite know *how*.

Until he looked at those compressed-air bottles floating in front of him. They used to be in a rack on the side and when he felt for it his fingers pulled out a metal strap that had been cut almost all the way through before the surging of the storm had broken it loose. Then he saw the other bottle . . . or what almost looked like a compressed-air bottle. It was six inches in diameter and two feet long; but it was painted green, the top that he knew had never been tightened down was gone and there was a glass liner inside the steel.

The only thing that bottle ever held was a deadly corrosive acid, and when it fell, its contents hit the bottom and began eating its way outside through the boat. It wouldn't have taken long to rot through the planking; then one hard thrust from the sea would finish the job and engulf the *Blue Tuna* before anything could be done about it.

There was a grim smile on Larry's face. He had seen bottles like that before. They were nested in forms outside the Jimson brothers' boathouse.

He grabbed the metal bottle and pulled it out. Then he heard Josh call him and his tone was urgent. He hauled himself back to the doors, edged through to the deck, his feet braced. "What is it?"

"There . . . see? Two of them. They're coming this way."

Larry squinted against the sun, nodding. "That's Bud and Joie, all right."

"What're we going to do, Larry?"

"Not stay here, that's for sure. We're only a couple of kids and they're not going to let us tell what we know." Josh gave him a sharp glance and Larry explained what he had found. To Josh, the death of a boat was a serious thing, and when it had been deliberately caused, with no concern for those on board ... He could feel a terrible anger fill his chest.

"For once, Larry, I wish I were grown up. I wish my father and yours could be here to meet them. I wish . . ."

"Wishing isn't getting us out of here," Larry said. "Look, let's go over the other side and keep the *Tuna* between us and them. If we head in any other direction right now they can cut us off, but if we get far enough away we can get lost behind the grass or one of those sand hills."

"You forgetting about our footprints?"

"We have to take that chance. If we're lucky the damp sand will fill them in. Let's go."

Keeping low, they scrambled up the slippery deck, then flipped over the side and let themselves down to the sand. They took off at a slow run, knowing they had to conserve their energy. Any pounding gait would drive their feet so deep in the sand they'd tire quickly, besides leaving behind an indelible path to their location.

Whenever they slowed they'd check back to make sure they were positioned properly, the *Blue Tuna* their shield from the Jimson brothers, but they knew they didn't have too long before they would be spotted. Their only hope was to cut down the incline toward the great drop-off where the seabed was darker and they could merge into its shadows. There they would be safe from the Jimsons. But if the sea came back…

Bud Jimson almost ran the last hundred yards to the *Blue Tuna,* his eyes on the other set of prints that were still evident in the sand. Joie was beside him, panting for breath, his eyes bulging from the exertion, but his brother was almost elated. He wasn't thinking of Larry and Josh as two boys … no, to him they were the *enemy* and enemies had to be destroyed before they destroyed you. He gripped the ax tightly and stopped, his fingers holding Joie back.

"Quiet now. They're inside. We have them."

"Bud…"

Without answering him, Bud pulled himself over the port railing. He looked at the shattered hatch doors and grinned, a mean twist to his lips. He knew what he was going to do and he wasn't worried about it at all, because when the sea *did* come back, it would dissolve all evidence and the boys' disappearance would simply be listed as another tragedy that happens to curious islanders.

But something was wrong. If they *were* in there he could hear them and there was no sound at all, absolutely nothing coming from the interior of the boat. He slammed the edge of the ax into the deck, grabbed the edge of the cowl and hauled himself toward the door. He said something nasty under his voice, then scrambled inside. It took only a minute to locate the tank and another to find the top. When he got back outside he grabbed the ax again, tossed the tank and the ax over the side and jumped down himself.

Joie had already found the footprints on the other side. He showed them to his brother, staying well out of the reach of his hand. When Bud got mad he'd take it out on him and he wasn't in the mood to get splatted again.

This time, though, Bud wasn't all that mad. He had gotten what he had come for and planned to bury it somewhere away from the boat That would take care of that. Then he could follow those doggone kids and take care of *them*. Right now, they could be standing between him and the dream of a lifetime.

Joie was dumb but not *that* dumb. He knew what his brother was planning and he was feeling sharp pangs of nervousness eating into his chest again. He grabbed hold of Bud's shirt before he could move off and stopped him. "Look, Bud, why you want to chase them kids now for? Gee, they get their fathers on us and we're in big trouble."

IT WAS time he told Joie, Bud thought. Joie wasn't much for bravery, but he was a greedy slob, wanting everything the easy way, and if he knew what the deal *really* was, Bud wouldn't have any trouble with him at all.

He made the decision, turned and looked at Joie with a cold, hard stare. "Do you think Vincent Damar went back to the mainland without telling his kid everything about the old salvage boat that located the *San Simon*'s treasure?"

"You mean . . . that little kid knows . . . ?"

"That kid's a smart one and don't forget it. His old man's got special permission to teach him and already he knows more than kids what go to the island schools. Right now those kids are after that wreck and if they find it first, we kiss it good-bye. All I know is that it's an iron wreck, a three-master about a hundred years old. I never got a chance to read everything Damar wrote down, but I got that much. Now, do you want us to have that new boat and the big times on the mainland with all the money we can spend or do you want them kids to do us out of it?"

Bud had called it right. His brother was seeing that big picture of city lights in his mind and the greed was clenched in his squinty eyes. "We're wasting time," Joie said, and when he started trotting beside the rapidly fading footprints he wasn't even limping any more.

Something seemed to have happened to the light. The sun was still there, moving slowly in a great arc across the heavens, but the odd texture of the bottom absorbed all the reflective qualities and Larry and Josh had the strange feeling of being on another planet.

The temperature had changed, too. Even the heat had gone out of the sun and there was a cold, clammy feel to the air, one that clung to the skin like an early winter's wind, a reminder that things wild and terrible were to follow.

They had gone into the dankness of the incline hoping to pick up a southerly path that would take them parallel to the great drop-off, then cut back to the west around the undulating hills of sand to stay out of sight of the Jimsons, but so far no solid path had showed itself.

Josh was to the right of Larry, peering around anxiously. Ahead was ever a deeper gloom than where they were, and the wet spots were getting more frequent. Somehow, the sun wasn't evaporating the water in this area at all. When he pointed this out, Larry said, "Most likely there's more water under the sand. If the sea were in, we'd be sixty feet beneath it right now."

"It's getting awfully soft, Larry."

"Yeah, I know." He paused and let his eyes drift toward the sky. "I wonder what time it is."

Josh followed his glance, peering through the unnatural gray haze that filtered out the usual sharp glare of the sun. He wasn't at all sure of the angle of the bottom he was standing on and couldn't position the sun the way he could on land, so he shook his head ruefully and said, "The morning has gone past, Larry. Right now we are at the halfway mark . . . the . . . How do you say it?"

"Point of no return?" Larry supplied.

Josh nodded, his face solemn. "From here we go back . . . if we want to get back before dark . . . or before the tide comes in."

Larry pointed toward the northwest. "Then let's take the upslope around the side of that coral ridge there. At least that will keep between the Jimsons and us for a little while." He turned and checked the tracks they had made a few minutes ago. "Although at the rate the sand is filling in," he said, "they're going to have to be awfully lucky to trail us."

"Larry. . ."

"Yeah?"

"Suppose they catch us."

A grimace passed over Larry's face. He didn't like to think about it at all.

"Would they . . .?"

"You know them as well as I do, Josh," Larry told him.

"Then we'd better hurry."

But out of sight, some distance away, Bud Jimson had anticipated their next move. He held out his hand to slow his brother down and said, "We'll lose those tracks if we go down into the drop-off."

"So what'll we do?"

"They have to come up. Sooner or later they have to head east again or the sea'll get 'em."

"Why don't we just leave 'em here and . . ."

"Because they know that as well as we do, stupid. Would you like to go wandering down in the big drop?"

"No . . . no, sir, Bud. I don't want any part of that."

"They don't either. Now, what we got to do is reach them or cut them off. I don't care who gets 'em, us or the sea, just as long as they are *got,* understand?"

"Sure, Bud."

"And as far as the law is concerned, the sea got 'em and who's to prove different?"

Joie nodded. "I hope we got enough time," he said.

"We have," Bud told him.

CHAPTER FIVE

BUT TIME WAS one thing that Larry's father had run out of. Vincent Damar left the office of the Lissop bank in Miami and headed toward Biscayne Boulevard. The Lissop people had been the third and last of his financial contacts and when they turned down his request for a loan, he realized that it was all over.

What he really dreaded was having to tell Larry. His son's faith in his ability to solve any impossible problem was so great he was afraid that news of their being utterly wiped out would be a terrible shock to the boy. It might not have been so bad if he hadn't had that solid gut feeling that they were closing in on the wreck that held all their hopes. Until the *Blue Tuna* went down, he could actually feel the nearness of that old hulk as if his body were a magnet, picking up emanations from that old steel hull. However, feelings weren't the things you could borrow money on. All that was left in the account was barely enough to get themselves and their limited possessions back to the mainland with enough left over to last about two weeks while he found himself a job.

Vincent Damar looked at his watch and frowned. As

long as he was here in Miami he might as well use his time as best he could. For a month or two he could take any job that would keep the two of them secure while he re-established his teaching contacts for something more permanent. They were going to need a place to stay, nothing expensive, and close to a school for Larry's benefit.

When Vincent had decided on his program for the rest of the day, he bought a newspaper to scan the job ads and see what was being offered in cheap housing. Luckily, it was off-season and something might be available right away.

He didn't realize how deep he was in his own thoughts until a couple of kids on bicycles almost ran him down. He started to yell after them, then stopped. For a moment he just stood there, wondering what had gotten into everybody. Not one person was coming toward him. Everyone was headed toward the water. The newsboy was closing his shop and Vincent said, "What's happening around here?"

"Got me, mister," the boy said. "They're all saying something's happening at the ocean."

"Now, what can happen to that?" Vincent asked in exasperation. "It's a beautiful day."

"Who knows? Maybe a whale got beached. Why don't you go see?"

There *was* something exciting about the way everyone was all worked up. There didn't seem to be any indication of a disaster—no whistles were blowing or sirens screaming and the police cars that went by were at normal speed. It was just that everybody else was hurrying and anxious to get down to the beach. Then suddenly Vincent grinned, tucked the newspaper under his arm and followed the crowd to see what it was all about.

Twenty minutes later Vincent *knew*.

Around him the crowd packed together as if looking

for mutual protection, their voices almost stilled. No one needed to ask what had happened; it was right there in front of them, so big and broad any explanation would be impossible.

Inexplicably, the sea had pulled back a full half-mile, laying bare the footings of that great city. Boats were tilted at crazy angles on the sand; ropes that had held them tied to docks snapped like threads. Shell-crusted pilings of the piers looked like giant insect legs all standing in silly puddles of salt water.

Except for the few boat owners trying to salvage their craft, nobody was yet venturing near the wet sand. The mild surf was twinkling out there as the gentle waves broke and receded, all as calm and serene as the lull in the eye of a hurricane.

Vincent glanced upward and scanned the sky. A good dozen airplanes were skirting the area and he recognized their military silhouettes. At least the Air Force had gotten on this sudden quirk of nature in a hurry. A pair of helicopters were cruising the shoreline and television cameras were recording the phenomenon for the evening's news.

The activity seemed to start at the southern end of the beach. The solid front of the crowd softened, then broke, Clusters of people getting over the startling sight and succumbing to their curiosity. Vincent saw them starting toward the vast emptiness, beginning to walk out onto the mushy bottom.

Unlike the others, Vincent worked his way back to the street. It was all too evident to him that the people regarded this as some local freak condition. They had seen unusual tidal action before, and wild situations where the ocean had gone berserk, and to them this was just some new oddity to add to their collection.

But Vincent was thinking scientifically and he was worried. He was familiar with oceanography and was positive this wasn't a simple local event. The ocean was a giant that didn't do things in little ways. Whatever had happened had to have had a start, and the origin of this oceanic display would probably be miles to the south.

And that's where Larry was!

Vincent looked at his watch and knew he'd have to hurry. The street and pedestrian traffic had thickened, all headed toward the water. He picked his way around them, cut west a block to where it was less crowded, and half-ran until he came to the Andra Radio Shop. A year ago he had purchased his marine and base radio from Bill Andra and knew he had good working equipment in his shop.

Luck was with Vincent. Bill was just about to close down and go see what all the shouting was about, but Vincent waved him back inside the store and told him what he had seen. Then he added: "Look, around here it's a curiosity. Everyone seems to think it's simply local, but who can tell what's happening in other places?"

"But nothing's been on TV yet," Bill told him.

"There hasn't been time."

"If the tide's out that far . . ."

"Look, it could go back pretty far before anyone would think anything about it, and the slope of the bottom is shallow enough to let it happen pretty fast."

Bill nodded sagely. "What can you do about it?"

"Let's see if we can raise Larry on the radio. That far south, the situation can be totally different."

"Okay." Bill nodded toward the transmitter on the desk. "You try to get him. I'll see what I can pick up on Air Force and Naval frequencies. And you might as well turn on the local radio Channel on my portable over there. Some news might be filtering through now."

Ten minutes later they were both looking at each other across the room, strange expressions on their faces. The local radio had played up the incident as if it were part of a Chamber of Commerce promotion for a new show. . . and how the public was enjoying the new view from an old ocean front. One thing the newscaster did mention, however, was that the tidal effect was felt north as far as Fort Lauderdale, where it seemed to fade out. Dozens of explanations were given for the occurrence, but no two were the same.

Vincent said, "Anything from government sources?"

Bill shook his head. "Negative. There are a lot of military planes being scrambled but all for Observation purposes. One thing is funny, though."

"What's that?"

"An awful lot of code is suddenly going out. Nothing I can make sense of. How about Larry?"

"No response. I tried a few others I know but can't raise them either."

"There's *got* to be radio traffic on those frequencies, Vinnie."

"Sure, and everybody is trying to talk at once. It's so scrambled you can't make sense of anything."

From the stricken look on Vincent's face, Bill knew what he was thinking. "Any way you can fly back?" he asked softly.

There was a somber note in Vincent's voice. "Only by seaplane, and under these conditions, I doubt any pilot would take the chance. If there are any choppers available, you can bet they'll all be chartered by photographers by now."

"It'll have to be by boat then."

"Any boats around here are all grounded on the sand." Vincent's hands knotted into fists with helplessness. "I'm stuck here, Bill."

"Look," Bill said, "Larry's a smart kid. He's not alone down there. If anything's happened, there will be a lot of people to help him out."

"Yeah," Vincent told him, "that's what I'm afraid of." For a moment his mind had envisioned an expanded picture of what had happened in Miami and he realized that the reaction of the island natives would be completely different from that of the city-bred people of this area. The world to the people of the islands was the water and any drastic change in it would provoke unusual reactions.

Bill watched him a moment, then suggested, "Why don't you try monitoring those marine channels until something comes through? If this thing has touched your area the base stations should be working overtime."

"Maybe not, Bill. Very little of the heavy marine shipping comes close to the islands. The small boats that do know the area so well they go on radio traffic."

"Won't hurt to try. At least it'll keep you busy."

Vincent nodded in agreement and sat down at the receiver. He fitted the headset over his ears, flipped the power switch to on, then began a routine search of the airwaves.

Five hundred and twenty miles to the southeast, the freighter *Emory Welsch* rolled slowly in the mild swells of the Atlantic. It had been an easy crossing from the African coast and the weather forecast had looked good for another two days. Captain Stephen Morelli relaxed on the bridge, anticipating their arrival in Jacksonville, Florida, and three quiet weeks at home, away from the vast emptiness of the ocean.

Not that he didn't enjoy a gentle passage. The only trouble was, a quiet trip was just too boring. He welcomed a storm at sea and even small mechanical difficulties— anything to break the monotony. Unlike the other officers and the crew, he had no hobbies to occupy his time, and the languid days had seemed to drag by.

For the past two hours he had been staring out the sturdy window of the bridge, his mind far away from the sea itself. But then something seemed to tug at the inner-most reaches of his thoughts, trying hard to attract his attention, and he frowned lightly, letting his mind come back to the present.

What was it trying to tell him? He gave a moment and start as he glanced outside a moment, then looked down at his watch. To be sure, he checked the position of the sun and the frown deepened. He looked across the maze of instruments to where his first mate was checking a chart. "Doug ..."

"Yes, Captain?"

"Come over here and take a look at the ocean."

The mate laid a heavy metal ruler and his dividers on top of the chart and walked over to the window. From the expression on his face he seemed to be viewing something for the first time too. Like the Captain, he peered up at the sun, then scanned the horizon. "Strange color, sir."

"What does it look like to you?"

"Like sunset, but we're far from that time."

"Ever see it before?"

"Only when we were under a very heavy dust cloud. There was that time off Aden ..."

The Captain interrupted him. "But there's no dust in the air at all. Now take a good look at the water. Since there's no dust and the sky is clear, it couldn't be an atmos-pheric reflection, could it?"

After a minute of deep study, Doug shook his head. "If I didn't know better," he said, I'd think we were seeing the bottom. . . deep down, but a bright, sandy bottom." He glanced at Captain Morelli quickly, turned and went back to his chart. When his tracing finger found what he sought, he nodded and rejoined the Captain. "According to the chart, we should have twenty-two fathoms under us."

"Let's be sure," the Captain said somberly. He went to

a side panel, switched on the Fathometer and watched the pattern of the ocean's bottom register on the screen. He checked the depth, and the frown on his face deepened.

Something had happened to six fathoms of water! If the charts were correct and their own position properly esti- mated, something had dropped the surface of the ocean thirty-six feet closer to the bottom!

"Mr. Andrews..."

Doug swung around, startled by the sudden formal use of his last name. "Yes, sir?"

"I'd like verification reports from any ships in the area. Contact the Coast Guard to see if any change has been noticed in this section or if any error could possibly have been made in depth soundings."

"Yes, sir."

"And bring back somebody to stand by the Fathometer every minute. I want to be informed of every change." When Doug hurried off to the radio room the Captain turned to the helmsman. "Ring for half-speed and hold a steady course."

"Aye, sir." The helmsman's hand shifted the position of the engine room telegraph and almost immediately the noticeable throb of the *Emory Welsch*'s Single propeller eased as the RPM's decreased.

Captain Stephen Morelli was feeling better again. Finally, some excitement had come into this drab ocean- crossing and a new spirit of challenge was surging through him. It might all be a false alarm, a simple error in printing on the charts, but at least it was something to think about.

Ten minutes later Doug Andrews was back with a Seaman, whom he stationed at the Fathometer before he went up to Captain Morelli. His face was grave as he handed over a typewritten report. "From the Coast Guard, sir. They want position and depth reports every half-hour."

"They've suggested a course change," the Captain noted.

"Apparently as a result of signals from other ships closer to the mainland. All vessels west of us have been ordered farther out to sea. From what I could learn, there has been a severe tidal drop along the southern part of the Eastern Seaboard."

Captain Morelli pushed his cap back and took another look at the ocean, as if he were seeing it for the first time. "Impossible!"

"I'm sorry, sir. I even intercepted signals from the Mexican coast. Nothing exceptional has happened there yet, but they were making inquiries. We even picked up a few panic calls from independent stations on the mainland who are trying to find out what's happening."

"Did the Coast Guard advise on the weather situation?"

"Not yet, sir. We've already notified those who asked what the condition was here, so they're alerted."

"What about emergency calls?"

"Nothing. So far all ships seem to be safe. The Jacksonville port is still open, but Miami is diverting all ships to other areas."

"Very well. We'll make this course change and head for Jacksonville. We can always stand offshore if necessary."

"Yes, sir."

"And Doug . . . please stand by the radio personally. I want all information brought to me immediately?"

In Miami, Vincent Damar slipped the headset off and leaned back wearily. Since he had come in, the back room of Bill Andra's shop had become more like a noisy bus station. Everybody was looking for information not available on the streets or from commercial sets and it took a good hour to get the crowd out and the doors locked.

Bill threw up his hands in a gesture of disgust. "With all the brains they're supposed to have in government, you'd think just one of 'em would have an answer to all this."

"It's never happened before."

"Let's hope it doesn't happen again. What did you pick up?"

Vincent shook his head. "I spoke to an officer on the *Emory Welsch*. They're in water shallower than it's supposed to be, so the condition is going out to sea."

"Any others?"

"Two more. They all reported the same thing."

"What were their positions?"

"All southeast of the Florida coast. Whatever it is, it doesn't seem to have any effect much north of here." He paused for a minute, his face taut. "I've got to get back some way, Bill."

"I wish I could suggest how," his friend said. "I just spoke to all the marinas in the area. Nothing's open and any boats out in the ocean are staying there. The Coast Guard is even planning a refueling run to keep anybody out there gassed up." He waited a moment, studying Vincent's expression, then said, "You did try *all* the islands, didn't you?"

Instead of answering, Vincent simply nodded.

"They wouldn't leave their radios, would they?"

Vincent let out a sour grunt. "You don't know that bunch, Bill. To them, the situation isn't a tragedy at all. It will be one big, grand opportunity to salvage anything that ever touched the ocean's bottom and they'll tear anybody apart who gets in their way."

"But. . . your kid isn't like that, is he?"

Vincent looked up slowly, his eyes meeting his friend's. "Bill. . . have you forgotten what a boy's curiosity is like? You think Larry could resist exploring an empty ocean bottom?"

"So let him, Vinnie. He's not going to get in anybody's way, is he?"

"Only if they figure out he knows more about a few things than they do."

It took a minute for it to sink in; then Bill realized what Vinnie was talking about. "Does he *really?*" Bill asked him seriously.

"I'm afraid he does," Vincent told him.

CHAPTER SIX

JAKE SKIDDO and Petey Betts had a sick feeling in their stomachs when old lady Betts told them the Jimson brothers were the only ones not safely accounted for. Every other boat was stranded beside the dock on the island, their owners accounted for and already out scrounging the great sea bottom for any booty they could find.

But the others didn't matter. It was the Jimson brothers who owed the most money to Jake and Petey, and if anything had happened to them, Jake and Petey would be out of business. It wasn't uncommon for the Jimsons to stay out overnight, but ordinarily they would have left word at the store. And to make it worse, there had been no radio contact at all.

Either the islanders had no imagination at all or they had too much of it, but they had gone to bed with the ocean in its usual place and awakened with the ocean almost gone, and how it had happened made their minds boggle. All Jake and Petey could picture was a giant outsurge of water sweeping all craft in front of it, making fish bait of any crews unlucky enough to be aboard.

Neither Jake nor Petey was adventurous enough to want to walk very far out onto that damp sand. Their lives had been spent by the sea and they knew what she could do and they didn't want to be in the way if and when she decided to return.

They were at their wits' end when old lady Betts got annoyed at their whining and told them they ought to get that crazy contraption of young Oliver Creighton's. She had seen him go through the swamp and across the beaches in the thing and since he was always out of money, a couple of dollars ought to rent it for a while. Jake and Petey didn't need any more urging. They ran for the pickup truck, hopped in and headed for the Creighton place before anybody else got the same idea.

What Oliver Creighton had was a homemade dune buggy. It wasn't much more than a VW chassis and engine with four outsize tires that not only would keep the rig going in soft sand but would actually float it if the need arose. It was ugly, but it was rugged and useful—and it was Oliver's prized possession. Not only did Jake and Petey pay heavily for its use, but they guaranteed in writing that Oliver would get the pickup truck if the dune buggy was lost.

Heading toward the ocean, Petey said, "If we find them Jimsons, you can bet I'm putting everything this cost on their bill."

"You think they'll pay it?" Jake asked.

Petey grinned and nodded. "They got any choice?"

For a scant minute, Larry and Josh thought they'd be plucked from this wild situation they were in. The faint drone they had heard from the sky grew louder and both boys looked up, their eyes searching for the plane that made it.

"Coming closer," Larry said. "Hear it?"

Josh was peering at the deepening color of the sky;

then he saw the speck in the northeast. "There it is!" He pointed excitedly, then began frantically waving his arms.

Larry followed the direction Josh's finger had indicated. The plane was there, all right, but much too far off for them to be seen by the pilot. It started to turn and for a moment their hopes faded, but when it turned back, sweeping in a wide arc, Larry said, "Bud and Joie Jimson won't want to be spotted, that's for sure."

"What do you mean?"

"They can't afford to let us get out of here."

"But. . . where can we go?" Josh asked. "If we go into the drop we'll never get back out. Look how wet it is already. There's no place left to hide!"

"We don't have to."

"Why not?"

"Because Joie and Bud will be doing the hiding. Right now I'll bet they're digging into the bottom like a couple of sand crabs to keep that plane from seeing them. If that's the case, then we can make a run for it."

"Larry . . . suppose they're still looking for us, though."

"That's the chance we have to take. You ready, Josh?"

"I'm as ready as I'm ever going to be." He looked at the plane that was getting larger as it neared their area. "Man," he said toward the plane, "just keep hanging around."

They couldn't really run. It was more like sloshing, like being in the middle of a bad dream with some wild monster chasing them. Their feet simply didn't want to move, sinking ankle deep into the muck before they came loose with a loud *slurp*. Their leg muscles tired, but they couldn't rest and their breath was like fire in their lungs.

Both of them fell twice but struggled up again and lurched toward the one small rise ahead. That monster behind them wasn't a dream—it was real and big and, right now, a deadly thing that wanted to leave them forever in the wet, salty sand far from the island they had left.

Overhead, the dull sound of the airplane was a comforting sound. It came closer each second, but the arc it turned in would keep it too far off for them to be seen. Larry turned his head once, slowing down for a quick look at where he thought the Jimson brothers would be. A pair of small dark areas could have been their forms, but the distance was too far to be sure. If the spots were the Jimsons, they weren't moving, just lying still with their heads down.

The boys looked at each other in silent recognition of the new problem facing them. The sand was firmer now, but to get to the protection of the sand hill, they had to cover a flat open distance the length of a football field, and if at any time during the run the Jimsons lifted their heads, the two boys would certainly be seen.

And that would be the end of them. With no trouble, the Jimsons could angle across and cut off any escape route toward the land. The boys were young and quick, but they were up against two strong men consumed with murderous hatred, a completely uneven match.

"Let's go," Larry said.

A brief rest had given them a second wind and they plodded ahead as fast as their feet could move. Behind them their tracks were in the drier sand but already filled in where they came up out of the drop. If the Jimsons thought they were still there and followed that path, the boys' chances of getting free grew better every minute. If they could only make the area where the bottom grew its mounds and hillocks and the weed lay between the great coral heads, their size and agility would even their battle against the size and strength of the men.

They were almost there, breath coming in huge sobs that choked and burned, feet like lead weights dragging them down. Only a little bit farther . . . but in the sky the airplane had turned away, its drone getting weaker and weaker and Larry and Josh knew that now the Jimsons would be getting up, and although the boys were close to the hill, they would be in plain view of the men.

Fingers clawed into the sand. They squirmed and rolled with a final effort, bodies so tortured with the pain of their exertion they couldn't even speak; then they were behind the mucky pile of sand that could well be made into their graveyard.

Behind them the Jimson brothers had risen to their feet. Bud was looking toward his left, a small scowl starting to appear between his eyes.

Jake Skiddo held the wheel of the dune buggy with all his strength while Petey was clutching at the upright of the rollover bar beside him. From the beach it looked like an easy drive across the open bottom of the ocean, but it was a deceptive vision and they were being tossed about worse than if they were in an open boat during a hurricane. The over-size wheels would sink in and drop them on one side, then just as abruptly carom off a half-hidden coral head and almost throw them loose. Unseen forces tore at the tires, wrenching the wheel in Jake's hands, and he was beginning to wonder how long they could keep it up.

They weren't alone out there at all. It seemed as if the entire population of the island was probing every mound and hillock for anything they could use, finding long-lost anchors, wrenching brasswork off sunken hulks, edging ever seaward, alert for the one thing they knew was there and all hoped to find— the treasure ship.

One other thing everyone was doing—they were looking for the Jimson brothers. The island was much too small for anything to go unnoticed or for any rumor to be squelched. They all knew that the Jimsons were hiding something ever since Joie Jimson had bragged a little too much to Arnie Snyder, and if anyone had an indication of where that ancient treasure ship lay, it would be them.

Or Vincent Damar. The islanders couldn't understand it, but Damar didn't even bother to disguise what he was doing. Not that he talked openly about his project, but the planned courses he sailed in the *Blue Tuna* spoke for themselves. Vincent Damar was clearly searching for something on the bottom and the only thing of any value as far as the islanders were concerned was the wreck of the *San Simon.*

Since Joie Jimson had hinted that they knew of Vincent Damar's plans, the islanders kept a wary eye out for what Joie and Bud were up to. The Jimson boat was fast and the brothers unscrupulous, but the islanders had their own schemes as well and they watched both Damar and the Jimsons.

And now, with Vincent Damar in Miami, they had to watch only the Jimsons . . . if they could find them. It wasn't until Jake and Petey showed up in that weird contraption of Ollie Creighton's that they cursed their luck for not thinking of that dune buggy first. Most of them were already laden down with articles that were junk compared with what the *San Simon* carried, but they didn't want to give up their new finds any more than they wanted somebody else to beat them to the wreck. For the first time they were beginning to learn how painful the disease of greed could be.

Only the original natives of the islands escaped the ravages of the disease. Discovering treasure was something they had never been interested in. To them, whatever the sea took to itself, there it belonged. The fish, the conchs, the crabs—all these the sea gave up, but she kept the treasure for herself. So the old-time islanders sat back and laughed at the mad scramble for baubles so long ago consigned to the sea's bottom.

Laughter, though, was not part of Jake Skiddo and Petey. Their bodies were stiff and sore from the jolting ride, their stomachs as sick as if they had been to sea in a skiff. For the past hour they had crisscrossed the area, eyes alert to any sign of the Jimsons, when Petey finally said, "Let's hold it awhile, Jake ... I can't take any more."

Neither could Jake, so he steered to the top of a weed-covered mound, the dune buggy vibrating over the strange, uneven surface. "Okay," he told his partner. "We need to gas up anyway. Grab that can out of the rack."

Wearily they poured the gas into the tank, emptying out their last drop. They both knew there was a limit on their exploration now. They could go just so far before the diminishing fuel supply demanded an immediate return to Ara Island. They both looked back at the buggy's tracks, noting the way water filled in the hollows in the sand. Any attempt to walk back from this point would end in disaster. The over-size balloon tires kept the dune buggy on the surface, but a man alone would go knee deep into the quagmire-like sand.

While they rested they squinted out at the vast empty bottom around them. There were moving dots of people on all sides and, strangely enough, their voices were carrying over that great wet plain.

"You think somebody will find the *San Simon?*" Pete asked.

"Ain't never gonna be a better time."

"They found other ships. How come the *Simon's* such a ghost?" Before Jake could answer, Petey added, "Maybe she's never even been."

Derisively, Jake said, "She's been, all right. Ain't they found the papers on her in Spain? And how about those cannon Reggie's pop dragged in?"

"Come on, Jake, that was fifty years ago and he never did remember where he got them."

"He just never found the spot again, that's all. But they were Spanish cannon and dated. The one in Miami even had the ship's name scratched into it."

Pete shrugged at that, still not convinced. "How about all the people who looked for that wreck so long? They shoulda found *something.*"

"Like what?" Jake countered. "The worms woulda eaten all the wood and the ballast rocks could get covered up. Even if there was cannon around, it would be so covered with coral you couldn't tell it from anything else." He eased himself off the dune buggy, stretched and said, "Like that stuff there, see?"

Jake pointed to a pile of coral at the bottom of the weedy hillock. Like most everything else, it was just a long, shapeless, coral-covered lump that smelled fishy now that it was exposed to the air. He stepped down the slope, tugged an open-end wrench out of his back pocket and gave the coral mound a whack. The whole side of it fell off.

Underneath was the pitted black cast-iron barrel of a cannon.

Jake couldn't get a word out.

Above him, Pete almost broke his leg clambering off the dune buggy.

Together, they stood there speechless, looking at each other, then back to the cannon again. Roughly, Pete grabbed the wrench from Jake and began hammering at the other sections of the coral, exposing more of the casting until there was no doubt at all about what they had discovered. Then the both of them attacked the other mounds. In fifteen minutes they had chipped away enough coral to realize they had nine separate cannon lying along one side of the mound.

Only then did it occur to them that the weed-covered hillock topped by the empty dune buggy was not just a plain sand hill at all. At close look, it had a definite size and shape. Without a word, they both scrambled to the top, took another good look, then began digging into the sand.

They didn't have to go far. No farther than a foot down they hit the first layer of large smooth rocks that could only be one thing. They were the ballast rocks of a Spanish ship.

Softly, almost in amazement, Jake said, "We found her. We found the *San Simon!*"

But Pete wasn't the quiet type at all. There was nothing important he could say in a whisper. He threw up two handfuls of sand, stood up with arms outstretched and shouted at the sky, *"We got the* San Simon!"

His voice traveled like all the other voices, and they all heard. And there he was standing, silhouetted perfectly for all to see, and when they dropped whatever they were doing and converged toward that sandy, weedy knoll, Jake was swinging at Pete for being so stupid as to give away the site of their treasure ship.

Had Bud Jimson studied that distant movement a moment longer he would have realized it could have been only Larry or Josh, but another bouncing movement caught his eye and he turned, squinting through the heat waves that bounced off the sand.

"What is it?" Joie asked, trying to find what Bud was watching.

"Somebody's got a vehicle over there."

"Can't no car go on that sand, Bud."

The look Bud gave his stupid brother made Joie pull away from him. "What's that thing then?"

Keeping one eye cautiously on his brother, Joie

studied the strange contraption a few moments. "Well, guess it *could* be *some* kind of car."

"Jughead," Bud said. "It's that dune buggy Ollie Creighton put together. Nothing else could go out here."

"You think . . . they're looking for . . . the kids, Bud?"

"No way," Bud told him. "That buggy came from Ara, not Peolle. If anybody's looking for anything, they're looking for the *San Simon*."

"What we oughta do . . . ," Joie started; then Bud gave him another fierce look.

"What we're gonna do is find those kids . . . Now, you hear?"

"Sure, Bud, sure. Let's go. All we got to do is follow their tracks."

Larry let out his breath with relief. He and Josh saw the Jimson brothers pick up their old trail and, for the first time in hours, they knew they might have a good chance of getting out of this enormous trap. Carefully they edged around the mound and, when they knew they were shielded from sight, took off at a fast pace, almost heading into a sun that was well on its way past its zenith.

The day had turned a more peculiar color of orange than before and the damp breeze had a chill to it that was completely out of season, but it was a comfort to the boys, who had worked up a sweat that dripped from their fingertips.

During a pause Larry noted the sun's position and estimated the time. His best reckoning gave them an hour's distance from the Jimsons . . . if the brothers had accepted the fact that they were still roaming along the lip of the coastal drop-off. As long as the boys could maintain that distance they were safe. Neither of the Jimsons had the stamina or the fleetness of youth, and each succeeding minute made the situation look better. In fact, Larry was already relishing the thought of telling his father what had happened. It wouldn't take *him* long to square things away with the crooks from Ara.

Larry's calculations would have been correct, too, if Petey Betts hadn't let out that joyful whoop when he and Jake Skiddo found the *San Simon.* The sound of his voice had rolled in an enormous wave across the barren ocean bottom, the peculiarities of nature amplifying and carrying it like a mirage all the way to where the Jimson brothers were standing.

"Bud . . . did you hear that?"

"I heard."

They were looking in a different direction now, at a 20-degree angle to the right of the sun. "Somebody found . . . the *San Simon."* Then Joie's eyes caught the wildly moving figure of Petey Betts on top of the mound, so far off that he was barely a speck. "There, Bud . . . see him!"

But Bud wasn't so concerned about that waving figure. He was looking at all the other dots starting their move toward the center of the action, and a slow grin started to play around his mouth.

"Let's go, Bud! We can't stand here and . . ."

Bud turned to answer his brother and by sheer accident his eyes picked up what appeared to be a pair of thin lines that circled around a dune an eighth of a mile away. He peered again, carefully, then nodded. Had the sun been overhead he never would have noticed those lines, but now, at an angle, shadows made them more apparent.

"Didn't you hear me, Bud? I said ..."

"I heard what you said," Bud said brusquely.

"Then why don't we get back there?"

"Because there ain't anything there, that's why."

"But the *San Simon* ..."

". . . *Was* a treasure ship," Bud finished for him. *"Was,* Joie. You know what that means? It means somebody else got that treasure a long time ago. It's on another wreck someplace out there and when we find that, we got the treasure. Now shut up. We've been movin' so fast we nearly got tricked."

"Tricked?"

Bud pointed toward the lines that etched the sandy bottom. "See that? Tracks, that's what they are. Those kids have cut back and are heading toward Peolle Island. We never would've caught them if we followed these tracks here."

Joie nodded eagerly. "Think we can do it now?"

"Yeah," Bud told him. "Now. They probably think they have plenty of time and they'll be slowing down. So we speed up."

Joie wiped the sweat from his face and was eager to get started. He had a better nose than his brother and he wanted to tell Bud how it was beginning to smell funny and the color of the sky was strange, but he didn't want Bud taking a poke at him. Whenever Bud had something on his mind, he couldn't think of anything else. Joie was wishing the visibility were better in the east. Someplace out there the sea was just doing something, but it sure was waiting to come back, and when it did, nobody had better be in its way.

That yell of Petey Betts had reached the boys too and when they had inched up a sand-slope as far as they dared, they could see its source and all the other islanders descending upon it.

"Do you think . . . they really found it?" Josh asked curiously.

"Probably. All the other known wrecks have been located; the *San Simon* was the last. It sure must have been pretty well hidden."

"There, my friend"—Josh smiled—" is where you will see one big fight pretty soon. From now on, everybody on Peolle and Ara will be enemies." He stopped, looked sharply at Larry and asked, "You think those Jimson brothers could have heard that cry?"

"Why not? We did."

"Then maybe they would ..."

Larry shook his head. "They wouldn't waste their time. I think they know very little will be on that wreck to start with. What they *really* want is to stop us. We're the ones who stand between them and the fresh air now. Jail is their next step if we make it back to the island."

"Don't say *if*, Larry."

"Okay. *When* we get back."

CHAPTER SEVEN

FOR THE PAST HOUR, Captain Stephen Morelli had kept the *Emory Welsch* on a steady course with depth soundings being given him at five-minute intervals. Each report was checked against the navigational charts by his mate, Doug Andrews, and radioed in to the Coast Guard at Miami.

There was no doubt about it now. The charts were right, and the sea was wrong. A whole section of it seemed to have picked itself up and simply disappeared. Until an hour ago, the depth change had grown more noticeable, the sea bottom steadily inching up toward them; then suddenly there was no change and the last few reports seemed to indicate a swing in the opposite direction.

Doug Andrews looked up from his charts, his eyes tired. "The last readings show a five percent rise, sir. Another thirty minutes and we'll know for sure."

"Any confirmations from other ships?"

Doug fingered through the top few radio communications beside him. "We're the outside ship, Captain. If there's any change, we'll feel it first."

"This can be bad news, Mr. Andrews. If there's any

sudden return of the ocean, the shorelines will be swept clean."

"They should have time to evacuate, sir."

"Perhaps the mainlands, but the islands will be devastated."

"If there is no wild tidal action," Doug suggested, "nothing might change at all. It might come back as quietly as it left."

"Does that sound logical, Mr. Andrews?"

The mate had to concede that it didn't. He had been at sea long enough to know how perverse nature could be when she wanted to. And right then, nature had a strange look. She was too quiet and very strangely colored, and when he stood outside in the breeze, she even smelt funny.

A runner from the radio shack entered and handed the mate a radio form. The Coast Guard was getting depth soundings from other ships now and caution was being urged for all ships in the area. Evacuation of the coastline population in endangered areas was already under way and an attempt was being made by military air and naval forces to alert people in remote areas of the possible hazard.

At the wheel, the young sailor looked anxiously at the skipper. Out of the corner of his eye, Captain Morelli caught his unspoken concern and said softly, "Keep a steady course, helmsman."

"Aye, sir."

The Captain looked at the Seaman beside the fathometer. "Any further depth change?"

"Still holding fast, sir."

"Mr. Andrews..."

"Yes, captain?"

"Get a couple of men to throw sounding leads from the port and starboard bows."

The mate glanced at him quizzically, saying nothing.

"Too often, electronic equipment can be affected by natural disturbances," the Captain explained. "A manual check will make any instrument change positive."

Doug Andrews nodded, relayed the order to a pair of seamen and waited for their report. In fifteen minutes he had it The manual measurement matched the depth readings on the fathometer. The only instrument that showed any noticeable difference was the thermometer. It was getting chillier than it should have been.

And now, a new silence seemed to have captured the ship. There were no jolting voices to be heard, no singing, and the only activities of the men off watch were staring at the strangely colored sky and listening anxiously to overhear any later news from the bridge. The pair in the bow throwing the leaded weights forward, letting the lines go out, then hauling them in to measure the lengths, had plenty of runners ready to relay the depth soundings to the Captain, eager to have anything to do during this strange day at sea.

Although nothing *appeared* changed since there was nothing to compare it with, everyone knew that the vast expanse of the Atlantic Ocean had shifted into a new configuration, and whether it was for good or for bad no one could tell. . . they could only hope.

The unnatural quiet wasn't only on the *Emory Welsch*. It hung over the thousands of people lining the beaches of Florida and the heavily populated islands to the south. It was the quiet of terror, the moment of facing the unknown and being unable to cry or scream for relief.

They heard the news first as a rumor... the sea was coming back in! A tremor went through the crowd, ears alert, waiting for further news. Every radio was tuned to the newscast, and the initial announcement of the new development gave the crowd an uneasy feeling. Some in the rear started edging back as if they expected a huge wave to engulf the whole coast, and here and there in the midst of the throng, others got the same idea.

Sergeant Arthur Lander of the Miami police was in charge of a command post where the crowd was thickest and he saw the first change in the attitude of people gathered on the edge of the ocean. He picked up the microphone in his radio car and hit the button.

"Lander here at post ten."

"Go ahead, Lander."

"Did you get a news flash on the tide?"

"Rodger, Lander. Coast Guard has reported a shift in the sea flow. All indications show it coming back in."

"They make a public announcement?"

There was a moment's pause, then: "Just a few minutes ago."

Sergeant Lander made a grunting sound of annoyance and said, "I thought so. They should have notified us first. You'd better alert all command posts to stand by. This bunch down here looks like they're going to break and run for it."

"Anything happening now?"

Lander shook his head. "Not yet, but if a couple of people suddenly get hysterical and try to cut out they'll start a panic like you never saw before in your life. It'll be worse than yelling 'Fire!' in a theater."

Again there was silence; then the base said, "We'll route some more cars your way, Sergeant. We'll institute all mob and panic control routines as best we can. Each command post will be on its own, however. It's a situation we never had to face before, so good luck."

"Yeah, swell," Sergeant Lander said before he tossed the mike back on its hook. But the Sergeant was a good professional cop and didn't waste any time. In his mind he recognized all the possibilities and called his men together. In five minutes the orders were given, all the equipment issued and the police assigned their positions. If they were lucky, they might be able to handle any sudden surge of the huge crowd.

It was a big *if*.

Like most radio shops, Bill Andra's had a receiver set to police frequency and when Ladner ended his communication, Bill looked at Vincent Damar, his face pale. "If there's panic . . ." he started to say.

Vincent held up his hand. "Don't speak about it."

"It could happen, Vince."

"Yes, I know. If one person flips out and screams or tries to run, it'll trigger the entire lot of them. It'll be a regular stampede and who knows how many will get killed in the rush. I hope the police have enough manpower to handle it."

"What about those areas where there are no cops?"

This time it was Vincent who went colorless. His mind was back at the island where his son was alone, and he was envisioning the worst. At least here they could go inland for safety, but on the smaller islands, there was no "inland."

"Look, Vince," Bill said, "don't sweat it too soon. So far there's no trouble at all, at least not from the water. Larry could be safer where he is than if he were caught in a mob scene here."

"Yeah, I know, Bill, but. . ."

Before he could get any further the door burst open and a big, tanned, burly guy came in totally out of breath and shoved a carton onto Bill's workbench. "You gotta help me, Bill," the guy said.

"Sure, Johnny . . . what's the trouble?"

"We're all set to go up in the chopper when the RB-510 went dead. And I mean dead. Started smoking, so I yanked it out of the panel and you got to do something, Bill."

"Come on, Johnny, I can't fix a radio in ten minutes."

"I know. That's why I want to borrow yours. Bill, I have to get that radio in. I got a contract to take this newsman south and without the RB-510 I'm shot down. He'll never get his story back and I lose a bundle of money."

"How far south, Johnny?" There was something quietly inquisitive in Bill's voice.

"The guy wants to range down to Triske Island."

"Isn't that past Peolle?" Bill asked him.

"Yeah, why?"

"How many you carrying?"

"Just the newsman."

"That chopper of yours seats four, doesn't it?"

"Uh-huh."

Bill looked at Vince and grinned. He said to Johnny, "I'll lend you my RB-510 if you drop my buddy off at Peolle."

The big flier didn't bother to argue. He just nodded, grinned and said, "It's a deal. Gimme the radio."

Five minutes later Vincent was in Johnny's truck, cradling the radio in his lap. In another half-hour they'd be in the air and on the way to Peolle Island.

Now it was all a matter of time, and every minute seemed an eternity.

"How far ahead do you think they are, Bud?"

The older Jimson brother paused and studied the foot-prints in the sand. Now the outlines were becoming more clear-cut and fresh-looking, and although the two men were tiring, Bud realized that little by little they were getting closer to the boys. He stood up and searched the area ahead, but there were too many sand hillocks in the way and with the strange orange setting sun in his eyes, he couldn't make out anything discernible more than a few hundred yards ahead.

Mentally, he measured the distance between themselves and Peolle Island. When they caught the kids they'd still have to be out of sight of any of the islanders, so that meant they'd have to make contact before the kids reached the weeds a quarter-mile offshore.

Bud's mean eyes squinted when he thought of the pleasure he'd have when his hands would be around their necks. Where he caught them was where they would stay, shoved well down under the sand where the sea life would gradually take any sign that they ever existed at all. It would just be a case of a couple of stupid kids who strayed away into the ocean when they should have stayed home. After that he and Joie'd have plenty of time to take care of Vincent Damar and the secret he had.

Joie said, "Well?"

"They can't be more than a half-mile ahead. They're going slower now."

"How can ya tell?"

"Because the space between their footprints is getting smaller," Bud explained. "The tracks aren't falling in so fast anymore."

"You think it'll be soon, Bud?"

"It'll be soon, Joie," his brother told him, looking at him with disgust. It would be nice to leave stupid Joie out here with the kids, too, he thought. Having him around all the time was like dragging an anchor. "Come on," he said, and the both of them picked up the pace again, paralleling the tracks laid down by Larry and Josh.

A fresh wind whipped across the wet sand and the men both shivered momentarily. It was an odd, disturbing wind, much too cool for this time of year, and riding on it were voices from a couple of miles away, voices so clear they could recognize their owners, voices yelling and screaming from the covered wreck of the *San Simon*.

They had to take a chance and make their way to the

top of the highest outcropping in the area. Unless they got a clear fix on their destination, they could wander off course and lose precious time in getting home to safety. The trouble was that they'd be exposing themselves dangerously if they were within sighting distance of their trackers.

"What do you think, Josh?"

"Back there," Josh said, "I think we gave them the slip."

"They aren't too dumb, though. At least, not Bud."

Josh looked at the sky again. The sun seemed to be buried behind an orangy-red haze and he couldn't be certain of its position at all. "We have to make sure, Larry."

"Okay, let's go. We'll stay in front of the crest and let it cover us as much as possible." He felt a chill go over him when the new wind hit his skin and he frowned, not liking what he felt. "Something's different, Josh."

His friend knew what he meant and nodded. "I feel it, too."

Quickly, they looked at each other, both with the same thought. "The sea is coming back in," Larry said softly.

And then it stopped being just a thought. It was something they both knew. Absolutely, definitely *knew*. They could hear the voices from far off, heard Jake Skiddo and Petey Betts trying to defend their find without any luck, the other voices mocking them, and Josh said, "I wonder if they know, too."

But it wouldn't be likely. That bunch would be much too concerned with scrabbling for gold or anything valuable they could carry to recognize any change in the situation at all. And behind them, the Jimsons would be too concerned with *them* to consider what was happening.

Maybe.

So they got in front of the slope, helped each other up

the loose sand and finally positioned themselves so they had an almost direct westerly view. For a good minute they sat there, knowing that if they didn't proceed carefully, the terror would get to them too.

They had expected to see Peolle Island. What they did *see* was a golden haze that obscured any physical objects more than a half-mile away.

"We could be too far south," Larry suggested.

Josh studied the terrain in front of them a good while before he was certain; then he pointed slightly to the right and said, "There, Larry. A point we passed earlier... where Pierre Combolt's two-masted schooner sank. We were north of it."

"You sure, Josh?"

"Yes, I remember it well. Peolle lies a little to our right. If we hurry, we can be at the island well before dark."

Larry nodded and began to ease himself back to the bottom. For the second time, both the boys were beginning to realize just how tired they were. Had they not been going at such a forced pace, they would have been fine; the past hours were telling on them now. They were hungry, they were thirsty and their bodies were aching from the ordeal. All they could hope for was that their pursuers were feeling the same strains of the chase as they were.

And up to that point, their pursuers *were* being beaten down. Bud and Joie Jimson were too tired to bother speaking to each other and their breath came in hard, hot gasps. A wetness had encompassed the area a few hundred yards back and the footprints they had been following were completely obliterated for a while, and it had taken them thirty minutes of fast cross-tracking before they picked up the prints again.

Twice Joie had stumbled and they had to rest to get their strength back, and by the time they found the trail again, they had been ready to assume the boys had gotten too far ahead for them to catch, but just at that moment Joie's mouth went slack and he pointed straight ahead. Bud followed the line of sight and felt the strength flow back into his body.

Ahead, on the crest of a hillock, clearly outlined against the sun was something that moved . . . and the only thing that could possibly move out there would be the target they were after.

"We got them now," Bud said.

His brother finally got his breath back. "They got to be tired, too."

Bud nodded his agreement. "Now we really push. They don't know we're here, so we got the edge on our side."

"You think it'll be long?"

"Another hour," Bud told him. "Then we got 'em."

Miles away, north of Peolle, a helicopter was taking off from its pad on the outskirts of Miami. It, too, was racing against time. From its cockpit an aerial broadcast of conditions on the sea below was being transmitted, the commentator giving a running account of what he was seeing, making the most of the last of daylight.

But to Vincent Damar, time was moving much too slowly. Even though he was airborne now, and enroute to Peolle Island, the slow speed of the chopper infuriated him. Inside himself was a knowledge too, and no matter what his friend Bill Andra had told him, he *knew* something was wrong back there on Peolle.

Yes, something was very drastically wrong.

CHAPTER EIGHT

THE MIAMI POLICE WERE LUCKY. The raw power of the bullhorns had kept the panic of the mob in check whenever unruly incidents started to appear, but it was the silent wonder in the minds of each person, the awe of the unknown, that really made them disperse without any difficulty. In the northern part of the state the water had already seeped back, rising slowly without causing any damage, but in outlying areas, this was to be expected.

It hadn't been until the last hour that the American Naval base at Guantanamo on the tip of Cuba had released news of the severity of the tidal drop. More than two dozen boats were stranded miles offshore, but so far there had been no reports of casualties.

But there was one alarming fact that seemed to go unnoticed. Although the ships at sea were beginning to radio the new changes in bottom depths, there was little visible sign that the sea was coming back in any great rush. What did get reported and was entirely overlooked was the degree of wetness in the formerly almost-dried ocean bottom. Two transmissions from ham radio operators in the southern islands relayed the message that the sand was getting soupy and dangerous, as if the ocean were trying to come back underground.

Not everyone was unaware of this fact, however. Hovering over the empty ocean bed, Victor Damar noticed the wet-shiny fingers on the sand, like unseen rivers making new paths toward the far-off shoreline. His mind could understand certain scientific principles that might cause this new condition, but it only added to his concern for his son's safety. Nature could work at incredible speeds if she wanted to, without being deterred by man's desires at all. Every day, in some areas of the world, there were tides that ebbed and flowed at speeds no man could match on foot.

Two others suddenly noticed their feet sinking deeper into the sand, and Joie Jimson said, "Bud . . . it's getting soft."

"I can see that, jughead."

"It should be dry here. Why is it getting wet, Bud?"

"How should I know." He raised his hand for a halt and studied the terrain. The footprints of the boys headed toward a hillock but were already beginning a swing to the right. "We're going to cut over that mound there and ..."

"That's a lot of work, Bud!"

"So's sloshing through wet sand. If those kids stay in the muck they'll slow down even more. Now shut up and save your breath. You're going to need it going over those dunes."

"Come on, Bud . . ."

"You want a rap in the ear?" Bud demanded aggressively.

His brother shook his head.

"Then move it!" Bud told him.

Together, they started off again, weariness dragging on every muscle in their bodies. They didn't know it, but if they could have seen what was not too far ahead of them, they would have run at full speed with the reserve energy the sight of victory gives.

Larry and Josh were standing stock-still, looking at a scene they never could have imagined. When they had approached it from the other direction coming out, they had taken it for just another long rise in the bottom, a natural seagrass-topped formation, but from where they were they saw what the configuration really represented.

It was an old iron ship lying on its side, half-buried in the sand, its coral-covered deckworks clearly discernible but invisible from a topside view. Boats must have passed over it a thousand times, but its position and the camouflage that time and tides had disguised it with, had made it just another section of the rolling bottom of the ocean.

It was too much for their curiosity. It was something that had to be seen a little closer. The fear of their pursuers was suddenly lost when they were under the overhang of the deck and could look up at the place where sailors once stood.

"How big do you think it is, Larry?"

Not all of the vessel was uncovered, but from the slope of her hull he was able to generalize as to the length. "A hundred eighty feet maybe. About an average size ship for those days."

"Would a ship this size have sailed this close to shore?"

"Only accidentally," Larry said quietly.

Josh caught the odd tone in his voice and his eyes searched for an answer.

"The ship wasn't under control," Larry told him. "There was a mutiny on board, they were drifting and when the boilers blew, it went down away from the regular shipping channel."

"How do you know this, Larry?"

Larry kicked at the coral that covered most of the old steel nameplate that was fastened to the top of what was the pilothouse. Part of the engraved "E" was visible, and when a large plate of coral calcium dropped loose, the word *"Belle"* stood out large and clear. "Under the sand is the rest of the name, Josh. We're looking at the wreck of the *Nantucket Belle!"*

Josh's face was a mask of astonishment. "You mean ... the one your father. . . ?"

Larry nodded. "The *real* treasure ship. The one that salvaged the gold and jewels from the *San Simon* so many years ago."

Silently, they stood there a minute: then Josh said, "When the sea went out it sucked all the sand from this almost-upside-down ship."

A funny little grin crossed Larry's mouth. "And when it comes back it might fill it up again."

"Maybe the sand will cover it so we'll never find it again."

"That's right," Larry agreed, "so maybe we ought to take a look inside while we have the chance."

"Do you . . . think it will be safe?"

"We'll have to be very careful."

But the closer they got, the more they began to regret their decision. There was something eerie about that old ship. Somewhere on board would be the bones of men who had gone down with her, and the others who were killed in the fight over the great riches not one of them ever got. There were sea creatures who made homes in the crusty caverns of old wrecks and some could still be hiding in the dark, wet corners of the hulk, terrified by the change in their surroundings and ready to attack anything that moved.

But it was something they had to do. Larry and his father had searched long and hard to locate this very ship and here was an opportunity to explore it under conditions that might never occur again. *If only his dad were here, Larry thought.* For a second his mind flicked back to the Jimson brothers and he mentally computed the time lapse between them. If he and Josh hurried, he figured, they could cover a good section of any interior that was exposed and get out with plenty of time to make it to shore. If they were lucky, they might even find the treasure!

Larry never figured it for a vain thought at all. He never considered that the treasure could have been scattered all over the ocean in the violence of the sinking, nor the possibility that hundreds of tons of sand might still cover it somewhere deep within the bowels of the hull. He was so full of the adventure and enthusiasm only young boys know that he completely dismissed all ideas of danger or failure and laughed out loud. He and Josh climbed up the rise of sand that led to the vacant windows of the pilothouse and wriggled inside its barely lighted interior.

Neither of them noticed the long, wet fingers of sand that were beginning to develop behind them, snaking around the hillocks, reaching out and growing, seeming to follow underground paths of new rivers.

When their eyes became accustomed to the gloom they took a good look around them. At first, it was difficult to realize where they were; not having any outside reference, they seemed to be sticking out from the wall of the pilothouse.

Larry knew what vertigo was and explained it to Josh. "Don't worry about what it looks like . . . just figure that whatever you're standing on is the bottom no matter which way the ship is tilted."

"I feel like a fly on the ceiling," Josh replied. He looked up at the way the brass binnacle and the crusted ship's wheel were pointed down at him from an angle.

Small pieces of old wreckage were sticking out of the

sand ... the remains of a stool, part of the iron framework from a window and a twisted and bent brass megaphone. The boys realized there was no time to look for souvenirs and when they made certain the area was devoid of anything important, they clambered out again, got on the topside of the pilothouse, worked their way aft, then dropped to a stanchion, where they stood long enough to get their bearings.

It was strange walking along a ship that was lying on its side. And even more than on its side, because the deck itself was covering them and they had a feeling that if they let go, they'd sail off into the sky. But the sensation finally cured itself and they went from one foothold to another until they had crossed the forward deck area and were standing on the raised housing amidships, looking down into smashed and open portholes.

Inside, it looked gloomier than ever and a chill swept over both boys when the thought of entering faced them. Oh, it wouldn't be any trouble to get inside at all. Right beside them the bulkhead door was twisted open and rusted solidly in that gaping position, an invitation for anyone who had the nerve to enter.

Ragged edges of metal projected out of the framework that had held the door, eroded into gnarled, deadly points. "This ship," Josh said, "looks like she wants to eat us."

"Scared?"

Josh nodded. "You?"

"I sure am," Larry said, "but if we don't go in, later I'll be more mad than I am scared."

"You're crazy, you know?"

"Aren't we both?"

"Sure looks like it. My father, man, right now he'd be telling me to forget this crazy thing and get out fast."

Larry shrugged, walked over and squatted down

beside the open door in the bulkhead. "There's just about enough light left to make a quick search."

"Then let's hurry," Josh said.

Larry took a deep breath, then gently let himself ease down into the opening, careful of the steel teeth on either side of him. When he dropped off into the sand he stepped aside and watched while Josh's figure was framed in the open door a moment before landing beside him.

They had expected an unusual quiet in this weird underwater tomb, but it wasn't so at all. The wind was making shrill whistling noises passing across holes where rivets had popped out of the hull. Strange crackling sounds of hard shells brushing together made them take note that this was an *inhabited* place. Things were here, hiding in darkness and lurking just under the sand...things with needlelike points and harsh, crushing claws.

"I wish we had a flashlight, Josh."

"Me ... I wish we were home." Josh half-tripped over something partially buried in the sand, reached down and extracted an old, blackened copper pot with a two-foot handle. "It isn't much, but in case we need a weapon ..."

"Against what?"

"Whatever lives here," Josh said. "Tell me, where are we on this ship?"

"Some sort of a stateroom or saloon. The *Nantucket Belle* was fitted to carry passengers and this would have been their dining area. If we go aft a little, there should be a stairwell going to the quarters below . . . only in this case, we won't be going down at all. . . we'll be going parallel to the bottom."

"You're thinking of something, aren't you?"

Larry nodded. Finally he said, "If there was any treasure, it would have been kept under guard by the Captain. Now ... when the crew staged that mutiny it had to be an attack on the officers, but the ship blew up so fast it's doubtful if anybody ever laid hands on the treasure."

"Then ... the Captain would have it in his cabin?"

"Or some other strongroom."

"We shall see, Larry. But let's hurry."

The stairwell was right where Larry had expected it to be and he was grateful that the ship was lying the way it was. The wooden steps had long ago been eaten away by teredo worms, and the two boys made their way toward the lower deck by simply walking along the steel wall.

Light was filtering down, making it brighter than they expected, but it wasn't until they reached the vertical barrier—actually the floor of the deck below—that they knew what caused it. The separation in the hull where the force of the boiler explosion had ripped the steel plates apart was letting the sunlight in. Ordinarily the opening wouldn't be visible at all, the weed barrier that grew upright in the sea water hiding the huge gap completely. But now the grass hung against the steel, damp and limp, outlining a jagged skylight.

"We're in luck again, Josh. We can see."

"I hope we like what we see," Josh said. "This isn't too good." He was indicating the evenly spaced holes in the "floor" ahead of them.

"Those are stateroom doors," Larry explained. "Don't forget, we're standing on the wall now."

After taking a good look, Josh asked, "Most of this ship is buried under the sand, isn't it?"

"I think so," Larry said glumly.

"Then if there is no sand inside, and we can find a way to get down farther, we'll really be far below the bottom of the sea, is that so?"

"Yeah, you're right, but don't plan on doing it. This old steel hull could still hold water, so even if there's no sand, we're inside a big basin of water."

"And no SCUBA gear," Josh said, grinning.

"Aren't we lucky," Larry laughed back. "Come on, let's see what we can find."

They had to help each other into the first two compartments, then stand until their eyes accepted the deeper gloom. Both places held the obvious remains of brass beds and scraps of what appeared to have been hand luggage. The walls and floor, being of steel, were still intact although well rusted and, in most places, coral-encrusted.

To get in the third compartment, both of them had to sit on the wall and kick at the door with their feet until the latch broke and the light metal door creaked on its hinges and slowly was driven back until there was room for the boys to drop down inside.

In this place there was no sand at all. Broken pieces of furniture were still recognizable for what they were and the broken bed lay piled in a corner. From the ruined door above, the filtered light came down with that strange orange glow and the boys were about to dismiss the place as being empty.

They turned, got ready to reach for the sill over-head . . . and they both froze with a sudden terror. They were being watched! From the murky shadows two grinning skulls were gaping at them, lying in a scattered pile of bones that hadn't moved since they had fallen there, the skeleton outlines of the bodies partially hidden under scraps of leather or heavy cloth, the bony hands of each still clutching the hilt of an old cutlass.

When he could talk, Josh said, "One must have been a mutineer. They fought to the death."

"But the bones . . . they're not disturbed."

"The door was closed on them, but there was no wave action and no sea life to bother them."

"But. . . shouldn't we have seen other . . . remains?"

"Nothing lasts long underwater. Nothing that once was alive, anyway."

Larry took the copper pot from Josh and pushed it among the wreckage, but there was nothing of importance at all, so he indicated that they should get back in the passageway again.

With a lift up, Josh grabbed the sill and hauled himself out of the room, then lay on his stomach

and grabbed Larry's outstretched hand. A quick pull while Larry pushed against the doorjamb and they were on their feet.

Now there was a more somber mood to the moment. Never before had either of the boys seen the bones of dead men and knowing they were likely to find even more made their bodies draw tight with nervous tension. In a way, as with the old submarine they had discovered, they were again at a tomb. No. . . not *at* but *in* it, with the dead of all those years ago.

Neither of them wanted to show anxiety, so Larry suggested they try the rest of the rooms off the hall and call it quits if they didn't find anything. Josh went along with the idea and they didn't waste any time. Getting back under the open sky was something to look forward to.

There was another room closed shut, but this time they couldn't open the door far enough to squeeze through. From what they could see, it was no different from the others, and if there were any relics of dead bodies in there, they were out of sight.

It was the last room that was different. It was twice as large as the others, the midwall being gone, so that the room went across to where it opened into the opposite corridor. Only in this case, the other corridor wasn't really *across* any more ... it was down, and in the dim light the boys could see the gleam of water below them.

"This could have been the Captain's quarters," Larry said.

"No good," Josh reflected.

"Why not?"

"The crew would have broken in and looted it."

"Think so?" Larry asked. "Look at the door again. See those dents in the metal?" He indicated at least a dozen four-inch scars on the panel, and in at least two cases the ends of the dents had opened into the metal. "Somebody used an ax trying to break in."

"How do you know they didn't?"

"Because we had to kick that rusted latch open to get in ourselves."

"Do you think..."

Larry shrugged. "We'll have to find out."

For a minute the boys thought it was a lost cause; then Josh suggested, "Those old beds back there, Larry. They had fronts and backs like a ladder. They weren't rusted, so they must have been made of brass...."

"Right! We could hook them together and ... Come on, let's get them!"

They were so enthused by the project that everything else left their minds. It didn't take long at all to get out the metal sections of the beds and arrange a make-shift ladder by hooking the frames together. When they were sure the arrangement would hold their weight, they grinned at each other with pleasure and Josh, being lighter, let himself down first.

What neither of them noticed was that the sun's rays were shifting and it wasn't as light as it had been, and more time had passed since they entered the hull of the *Nantucket Belle* than they thought.

CHAPTER NINE

AT FIRST BUD Jimson figured the kids had taken a wrongly angled path and would cut back north and he and Joie could save time by shortcutting the route. There shouldn't have been any reason at all why the kids would want to climb over that big mound off to the left. He was all ready to follow his plan when something about that mound made him look twice. He didn't have to do it again.

"What is it, Bud?"

He pointed. "What do you see there?"

"Only a . . ." Joie started to say. Then: "That's a ship!"

"We almost missed it."

"But..."

"See where the tracks go, Joie?"

His brother frowned and nodded; then he looked up, grinning evilly. "We got 'em, Bud. We sure got 'em good, all buttoned up inside a dead ship."

Bud's grin was just as evil. "Now we can make 'em part of a dead crew . . . and no way anybody's ever gonna find what happened to 'em."

They were terrified, all of them. Most were half-way up to their knees in wet sand, barely able to walk, and the whole ocean bottom to the east was starting to glisten. Miles away the setting sun was doing a sparkling dance off something very familiar to them and nobody had to tell them what was happening.

The sea was returning!

Gone were the pieces of junk they had scrounged out of the pile of ballast rock and rotted timbers that had been the *San Simon*. Nothing was of value that would drag them deeper into the sand. Without exception, all were clawing their way toward that distant spot on the horizon that was Ara Island, hoping they would make it in time. A quarter-mile ahead the bottom still showed itself to be dry, and if they could only get that far, their chances would improve.

On the side of the wreck, Jake Skiddo and Petey Betts were trying to right the dune buggy. They shoved and heaved, finally getting it back on its wheels again, and they clambered aboard. Petey gave Jake a dirty look and said, "You watch what you're doing, y'hear?"

"Oh, shut up and hang on."

Jake hit the gas, and with a jolting rush the buggy jounced down the pile of rocks, hit the bottom, and the mud cleats clawed for traction. For a few seconds it didn't look as though they were going to make it; then the buggy pushed loose and began a crawl toward Ara, gradually picking up speed as it went. They passed a few of the others that were fighting through the sand but ignored their pleas for a ride. All they were concerned about were their own skins and nothing was going to stop them.

Nothing, that is, except a sinkhole in the soft sand. One second they were riding. The next they were splashing their way out of the sand-soupy puddle that was swallowing the dune buggy. Bitter about their luck, they joined the others, wading mightily toward shore to keep from being gobbled up by an angry sea.

From the chopper, Vincent Damar could see the silvery sheen of the Atlantic, the sun glinting off it like diamonds. They were at five thousand feet and the sky was brighter here than at ground level, with less of that strange orange tint.

Occasionally they passed over small boats that had been left stranded on the bottom, their captains and mates still with them. Most were chartered fishing boats and they were too far off shore for their crews to attempt a walk back. Apparently they were simply awaiting a return of the ride to float them and as long as they still had radio contact, they weren't too worried.

The pilot of the chopper was in constant communication with ships at sea and the Coast Guard base and as far as could be determined, there still was no damage. Ships lying well offshore had already recorded a four-foot rise in depth from their lowest point and the coastline cities were breathing with relief in the northern sectors because the basins were filling up and very little damage had been experienced anywhere.

But farther south the question was still unanswered. The oceanography services were being canvased to get their opinion, but as yet none was forthcoming.

Although the ocean had receded quickly and passively to the north, in the south it could sweep back with a rush that could destroy anything in its path. There was no way anyone could form an opinion, for what everyone was seeing was something that hadn't happened before in the written history of America.

Vincent Damar kept watching below, eyes anxiously searching the east where the sea lurked, coming back at a still undetermined speed. The bottom was uneven, so the major depths would be filled in first without too much forward motion, but when the bottom leveled off and the sea reached the shelf, that forward motion could be increased a hundred-fold. There was just no way of telling what it was going to do.

The pilot reached over and tapped Vincent on the shoulder, then pointed ahead toward the horizon. "Peolle Island." he said. "We'll be there in twenty-five minutes."

"Any radio from the island at all?"

"None."

Vincent Damar looked at his hands. They were knotted into tight fists. There wasn't any doubt about it in his mind at all. . . his son was somewhere on that vast reach of wet sand, and getting ready to engulf him was that shiny, silvery ocean in the background.

The boys took a deep breath of relief. The water around their feet was only about four inches deep. When they had dropped from their makeshift ladder they had only been able to guess at the distance and had figured no more than a foot. Had it been any more, they would have had trouble reaching the ladder to get back out again.

The rubble of the room lay about their feet, rotted wood and more metal, rusted and bent out of shape. But not all the metal was indistinguishable. Josh saw a handle projecting from the silt, worked it loose and came up with a cry of triumph. "A mug, Larry ... look, it's silver!"

Larry took it from him, turned it over and rubbed some of the muck off its surface. "It's silver, all right. Luckily it was stuck there alone. If it had been in contact with any other metal it would have oxidized."

"Like that clump of metal we found on the beach . . . the one that used to be silver coins?"

"Exactly." Under the heel of his hand Larry could feel lines on the mug and scrubbed a little harder. After a minute he held it in the fading light and studied what he saw. "We're in the Captain's cabin, that's for sure. This was his cup. Look at this."

His finger underlined the printed *"Captain Henry Logan, Nantucket Belle."*

And as though that were a hidden signal, both the boys felt a cold, clammy sensation and looked to their left. The skull was near what had once been a metal table. It was grinning like the others, although nothing was funny at all. Around the bony forehead was a metal band that used to be part of a cap, still attached to it the brass insignia of master's rank. A small salt water crayfish was crawling out of one empty eye socket, waving its antennae in the air.

And the Captain himself was there to greet them, the remnants of two pistols still lying there among the bones of his hands.

"He was waiting for them to break his door down," Larry said.

"But the sea got them all," Josh added. He tore his eyes away from the gleaming skull, peering into the gloom of the room's corners. "Could there be anything here?"

"It'll be on the bottom if there is. Why don't you take one side and I'll take the other. See what we can find."

Two minutes later they met at the forward wall. "Nothing," Josh said. "How about you?"

Larry was about to shake his head, then stopped. "Look at this." He wiped at what had looked like a plain wall panel.

"What is it?"

"A door." He saw Josh's surprised look and added, "Don't forget, we're standing on the *wall*. This part of the door is its *bottom*."

"Crazy, man."

"Give me a hand. Let's see if we can get it open."

It didn't take much prying. The handle of the copper pot Josh had kept with him made short work of the latch, and their feet did the rest of it. The door flew off, breaking at the hinges, clattering noisily across the room. Inside was a small area, piled with pieces of what once had been boxes of tools still recognizable heaped where they had fallen when the ship went down.

Even now, there was so much loose debris under their feet that the boys could hardly walk. "What is that stuff, Larry?"

"Beats me." Larry bent down, scooped up a couple of golf-ball-sized objects and said, "One's a hunk of coal. The other looks like a rock."

"Coal? In here?"

There was just enough light seeping in for them to see it, a section of the side that was decking when the ship had been upright having been wrenched loose and bent out. "The boiler explosion," Larry explained. "It blew coal from the bunkers right through the wall." He tossed the chunk of coal back and stuck the other rock in his pocket. I'll keep this souvenir with the other rocks in my tropical fish aquarium."

"You got more rocks in there now than you need."

Gently, they picked their way forward, stepping carefully. Then Josh tripped, nearly fell and caught himself just in time.

"Trouble?"

Josh shook his head and reached down to his feet. He let his hands run across the objects that he had stumbled over, then drew back as if they were hot. "Larry . . . come here."

"What have you got?"

"Feel here . . . at my feet."

Larry's hands went under the water; then he touched the smooth, cold oblong objects, moved one, finally got it tilted enough to get his fingers under it, then came up slowly, the small object a massive weight in his hands.

They didn't have to be told what it was. Even after

having been under water all those years, the yellow sheen was still there. Nothing else that small could have weighed that much . . . and in Larry' s hands was the wealth of a lifetime.

With the same breath, the boys said, *"Gold!"*

They had found the treasure!

But the excitement of their discovery faded to nothing compared with the incredible terror that came with the sound behind them, a harsh metallic sound they both recognized at once. As though it were nothing but junk, Larry threw the gold bullion down and they scrambled for the door of the room. They made it together, just in time to see their "ladder" being pulled up out of sight.

They had found gold, all right, but the Jimsons had found them! They knew it when they heard Bud's harsh laughter and the stupid giggle from his brother, Joie.

For a stunned second all the boys could imagine was that they were trapped, sealed in a dead ship with dead men they would soon join. Only now did they realize the time they had used and sense how low the sun was by the dim light.

Above them they could hear the feet of the Jimson brothers treading the steel, heading forward. There were no more tracks to follow. They had ended at the *Nantucket Belle* and once more that nasty laugh rang through the tomb of the ship like a hollow echo.

"Larry..." Josh was looking down at his legs. The water wasn't inches deep any more. It was closer to his knees now.

"The sea is coming back in," Larry said.

"We could float out," Josh suggested.

"By then it will be dark. No . . . we have to get out now or we'll never make it."

"I'm afraid, my friend, that it won't be. There's no way

we can reach that door up there, not even if I stood on your shoulders."

"But there's a way, pal."

Josh looked at him hopefully. "Where?"

"The next room," Larry said. "You know that hole the explosion blew in . . . where the coal came from?"

"It goes into the next room ... the one we already explored."

"You can get through, Josh. You're small enough."

Suddenly it dawned on him what Larry was suggesting. "No! Larry, without you ..."

"Don't be stupid, Josh. If I can't get out at least you might be able to find something to help get me up, understand?"

The logic of it calmed Josh down and he nodded his agreement. Together, they went back to the small room, shoved their way to the rip in the plating; then Larry helped Josh up. He had to twist and squirm, but he made the other side. "Try it, Larry," Josh said. "You might make it."

"It's pretty small, Josh."

"Try it anyway! Here, give me your hand." He felt Larry's fingers lace around his wrist and hung on. He could see the effort his friend was putting out, the way he was trying to force himself through the narrow opening. The metal had already scraped Larry's skin and for a minute it didn't look as though he was going to make it, but with one last effort, flattening himself as much as possible, with Josh hauling on his arm, Larry broke through the slot and lay gasping for breath in front of Josh.

There wasn't time to waste gathering strength. They had to use what they had left. Someplace above them, the Jimson brothers would be plotting the position of the *Nantucket Belle* and they would have to get away from them unnoticed. The sand was dry enough outside, the hillocks getting smaller, so they would be fair game if they were chased by the larger men. No . . . now it would be stealth that counted . . . if they were lucky.

Unlike on their entry, this time the boys made as little noise as possible. They picked their way back carefully and when they reached the end of the corridor, the voices of the Jimsons came to them. Quietly, the boys edged back into the large saloon compartment, spotted the Jimson brothers and held themselves motionless until the men moved on past their position.

When they were sure they were clear, Larry and Josh squirmed through a section that had been wrenched out, stood there looking down, then made the eight-foot jump into the damp sand. Except for the *whoosh* of their breath when they landed, there was no noise at all. Larry nodded for Josh to follow him, scuttled forward on all fours, got to the end of the ship and took one last look around.

He knew the Jimsons were close, all right, but at that moment they weren't to be seen.

"Now!" Larry whispered, and both boys took off in a fast sprint, heading toward Peolle Island as fast as their feet could carry them. The sand was still firm and the going flat and straight. Ahead was another small hillock and if they reached it, the protection might just be high enough to shield them for another hundred yards or so. All Larry knew was that they needed a distance of at least two football fields between them and the Jimsons to keep from being caught.

Right then there was *one* football-field length between them . . . and that was all they were getting. They heard Joie Jimson's voice bellow out, "Bud ... there they go . . . they're getting away!"

And Bud's coarse holler right behind him, "Get them . . . chase them, you dumbhead! We can't let them reach Peolle!"

Joie was closer than his brother and his feet were plowing against the sand as he took huge strides toward his quarry. "They won't get away," he called back.

Larry took a quick look over his shoulder. His heart sank and try as he could his legs wouldn't go any faster. Joie was right. He was fresher and quicker. They weren't going to get away after all. He could almost feel Joie's hand closing around his neck.

VINCENT DAMAR RAN from the chopper, shielding his face against the blinding sand the rotors threw up, and the chopper moved up and away. When it was clear, Vincent spotted the house and got there as quickly as he could.

His worst fears were realized. The house was empty. There was no note—nothing to tell him what had happened. Just a missing son who had given in to childish curiosity and roamed off into the unknown.

For Vincent it was the end of everything ... his son lost to him, the boat gone, all his savings wiped out. He looked toward the still-empty ocean with dull eyes. Nothing was moving out there. Nothing at all. Another few minutes and darkness would close in, the sea not far behind.

Idly he flipped the radio on and set it to his common frequency. Steve Percy over on Ara was on the mike, talking fast to someone on the beach. Half of the bunch who had gone out on the ocean bottom that day were already back and the other half were in sight, struggling against the wet sand. Some of the stragglers still a half-mile out were being helped back, their strength gone from the effort of wading through the muck. There were no casualties except a lot of bitterness and hard feelings and some kid named Oliver Creighton was having a fit because Jake Skiddo and Petey Betts had lost his dune buggy.

If the strong could barely make it, Vincent thought, how could a kid?

"Sar. . ."

Vincent heard the voice without realizing it was there.

It came again. "Sar?"

He spun around, startled, until he recognized Timothy, Josh's father. "Come on in, Tim."

"Thank you." There was a fear in his eyes. "Have you seen Larry?"

Vincent sensed what was coming. "No."

"He and Josh were together."

With a horrible sense of foreboding, they both looked out toward the sea.

"It has them, Vincent," Tim said.

Vincent put his arms around his friend's shoulder, leading him to a chair. Just for something to do he filled the coffeepot and put it on the stove. There wasn't much anticipation in his voice when he said, "All we can do is wait, Tim."

"Josh is so little."

"So is Larry, but they're smart."

"The sea is smarter," Tim said.

"All we can do is wait."

They were tiring now, their breath like fire in their chests, legs pulling as if they had weights attached to them. Behind them the Jimsons were shouting to each other, their voices coming closer and closer. Peolle was still a good mile away, a dull smudge on the horizon with the wild orange sun sinking down behind it. Even the chill in the air didn't help them, nor the ocean that was coming in so fast that you could smell its saltiness.

Another thirty seconds and the Jimsons would have their hands on them and it was hardly worth-while running any longer. For a brief second both the boys wanted to give up completely; then they both saw the same thing at the same time.

Directly ahead of them was that long, narrow trench they had had to cross that morning, the one with the deadly occupant who was trapped in that Channel, the one who would respond to any sound and motion he could feel and tear it apart with mad predator teeth.

It was either the Jimsons or the shark and their only chance lay with that gruesome monster whose speed was incredible and whose aim would be perfect in the trap of that narrow valley in the ocean's floor. But if they could get across it before the shark reached them . . .

And it was that single thought that lent wings to their feet, so that for the last few yards the Jimsons didn't gain on them at all. With one final, great leap the boys dove headlong into the trench, their arms flailing with a last, desperate effort. They could almost feel the vibrations of the shark's charge; then their feet hit the incline on the other side and they were clambering up it as fast as possible while Bud's voice was shrieking hoarsely at Joie and when they looked back, Bud was holding onto his brother in near panic on the opposite bank while their eyes bugged out at the sight of a fifteen-foot shark waiting directly below for them.

Across the trench, Larry and Josh were trotting away, knowing that there was no way the Jimsons could catch them now. All they had to do was beat out the return of the sea. The Jimsons knew it too. They knew they'd never be able to get back to Ara again without facing a prison sentence. Now, the only thing open to them was getting back to where their boat lay on its side in the wet sand. If they hurried, they might make it. After that it would be some dirty little village in some remote, forgotten island.

Vincent and Timothy heard the shouts from the beach

and with a yell of pure joy they ran out side by side. There was so much hugging and backslapping that the boys couldn't get a word in, so they waited until after they had eaten and everybody had settled down before they began their story.

Outside, the sea had returned, not violently but as quietly as it had left, seeping up from the bottom and rolling in on the tide from the west. It was well into the night when all the questions had been asked and the answers given; then Larry had one of his own to ask. "But Dad," he said, "isn't there some way we can get to that treasure ship?"

"Sorry, son, but you never triangulated the position. It might take a long time to find it again."

"Not if you had the equipment..."

"That takes money, Larry, a lot of money. We haven't got it any longer. Now we have to give up the island . . . everything . . . and by the time I could get another stake, who knows what would have happened to the *Nantucket Belle?* Believe me, if I could finance an expedition, all of us would be rich, even the people on Ara. Between the artifacts on the *San Simon,* that old submarine and the *Belle* herself, this would be one prosperous area indeed."

"Too bad," Josh said.

"Too bad what?" Larry asked him.

"Too bad we didn't bring home one of those gold bars we found."

Larry let out a laugh. "That sure would have been great all right, but at least we came close. *We felt* the stuff." He reached in his pocket and brought out his rock. "And at least I have a souvenir. I hope my tropical fish enjoy it."

"What is it?" his father asked.

"Just a crazy-looking rock that was in that room." He

tossed it to his father, who held the golf-ball-sized rock between his thumb and forefinger.

Vincent spun it around, looking at it casually and was about to toss it back when suddenly he frowned, looked at it closer, then ran to his desk and pulled out a magnifying glass and studied the specimen carefully.

For some reason everyone in the room was strangely silent, as if waiting for something tremendous to happen. There was an electrical tingle touching all of them and as Vincent Damar's eyes began to light up, the tingling got even stronger.

Then he began to laugh. He laughed until the tears were rolling down his cheeks and the others were laughing too, even though they didn't know what they were laughing at.

Finally words came to young Larry and he said, "For pete's sake, Dad, what's the big joke?"

Vincent Damar wiped his eyes and put Larry's "rock" in the middle of the table. He looked at each boy in turn, then winked with pleasure at Timothy, telling him to get ready to be real proud of his son.

"Larry," he said, "that crazy rock of yours *is one of the biggest uncut diamonds in the world!*"

And they all started to laugh again. . . easily at first, then harder and harder . . . and kept it up until they thought they would never stop.

THE SHIP THAT
NEVER WAS

CHAPTER ONE

THE OLD MAN was a gaunt wreck, barely able to speak. The sun had leathered his skin and his mouth was a dry, parched thing, moving slowly, speaking without being able to be heard.

Larry and Josh pulled the old gray skiff all the way up on the sand and Josh said, "I'll get some water."

Larry nodded and looked back at the man they had just dragged out of the sea. "Take it easy, my friend. You'll be all right."

The man tried to smile, but his face was weathered tight and the skin tightened on his face. When Josh came back with the thermos of water from their boat, Larry let it dribble into the man's mouth slowly, then wet his face and hair.

Appreciatively, the man nodded and his voice croaked out a sound.

"What did he say?" Josh asked.

"I think he said thanks."

The occupant of the old skiff blinked, acknowledging. He took another sip of water, let the boys wet him down again, then smiled slowly and fell asleep.

As gently as they could, Larry Damar and Josh Toomey lifted the old man from the bottom of the wooden boat and wrapped him in the blankets from their own craft.

One hour ago they had been out on a leisurely cruise in the *Sea Eagle* with nothing on their minds when they spotted what they had thought to be a deserted boat floating low in the water.

Josh had said, "Hey, look at that over there."

"It's some kind of a boat."

"And it's sinking."

"Josh," Larry had said, "I think it's already sunk."

"Only halfway." Josh laughed. "Should we pull it in?"

"You want an old wreck?"

"That thing has pretty good lines on it. I bet your dad could tell us what it was modeled after."

"Maybe." Larry grinned. "Let's go look."

The skiff was old and it was sinking, but it had an occupant whose eyes looked at theirs and they had brought the boat to shore. Now they were fifty miles away from civilization with the survivor of an unknown wreck and they weren't quite sure what to do.

It took quite a while, but they made the old man as comfortable as they could, slinging him on a canvas hammock made from their motor cover, with a shade of palm fronds to keep the sun from him. When they were sure he was asleep, they went back to the skiff they had found him in and reread the name printed on it.

H.M.S. *TIGER,* it read, in faded black with a red-and-gold border. "This can't be real," Larry said.

"What does it mean?"

"The initials stand for *His Majesty's Ship,* but the British haven't made wooden boats like this for oceangoing ships in ... well, a couple of hundred years."

"But it's only a skiff," Josh insisted.

Larry walked around it, studying its size and construction. It was an oaken lapstrake job, with cedar ribs and remnants of pine seats. In the bow, an open copper water cask had a green patina on its surface, and the forged iron fittings of the rudder were pitted and rusted with age.

"This isn't a skiff," Larry told his friend. "It's what they called a 'longboat,' a working utility boat they kept on the decks of galleons."

Josh seemed a little incredulous. "Larry ... don't tell me this ... this longboat has been floating around with that old man in it for a couple of hundred years."

"Not likely. You notice something funny?"

"What?" "

"No wormholes. If this *had* been in the water any length of time, the teredo worms would have eaten it up."

"But it *had* to be left in the water. The seams leak, but not all that much." Josh paused and looked at his friend quizzically. "Unless it's been in fresh water."

"Here in the Caribbean?"

"Then what do you suggest?"

After a few moments' thought, Larry said, "They used to make movies down this way. Oh, the ships they used for British ships of the line and Spanish galleons were all converted from more modern hulls, but smaller boats like this would have been duplicated almost exactly."

Both of them fingered the aged wood, examining the cracks in the close grain and the warped ridges of the joints. Josh grinned slowly and said, "You don't really believe that, do you?"

Larry felt silly, but he shook his head. "No."

Then he let out a chuckle and added, "Maybe our passenger can give us some information."

But that didn't seem likely, not for many hours anyway. The boys managed to have him drink a little more water, but the old man went back to sleep immediately afterward. "I think we'll be camping out here tonight," Josh said.

Larry nodded. "I'll go radio Dad on Peolle Island and he can get the word over to your place."

"Should we call for help for the old man?"

"It would be dark by the time anybody got here," Larry replied. "Besides, he seems to be okay. Pretty worn out, but not in serious condition. Tomorrow we'll move him back to Peolle ourselves."

"What about his boat?" Josh asked.

"I have an idea that old boat is important somehow. Let's rig up a tow on it and get it back."

"You think it will stay in one piece?"

"Well, it has so far ... and it looks like pretty sturdy equipment."

"Larry...?"

"Yeah?"

"You remember those funny feelings I used to get when something strange was going to happen?"

Larry let out a grunt and said, "Look, how many times do I have to tell you that . . ."

But Josh cut him off. "My friend, you are a main-lander and I am an islander. We think different ways. In Miami, you were at home. Here, I am at home."

"Okay," Larry grinned, "I remember your funny feelings."

"Good, because I have them again."

Getting their survivor aboard the *Sea Eagle* wasn't as easy as the boys expected. Even as frail as he was, the old man was difficult to handle, but using their canvas and ropes, they managed to hoist him to the back deck and make him comfortable.

All this time he had kept his left arm pressed closely to his chest, and until they had him in the deck chair, they thought he had been injured. But in this new position, they realized what he was doing: Under the tattered rag of a shirt, he was pressing an old, dried-out leather purse against his ribs. When Larry went to move it, the old man's eyes filled with terror.

He made some guttural sounds, said some faint words in protest, and Larry smiled to show him no harm would be done and pulled a blanket around him.

"What did he say?" Josh asked.

"Beats me. It sounded like a foreign language."

"That last time he spoke ... when he said thanks . . ."

"I said I *think* he said thanks. It wasn't what he said, but the way he said it. He sounded grateful."

"He sure thinks a lot of whatever's in that leather folder," Josh remarked.

"Probably all of his possessions."

"Yeah. Well, we better get going if we want to get home by evening. I put a snubber on the tow-line back there to ease the strain on the nylon. Now, if that boat just holds together ..."

"Only one way we'll find out," Larry said. He threw the clutch lever to forward, eased the throttle on, and pulled away from the beach. In their wake, Josh hauled the boat forward until it was riding the second wave. It held its position perfectly and Josh tied it in place.

Together, the boys watched it riding proudly back there, the water peeling back from its prow. They were both thinking the same thing ... that long-boat *could* be old and it *could* be hiding a great secret, but they didn't build boats like that anymore.

Vincent Damar and Timothy Toomey made sure the old man was in satisfactory condition and asleep before they made coffee and looked out at their sons, who were pulling the longboat up above the high-water mark.

"What I can't understand," Vincent said, "is how two

kids like them can get involved in so many unusual circumstances."

"They are curious, my friend. You, me ... well, we might have figured that boat for a derelict and never have bothered to look inside it."

"At least this time it was a simple rescue and not something that sets the entire Caribbean on its ear."

"You never can tell, Vincent."

"What's that supposed to mean?"

Timothy nodded toward their sleeping guest. "We still don't know who he is. His language ... so strange. Do you know it?"

A frown creased Vincent's brow and he chewed his lip a moment. "There's something strange about it. . . and something mighty familiar too."

"Have you heard it before?"

"I don't know, Tim. It seems like I have, but I can't tell where."

"Those papers ... the ones in the old leather case ..."

"From the edges I saw, it's very old parchment. They are handwritten documents done with a split quill point, but unless I examine them carefully, there's no way I can tell what language they're in."

"I wish I had your education, my friend."

"You have," Vincent told him, "but your education is in the ways of the island. Look at how much I've learned from you."

"We all learn from each other." He paused a second, then: "How do you plan to learn the old man's identity?"

"There is one way," Vincent said. "We'll wait until he's strong enough to talk, then make a tape recording of him and send it to the Language Institute in Miami. Somebody there will certainly identify it and after that, it's just a case of getting an interpreter here."

"We could sail him there."

"Let's wait until he's awake. We don't know what nationality he is and we sure don't want to cause any immigration problems. What do you say ... let's go take a look at the boat the kids found him in."

An hour later, Vincent Damar was more baffled than ever. Old wooden sailing ships had been a pet project with him for a long time and he was familiar with the merchant and naval vessels from all the major nations of the world.

Now, after a close examination of the antique construction of the boat the boys had towed home, he was absolutely dumbfounded. "There's no doubt about it ... this is a longboat, all right, and it's exactly the same type carried by English naval ships for a good eighty years."

"It's not a copy, Dad?"

"Son, you found yourself an original. Even with aged wood, nobody could make a duplicate like this." He pointed to a few spots in the hull. "See there? Boat-building details like that have been long lost. Why, they don't even make tools to do it like that now."

"We didn't find it, Dad. That old man did."

Vincent was silent a minute, still studying the boat. "I suppose you noticed what's odd about it, didn't you?"

"No wormholes or barnacles?"

"Exactly. And that boat hasn't been lying up out of water either."

"Vincent ..."

"Yes, Tim?"

"There are boats in the island that are over a hundred years old."

"But this one is over two hundred and seventy years old."

"It doesn't seem real."

"Dad . . ." Larry said, "you said they carried these longboats *on board* on those naval vessels, didn't you?"

"That's right."

"Could there be ... could the ship that carried *this* longboat still be in existence?"

"Larry ... why would you ask that?"

"The name on the transom ... H.M.S. *Tiger*. It's barely worn at all. Why, the gold leaf is still intact."

"Son ... there can be reasons that a small boat like this could still be serviceable, but forget about the rest. The *Tiger* ... the mother ship of this longboat. . . is long since gone."

The silence was long and the boys' eyes watched him carefully. Finally Vincent Damar grinned and said, "Okay, kids, you win. We'll photograph this longboat and send a copy to the British Naval Archives and see what they can come up with on the old ship."

Both the boys let out a loud whoop of pleasure and set about finishing the job of chocking the longboat into place. Timothy looked at Vincent, a broad smile on his face, his teeth flashing white in the sunlight. "I am beginning to think that you have a curious streak too."

"I'm beginning to think those kids can talk me into anything," Vincent retorted with a laugh. "But. . . at least it will be fun getting back into some research material again."

"Don't set the Caribbean on its ear, my friend."

"Ha! No way, Timothy. This is nothing more than a wild goose chase."

CHAPTER TWO

EIGHT DAYS after receiving the letter and photographs from Vincent Damar, Sir Harry Arnold, head of the antiquities department of the British Naval Archives, arrived at Peolle Island by helicopter. He carried two bags, one for a small selection of clothes, the other filled with photos, documents, and certain devices for determining the age of wood and metal.

When everyone had been introduced, Sir Harry said, "You have no idea what excitement your photos have caused, Mr. Damar."

"Well, they're not exactly mine, if you recall my letter." He nodded toward his friend Timothy and added, "It was our boys who found the longboat, which was found even earlier by the survivor it carried."

"Ah, yes, and what about that old man?" Sir Harry asked.

"He's better now. Up and beginning to eat well, but we have a communication problem. He speaks a language I don't understand."

"That will make things difficult."

"Not really," Vincent told him. "I sent tapes off to the

Language Institute of Miami and we should be hearing from them shortly. So far, they've been able to sort out just about every native tongue and dialect in the entire Caribbean. In one way we're lucky ... he has some hand-written parchment Information on him that he refuses to let anyone see, but I managed to photograph one corner that held a dozen words. At least we're not dealing with some dead language."

"Sir Harry ..." A pair of youthful faces were looking in the door. "Yes, Larry?"

"You want to look at the longboat?"

"More than anything you can imagine."

"It's all set up for you on the beach."

"Wonderful. Now we'll see what this is all about."

Sir Harry Arnold was an expert in his work and for the next three hours he went over the longboat, examining every detail inside and out. He measured dimensions and curves, matching them against specifications in an official handbook. Metal and wood underwent chemical tests, and the longer he searched for the identity of the old hull, the more concerned he seemed.

When he finally put down his equipment, he turned and looked at the two fathers with their sons, who had gathered to watch him. "Gentlemen," he said, "as far as I can determine, you have in your possession a genuine, original longboat from His Majesty's Ship *Tiger*, a three-masted naval ship of the line mounting forty-eight guns that was built at the Cremington Boatyards, England, in the year 1791."

"Wow," Josh said softly.

"It's in awfully good condition to be that old," Vincent Damar said doubtfully.

"Nevertheless," Sir Harry insisted, "it is an original. I'm not concerned about *how* it stayed this way ... I'm simply overjoyed that it did."

"You have any idea how it could have happened, sir?"

Sir Harry nodded. "Possibly, Larry." He paused, looked back at the longboat, and turned around again.

"At the time this boat was built," Sir Harry started, "England had no shortage of lumber. On her shores were some of the finest and longest-lasting woods for a keel, ribs, planking, masts ... anything necessary for a military ship, and fashioning that wood into British ships were the best workmen in the world."

"Wood, once it's cut, is perishable," Vincent told him.

"True, but with limited use and proper attention, it can last a very long time."

"Sir Harry ... in those years British naval vessels certainly weren't in 'limited use' ... in fact, the British navy was the busiest one in the whole world, especially the galleons."

"Correct again, Mr. Damar." Sir Harry smiled and peered at them over his glasses. "However, with the *Tiger* we must make an exception. Her use was *very* limited."

"The *Tiger* never put to sea?" Larry asked hurriedly.

"Oh, she put to sea, all right. In fact, she put to sea twice. The first time was her maiden, shake-down voyage." He paused and smiled again.

Impatiently, Larry and Josh said the same thing at the same time. "What happened?"

"You Americans have a rather strange saying ... yes, ummm, a law. Murphy's Law, I believe you call it."

Larry looked up at his father, frowning.

Vincent told them all, "Murphy's Law states that no matter what you do, if anything can go wrong, it will." He let out a little laugh at the odd expressions on the faces around him and glanced at Sir Harry. "What's that got to do with the *Tiger?*"

"I'll have to tell the story in my own way," Sir Harry said. "It's a very odd tale, but absolutely true, and I'd be very grateful if you didn't laugh. You see, it has to do with national pride, something we British are quite strong on. And too, there's a degree of superstition involved, plus all the unknowns ..." He stopped and chuckled. "As I mentioned, it's a very strange story indeed."

Under his breath, Larry told Josh, "If he doesn't get on with it, I'm going to pop!"

"When the keel of the *Tiger* was laid, the Cremington Boatyards were, perhaps, the best in all England. Presiding over the construction of His Majesty's ships was Ashford Hampton, the finest shipwright in the land. He had a force of eighty of the most skilled craftsmen at hand, all well experienced in their work, along with the best materials that could be found. Therefore, you see, no one, not even the king, had any reason to doubt that the *Tiger* would be anything but the finest ship afloat.

"I imagine that it was Ashford Hampton himself who felt the twinges of doubt first. Chocks would slip, tools would break, exactly measured parts refused to fit into place. At first, it was little things, annoying things, but as those were overcome, bigger, more irritating things began to happen.

"The Cremington Boatyards had always prided themselves on being able to adhere to a schedule, but with the *Tiger* ... well, this was a different matter entirely. They began to fall behind, first by days, then weeks and months. Ashford Hampton even put on more men, but that didn't help either.

"Finally, six months behind time, the hull was finished and the *Tiger* was ready to be floated and finished while moored to the main dock. That was when the first workman was injured. After that there was one injury after another, and now they were calling the *Tiger* a jinx ship. Everyone was afraid to work on her, and if it hadn't been for Ashford Hampton they all would have left the project. Somehow he appealed to their pride and they kept on the job ... but one thing they kept to themselves was the fact that they considered the *Tiger* to be carrying a built-in jinx it would never lose, and anyone sailing on her would have nothing but bad luck.

"Now, at this time, England was the greatest naval power in the world, and she needed ships, ships, and more ships. The king himself grew insistent that the *Tiger* be finished, and despite the fear of the jinx, they hurried the job, and at long last she was done and fitted, guns installed, and a crew drawn to man her. Oh, it was a great day when she sailed downstream to the mouth of the river and headed out to sea. It was to be a journey of three months to make sure all was in proper working order. Then the *Tiger* would put back to port for a fresh supply of water and food, get her sailing Orders, and be off to some foreign lands."

For a moment, Sir Harry paused, scowling off into the distance. "That maiden voyage only took one month," he said. "It was the worst month in England's history. Abroad, there was nothing but trouble, our ships running into difficulty no matter where they were. In England itself there were great fires and some strange disease that put a quarter of the population in their beds ... and that was when those men who worked on the *Tiger* mentioned the jinx ship.

"That being a time when believing in superstition was common, you can imagine how the people reacted. The story spread like wildfire until all England was blaming everything that went wrong on the ship the king had sent to sea. In fact, it got so bad that mobs were forming to force the king to send out a squadron of ships to find and sink the *Tiger!*

"Well, he never had to do that, because one day the sails of that jinx ship showed on the horizon, and in came the *Tiger,* her canvas storm-ripped, her crew sick, the captain in his bunk with a broken leg, and a bandaged first officer at the helm.

"There was no noise, no shouting and whistling to welcome her back. There was just a deadly, wide-eyed quiet, with everybody too afraid to speak. When the injured were taken off, the shipyard crew went back on board to survey the damage and couldn't believe what they found. Cannons had split open on their first round. Some had lasted longer, then blown up. The water casks had sprang leaks and all the crew had to drink was rainwater they managed to save. Food had spoiled, water seemed to come into the hull from every seam, and they had to work the pumps constantly to keep the ship afloat. Even the weather went against them. A small squall that never should have bothered them a bit ripped their sails apart.

"My story about the *Tiger* hinges on what happened next. From the minute they took the ship out of action, everything seemed to change. There were no more fires, the sick got better, news from other areas improved, and now all of England seemed to know something special.

"*It was the jinx ship that had caused all the trouble!* The delegation from the city didn't have any trouble getting their petition before the king, or having him sign it. You see, the king was one of those who got sick too, and a nearby fire had almost spread to the palace itself. In fact, as much as he needed ships, he was glad to get this one off his hands.

"The only trouble was how they were going to do it. Nobody wanted to dismantle a jinx ship, and burning it could be dangerous. It was Ashford Hampton who came up with the final idea. You see, he didn't believe in this superstition business one bit, and being a lover of fine boats, he didn't want to see this one destroyed ... especially now, since not one thing had happened to her the past two weeks at the dock. There was no more leakage, the water casks were holding fine, and the new casks and cannon they had installed made the *Tiger* a proud beauty indeed ... but not a beauty the people wanted in their city.

"So ... because they were afraid to offend the jinx that inhabited her, Ashford Hampton and a small crew took her down the river again, set the sails with her prow headed out to sea, lashed the wheel in position, and climbed over the side to their pilot boat. From there they watched the *Tiger* sail west to an unknown fate, fully provisioned, armed to the teeth, a brand-new fighting ship of the line sailing into a setting sun with a ghost crew on a journey no one would ever record in a logbook."

Slowly, Sir Harry turned and looked at the long-boat nestling in its chocks. "Until this moment, gentlemen, the *Tiger* had never been heard from. It was assumed that she had succumbed to the elements and sunk."

Vincent Damar caught Sir Harry's attention. "She *could* have sunk. It isn't unusual for ship's boats to float loose from a sinking ship."

Sir Harry shook his head. "Are you familiar with the old shipboard practices of the British navy?"

"No, sir. I never got into those details."

"Let me tell you then ... the way the longboats were lashed down, there was no way they would have come loose accidentally." He smiled and said, "But we're back to Murphy's Law again, aren't we?"

"How's that?"

"Whatever could go wrong did. We have the *Tiger's* longboat right here with us." There was not much they could add to that, so they just looked at each other and shrugged. "Now ... there is one thing you could do." He looked at the two boys and went on. "You can sell this boat back to the British government. It would make an excellent museum piece."

"It isn't ours,", Larry stated. "You'll have to ask him ... but what can he say? Nobody understands him."

Sir Harry smiled and put his arms around the boys' shoulders. "Well, there's always sign language. What say we go in and speak to the old gent?"

As he watched the three of them go toward the house, Timothy flashed his teeth in a broad, white smile and said, "Vincent, my friend, I have a feeling that your wild goose chase is getting a good start."

Vincent didn't answer him. He was beginning to get that same feeling too.

In Miami Beach, one block east of Biscayne Boulevard on the fifth floor of the Wallace Building, three men were seated at one end of a Conference table, intent upon the voices coming from the tape recorder in front of them. The one operating the machine was short and balding, his skin tanned from the Florida sun. Behind his glasses his eyes were narrow and shifty, greed set deep inside them.

At first glance, the other pair seemed to be well-dressed businessmen, but there was something different about them. For one thing, neither was burned from the sun, and their clothes seemed strangely out of date. Both of them were big, with wide shoulders and powerful hands. The one called Aktur Cilon had a fine red scar down his left cheek, while his friend, Embor Linero, had the first joint of his right pinky finger missing.

When the tape ended, associate language director Herbert Mackley turned off the switch, leaned back, and looked at the two men across from him. "Are you satisfied?" he asked.

"How do we know that the recording is authentic?"

"Since when has that language been in use?" Mackley demanded.

"You knew it," Embor said pointedly.

Mackley shook his head. "Not like that. Nobody on the outside can speak it like that. All I did was recognize it. Oh, I understand it, all right, but you know as well as I do *nobody* can speak it anymore."

"That person on your tape can."

The crafty smile that crossed Mackley's face said a lot. "Exactly, gentlemen, and as hard as your government tried, it wasn't able to erase the original language of the country of Grandau after all. Over two hundred and fifty years, and it's still there in its original purity."

Aktur shrugged. "After all, Mr. Mackley, it is still only a recording."

Mackley knew he had them then. Deliberately, he poured himself a drink of water, took his time about finishing it, then put the glass down and made wet rings on the tabletop. "Your new country has always been in a state of unrest. The people give you nothing but trouble and you know as well as I do that if they decide to get from under the control of your government, there is no way you can stop them."

"I doubt that," Embor Linero said firmly.

Mackley smiled, a hard, nasty smile. "Even if a descendant of their good King Tynere suddenly appeared with positive documents to show he is the true heir to the crown? You forget ... the nation of Grandau was a free, wealthy, and happy place until your ancestors grew jealous and ran an army through them and stripped them of all their possessions."

"They were weak," Embor said.

"They were ambushed," Mackley told him. "Now they have a chance to get back at you people."

Both the men knew the time for talk had ended. Embor Linero leaned forward, his hands folded on the tabletop. "How much will it cost us to know where this tape came from?"

"One million dollars," Mackley said evenly.

"That is a lot of money."

Mackley shrugged. "That is a lot of information. After all, you are paying for ... the elimination of certain people."

"Quite right," Embor said. "Now, shall we do business?"

The associate director of languages of the institute nodded and began to lay out his demands. The tape recording itself didn't mean a thing. It was the letter giving Vincent Damar's address that was valuable. And now he had to act quickly before Vincent Damar got impatient and possibly contacted another language expert.

An hour later the arrangements had been made. Herbert Mackley was taking no chances on having Aktur or Embor eliminate *him,* so that when the money was put in the bank under *his* name and the passbook was left with the head cashier (who would verify the transaction by phone and hold it until told where to send it), only then would the two men be given the name and address of Vincent Damar.

They left the building at ten-minute intervals, then Aktur Cilon and Embor Linero met in a small foreign restaurant. After coffee Aktur said, "Will it be easy to handle the man Mackley?"

His friend nodded. "Certainly. He is a fool."

"And the others?"

Embor's shrug was eloquent. "Simple. We do as our ancestors did to the people of Grandau ... we ambush them."

CHAPTER THREE

THE SMALL GROUP in Vincent Damar's house on Peolle Island were gathered around the old man who was sitting smiling in the rocker, for the first time able to communicate with his new friends.

"You did a great job, Sir Harry."

"Simple sign language to start with," he told Vincent. "We may not be able to *write* his language at present, but we know how to match words and objects now. At least we know his name ... Vali Steptur, and by finger count he is seventy-two years old."

Supper was a laughing time with everyone trying to add to the conversation. Before it was over Vali had managed to convey to them with a pencil drawing that he had come from another island in the southern chain and the number of people on it amounted to forty-six. He drew a lot more stick figures and showed with gestures that at one time in the past there had been a great deal more of them. But he rocked in his chair to indicate an earthquake and blew hard at the paper with one finger pointing toward the sky to mimic a great storm, then ran the pencil through most of the drawn figures to show how many had been lost.

It was Larry who finally got a sense of distance through to Vali, pointing first to his island, then to the others, and looking curiously at the old man.

Vali's face tightened and he looked scared. Slowly, he shook his head in the universal language that meant "no." Then carefully, he took the pencil and drew another picture. It wasn't a stick figure this time. It was rough, but a lot of detail went into it, and when he was done he turned it around.

"What do you suppose that is?" Sir Harry asked.

Only a few seconds were spent studying the sketch, then Vincent nodded with understanding. "It's a young girl."

"But there's something important about it, isn't there?"

"There certainly is," Vincent told him. "She's wearing a crown on her head."

The old man knew that his message had been understood. Then, with a simple gesture, he took the leather folder from his lap and passed it to Vincent.

There was no need for Vali to tell him exactly how valuable his treasure was. The fine lambskin parchment so beautifully decorated with artwork, inscribed with magnificent penmanship, and stamped with an aged waxen seal that fixed red, blue, and gold ribbons to the document said it all.

Something else was in the folder too, carefully wrapped in old yellowed linen. When Vincent unwrapped it, a magnificent gold ring, faced with a royal crest and surrounded by diamonds, dropped into his palm.

And now, Vincent Damar didn't have to wonder about his guest any longer. His research into the histories of European countries had supplied him with everything he needed to know. Pictures of that crest on the ring were well known to students of the times and events that turned Europe upside down those many years ago.

"What is it, Dad?"

His dad held the ring up in his fingers for all to see. "This is the royal seal of the nation of Grandau that was crushed by an oppressor nation when Tynere was its king."

He looked at Vali, saw his shining eyes because the old man recognized the name of his country and king, then everything made sense. "Sir Harry," he said, "I think we have something of international importance here."

The Englishman said nothing, his face serious.

"It's more than just a longboat from the *Tiger* now." He rewrapped the ring and put it back in the folder. "If I'm not missing my guess, on Vali's island are the heirs to the throne of Grandau and these are the documents to prove it."

Sir Harry seemed confused. "But Mr. Damar ... how could they possibly have gotten there?"

This time it was Vincent's turn to tell a story. Carefully, he sorted out the facts in his mind, then said, "When Grandau was overrun by that neighboring country, certain members of the royal family and their servants managed to escape. They got to the coastline with the enemy in hot pursuit and purchased an old fishing boat to take them to safety in England. They never arrived. Folklore has it that the boat left the harbor hours before their pursuers showed up, but there was no chase after that since a vicious storm came up that would have put such a small boat in terrible danger. As far as the enemy was concerned, that small band of people were as good as dead, and they went back and reported it that way. Afterwards, there was no longer any royal family to rule over Grandau. Since that time there has been nothing but one dictatorship after another."

"Yes, Mr. Damar, that puts them off the European coast in a small, ill-equipped, and rickety boat, but not here in the Caribbean."

"There is one thing here that fits both pictures, Sir Harry."

"Oh, and what is that?"

"The *Tiger's* longboat."

"Certainly ... you don't mean ..."

"Yes, I do mean, Sir Harry. It's quite possible that the storm drove that small boat out to sea, and no doubt that eventually it would have foundered and sunk, but before it did another ship came by at exactly the right time, a fully equipped, brand-new ship with no captain, no crew, and no place to go at all."

"The H.M.S. *Tiger!*"

"Right."

"But ... those were people from inland, not seafarers!"

"I don't think they cared much. The *Tiger* was there, they went aboard, and they just let it sail. The trade winds did the rest. They blew them right smack into the Caribbean and they've been here ever since. On some island south of Peolle, probably in the Cardiff Chain, are an ancient people speaking an ancient language no longer in use, and in their midst is a young girl, a princess to the crown of Grandau."

Larry glanced up at his dad, a thoughtful expression on his face. "Would it make any difference if they got back to their home in Europe?"

"Son ... that's a strange section of the world. They have long memories and they have never given up hope of becoming an independent kingdom again."

"But now that neighboring country controls the whole area."

"No matter ... if Grandau was independent again, or had a reason to rebel, it is so strategically placed that it could cause more trouble than it's worth. Frankly, I think they'd simply let Grandau alone if a descendant of King Tynere showed up, but if they found out about the heir ahead of time, they'd do everything in their power to destroy what is left of those original survivors."

"Well then, Mr. Damar, that should be no trouble. Apparently no one but us knows of their existence."

Vincent frowned and gnawed at his lip. "That may not be so, Sir Harry. It all depends on what Vali here said on those tapes when he was trying to make himself known to me."

"But "I'm certain the Language Institute is reliable."

"No doubt, but greed can do strange things to people. Let's hope that everyone at the institute is honest."

Until now, Josh had been silent. Finally he said, "There is one thing we do not know. The stories you tell are great adventures, but one thing is missing."

"What's that, Josh?" Vincent asked.

"What happened to the *Tiger?*"

"Yes," Sir Harry stated. "What *did* happen to her, do you suppose?"

"Can I guess?"

"Of course."

"The *Tiger* probably grounded off that island and the passengers let the longboat down and rowed to shore. They might even have had time to take off enough supplies to get them started in a new life before the tides and wind floated the *Tiger* off to some burial spot in the ocean. Until Vali here used it, that longboat has been in their hands."

"I'm glad you're guessing, Dad," Larry said.

"Why?"

"Because it's not the way I'd guess."

Vincent smiled at his friend Timothy and then he looked back at his son. "Then how would *you* guess?"

Larry let his eyes watch Sir Harry intently. "Remember ... you said the *Tiger* was a jinx ship?"

"Well, that was what they called her *then*. Of course, with the strange things that happened to her, they had reason to."

"She wasn't a jinx ship, Sir Harry," Larry told him. "I think the *Tiger* was a special ship. She didn't want to go to war or police the seas. She had one special job to do and she was determined to do it." He paused, then said firmly, "I think the *Tiger* knew the reason it was built was to rescue the royal family of Grandau, and right now it's waiting to finish its job."

The envelope was delivered to the hotel suite of Aktur Cilon and Embor Linero in the afternoon mail and when they opened it they found a photo-copy of Vincent Damar's original letter to the Language Institute of Miami. Aktur read it carefully, got out a small book of maps, and opened it to the Caribbean sea. He studied it a moment, then circled a small spot with his pencil. "Here," he said. "Peolle Island."

"How far from the mainland?" Embor queried.

"There is no airfield indicated, so if we fly it would be by helicopter and I would estimate a four-hour trip."

"A helicopter would alert them, I'm afraid. We would do better to hire a boat."

"That is a problem too," Aktur replied. "Those boat captains stay on the radio. The answer is, I think, an outright purchase of a sailing boat. It will be no trouble to fake a breakdown and give us a good reason for landing on Peolle."

"Excellent, comrade. At least this will be a pleasurable assignment for us. At home they will be buried in snow and here we are warm and comfortable with a nice sea voyage Coming up. It makes, ah, eliminating the others a real pleasure."

"Embor ... we can make this assignment even more pleasurable if we wish to."

"Oh? And how would that be?"

"Our government has given us the million dollars for the purchase of this information from the man Mackley, has it not?"

"Yes, that is true."

"It expects no return, does it?"

"The information and elimination is worth much more than a million dollars to them," Embor said.

Aktur Cilon smiled grimly. "Then if we take back the million dollars from Mackley and eliminate him too, our government would think nothing of it, would they?"

With a conspiratorial grin, Embor nodded. "Not as long as they knew nothing of it. But tell me, comrade, where will we spend all that money?"

"Simplicity itself, my friend. We do just like so many others. We just disappear at sea after our final report to headquarters when the elimination is accomplished. They will think we perished at sea and will never realize that we have become part of the great population of the United States."

"You know, comrade," Embor said, "you are more clever than I ever thought. If nothing goes wrong, we can spend the rest of our lives in absolute splendor."

Aktur Cilon laughed humorlessly. "Comrade ... what could go wrong? We are dealing with nothing but simple islanders and a schoolteacher and a couple of kids. What trouble could *they* cause?"

Everything was an exciting surprise to old Vali Steptur, from photos in the books and albums to the shortwave radio on the shelf. But he was an intelligent man and these things came easily to him. Many times he had seen the faraway specks of sailing ships on the horizon and occasionally airplanes would go by overhead, leaving long thin cloudlike forms behind them. Often, he had known there was another world outside that on the island they had named Halu, but it was a world they were all afraid of.

For generations they had let it be thought that Halu was totally uninhabited, shielding their fires and living in hand-built houses that looked exactly like the rest of the landscape unless you were standing right on top of them.

They had always been a proud people and smart, keeping their heritage intact, everyone being able to read, write, and count. From mouth to mouth the story of Grandau and the escape from the enemy had been handed down without any detail being lost, and always they had planned for the day when they would return.

But that day never seemed to come. The prince that had come in the original party had married and had had a son, and in time that son had married too, his wife giving him a daughter. With each generation, the royal house had been preserved, the lineage kept on a hidden scroll for future use ... and even now on Halu, there was a royal princess, heir to the throne of Grandau.

Vali Steptur's ancestor had been the teacher and good friend of King Tynere. He had given his pledge to the king to protect the prince, even with his life if need be. That pledge had been handed down from father to son throughout the generations, and now it rested in Vali's hands.

And after all this time, it was Vali Steptur who knew that if something didn't happen shortly, there never would be a return to Grandau; so as the sea brought them there, he let the sea bring them back. He found the secret place they all thought was only a silly legend, pulled the long-boat out into the sun, then filled the water cask and shoved off with the leather folder under his arm to prove his story.

Looking back toward Halu Island, he could see the dark shadow of the opening in the cliff. It had been dark and scary in there. He knew there was something else there too. It was a huge, awesome thing, a deadly menace that seemed to be waiting there, ready to pounce. He shook the idea out of his head. He was getting old. What he saw was probably nothing more than shadows in that enormous cave.

Now he knew that he had made the right move. He had found friends, true friends among these strange people. They had taken care of him, fed him, and now they were actually able to talk to each other, even if most of the talk was with signs or drawn pictures. When the white-haired man who was so interested in his old boat showed him the pictures of that same boat in a large book and indicated what he wanted, Vali laughed and showed that he understood by pointing to the longboat and making a gesture of giving it to him.

He didn't quite understand why they seemed so happy about it, but the white-haired man waited for the other to do something to the machine-that-talked on the shelf, then he spoke into the funny block tied by a coiled string to the main machine.

What Sir Harry was doing was contacting Miami on the shortwave radio, and when he got Kevin Smith he said into the microphone, "Harry Arnold here, old boy. Good news ... the longboat was authentic."

The voice from the Speaker said, "Wonderful! Have you been able to buy it?"

"I'm afraid not, old chap."

"Oh, no." The voice was totally dejected.

Sir Harry laughed. "Don't worry, chap. The owner gave it to me. As soon as we make arrangements, it will be on board a freighter and into the British Museum."

"And ... it was from the *Tiger?*"

"No doubt about it, Kevin. The original longboat."

"I wonder what really did happen to the old lady."

"Well, I'm afraid we'll never know about that, but at least we have part of her. Can you get one of the interisland boats to make a stop by here as soon as possible?"

"Right, Harry. The *Gull* is in port now. I'll contact the captain and he should make the pickup by Wednesday. Will you be coming back with the longboat?"

"Old boy, after all this, there's no way I'm going to let it out of my sight until I see it safely in the museum. By the way, I have a great story to tell you in connection with the *Tiger*. Probably all legend and speculation, but mighty interesting. And too

. . . it could be true, you know."

AKTUR CILON HANDED the briefcase to his partner and let him examine the packages of money that were stacked so neatly inside. "A million dollars," he mused. "Was it difficult?"

"The man Mackley was in too much of a hurry. I knew he would not be able to wait very long before taking the money out of the bank. He would want it where it would be out of sight of the tax men. It was a simple matter."

"He is, ah ... eliminated?"

"Permanently," Aktur said.

"Then shall we look into the matter of obtaining ourselves a boat and learn the ways of rich men before we finish our assignment?"

"Excellent thought, comrade. It shall be business with pleasure and no need to hurry at all. Those people have been here over two hundred years and I am sure a few days or weeks longer will not matter at all."

"There is a small problem, however."

"And what is that?"

"This schoolteacher ... Vincent Damar," Embor said. "Supposing he does not believe that letter we sent him?"

"Why shouldn't he? It was on the stationery of the Language Institute with Mackley's signature at the bottom. It was a clever forgery."

"I mean the contents ... he may not believe it."

"Nonsense. He asked for the origin of the language, and we told him the truth. The message was very simple, just the plea of an old man looking for help, that his boat had been wrecked and his papers were old family documents that he fancied. Besides, what would an island schoolteacher care about it anyway? All he probably wanted was to shove the old man off on some government agency to take care of him. Anyway, we'll have them all eliminated before he knows what has happened."

On Wednesday morning the interisland steamer dropped off the mail and hoisted the longboat from the H.M.S. *Tiger* on board. From the dock the small group waved at the departing figure of Sir Harry Arnold until he was out of sight.

Only then did Vincent Damar open his letter and read it. Something in his face made Larry ask, "Bad news, Dad?"

"No, just puzzling."

Larry saw the postmark on the envelope. "The institute couldn't figure it out?"

His father handed him the letter. "Apparently they did. It just doesn't seem to tie in somehow."

When he finished, Larry handed the letter back. "Dad ... if the old man was on *another* boat, he could have told us that when he was drawing those pictures."

"I know."

"Would he lie to us?"

"Son, I sure don't think so."

"Then why..."

"It's an old language, son, a dialect that hasn't been spoken in the civilized World for a couple of hundred years. It wouldn't be hard for a translator to make a mistake at all."

"You don't think that, do you, Dad?"

"Right now I don't know what to think. Let's go take Vali back to the drawing board again. If he can sketch an outline of his island, maybe we can find someone who can recognize it."

It took fifteen minutes to get the idea across to the old man, but when he knew what they were after, he went at it eagerly, sketching Halu from several different directions, indicated by the position of a model sun in the sky. When he finally decided that he could do no more, he handed the paper to Vincent.

Knowing he wasn't that experienced in the islands, he let Timothy take a look at it. And Timothy *was* experienced. He looked up, puzzled. "This is Montique Island, Vincent."

Quickly, Vincent found it on the map. "The southernmost in the Cardiff Chain."

"But something's wrong, my friend."

"What's wrong?"

"No one lives there," Timothy told him. "There is no water, nothing will grow, and to the islanders it is only a place of the old dead. They will not go near it."

"So that is why they have never been discovered," Vincent half whispered to himself. "How long will it take to get there by boat?"

"Three days by sail," Timothy said, "if the winds blow well and there are no storms to fight."

"Day cruising only?"

Timothy nodded. "It is better to anchor in a cove at night."

"Okay," Vincent decided, "I'll start outfitting the *Blue*

Tuna II in the morning. We'll get two weeks' supplies on board, have the depth finder fixed, and go see what this is all about."

"Dad..."

"What, son?"

"You'll be a week getting the *Blue Tuna* ready again."

"I know, but there's no way to shorten the time. Why?"

"Josh and I have the *Sea Eagle* all ready. We could go ahead and you could follow when you're outfitted."

With an annoyed tone of voice Vincent said, "Son, that's a three-day trip. I can't let you two kids..." Then he stopped and grinned slightly. "I keep telling you the same thing, don't I?"

"That's okay, Dad."

"Sorry, son. I just keep forgetting that you two keep growing up. You sure you can handle a voyage like this?"

"Remember our trip to the Shrinking Island?" Larry reminded him.

"How can I forget it?" He glanced over at Timothy. "Is it all right with you?"

"Island boys must learn the ways of the sea early," Timothy said, looking at his son fondly.

"Okay," Vincent agreed. "When do you want to get started?" Before the kids could answer he cut in, "Yeah, I know, right now." He let out a laugh and handed them the charts they would need. "Go plot your course, get your gear aboard, and move on out."

Larry gave him a big grin and a hug. "You're great, Dad."

On the other side of the room, Josh was doing the same to his father.

By the time the sun was centered over Peolle, the *Sea Eagle* was out of sight. Idly, Vincent picked up the Miami paper that had been dropped off by the interisland steamer. He flipped the pages, looking at the two-day-old news, then he paused at an item and frowned.

Timothy saw the look on his face and said, "Are you troubled, my friend?"

"I don't know." He reached in his pocket and took out the letter from the Language Institute of Miami. He checked the names and put the letter back. "Timothy, something is *very* wrong. I've received a letter written by a man a day after the police found his body in a mangrove swamp."

"But...that's impossible."

"Exactly, but Herbert Mackley, the man I sent the tape of Vali Steptur's voice, was found murdered."

"Who would do such a thing, Vincent?"

Seriously, Vincent said, "Someone who knows the true importance of the survivors of Grandau nobility ... and the trouble they could make for a modern dictatorship."

"Then they'll be looking for Halu ... or Montique Island too."

"I'm afraid so."

"We should recall the boys."

"There's no way now, Timothy. They won't be wasting the battery charge listening in all day. We'll have to get them at sundown when we planned the contact."

"We must trust that the boys can take care of themselves then."

"They always have," Vincent said.

But in his heart, Vincent was scared. They were only boys, half grown and adventurous.

There were others who were killers.

Vincent Damar wasn't going to take any chances. He flipped the switch on the radio to the ON Position, let it warm up, then tuned in the frequency of his friend's marina on the Florida keys. He gave the call letters three times, then a crisp voice repeated them with "Herman's Marina Service, can I help you?"

"Hi, Herm. It's Vincent Damar."

"Good to hear from you. What's up?"

"I need some Information. Did you see where a man named Herbert Mackley from the Language Institute was found dead? The police think he was murdered."

"Yeah, Vince, I saw that. It's in today's paper again too."

"Really? What's it say?"

There was a crackle of static, then Herman said, "Just an item of how the police have his suspected killers in custody. They were two escaped convicts hiding out in the swamp."

"They say what Mackley was doing there?"

"Sure. He had rented a boat and a shack out on one of those islands. He had plenty of provisions ... fishing equipment and all that, so apparently he was going to take a good vacation." He paused, then added, "He just picked the wrong spot. Those convicts had been on the loose for ten days when Mackley turned up with the perfect answer for their escape .. . a boat and plenty of food and clothing. Hey ... what's all this about?"

"Mackley was somebody I wrote to, that's all."

"Well, if I can help any other way, just let me know. When are you bringing the *Blue Tuna II* for the valve job on the port engine?"

"Next month, Herm. See you then."

"Roger and out, Vince."

Timothy had overheard the whole conversation and saw the relief in his friend's face. "Feel better now?"

"Much," Vincent told him. "At least we don't have to get the International Patrol Squadron out to chase the kids down."

Forty miles away, the two men in the sailing sloop

Dragonfish had given up trying to navigate against the wind. They had begun to realize that even in a calm sea with a gentle wind, there was more to handling a boat than they had thought.

Aktur Cilon had gotten disgusted with their progress, so he and his partner lowered the mainsail and jib, let them lie in a sloppy pile on the deck, and Aktur started the small diesel engine. Now there was no trouble at all. He simply followed a compass course and enjoyed the day while he could. Peolle Island and those to be eliminated were only a short way off. On their starboard side was the outline of a power cruiser. One of the island boats, Aktur suspected.

Had he been closer, or used his binoculars, he could have read the name on its transom ... the *Blue Tuna II*. Of course, he wouldn't have known it was heading north to Ara Island for a full refitting and on board were the targets of his planned "elimination."

CHAPTER FOUR

FOR THE BOYS, the first day out had been filled with the exciting planning of their visit to Montique Island, or, as Vali had called it, "Halu." At their first landfall, the islanders of Peke had come down to greet them, roasted many fish in their honor, and sat by the fire the early part of the night to tell them about Montique.

None of them had ever been there, or even planned to go. As far as they knew, it was a barren place without water or plant life, unhospitable and of no use at all. However, they wished the boys luck before they left, certain they would find nothing more than they had been told.

Just as the last embers of the fire were going out, Josh asked, "What do you think about Montique Island, Larry?"

"I think Dad was right," Larry answered. "If the old man *did* come from there, then there has to be water and vegetation. All these islands are volcanic in origin, and there could possibly be a bowl inside the rim of Montique nobody knows about."

"The islanders have been here a long time."

"Yes, I know, but they have their own legends. If their ancestors said it's an empty island, then they say it too and pass it down to their kids. So who wants to go to an empty island anyway? They have everything they need or want right here."

Josh nodded in agreement. "I guess you're right." He looked across the fire at his friend. "What will we do if it is empty?"

"Old Vali Steptur came from somewhere."

"Maybe it wasn't Montique Island."

"The pictures he drew of it sure looked like it. Your father has even been around it and he said it was Montique, all right."

"Well, pal, we'll sure find out pretty soon, won't we?"

"One way or the other. Good night, Josh."

" 'Night, Larry."

Montique Island seemed to simply grow out of the sea like a giant barnacle. Its sides were irregular craggy cliffs and there was no place to make a landing except on the southeast quadrant, where a small white beach glistened in the brilliant sunlight. Behind the beach were a few scraggly palms struggling for existence in the sands before the slope edged upward at a lesser angle, the dull face of the rock etched by the winds of time.

To all the world, Montique was nothing but a rock, a great barren rock not worth climbing because nothing would be at the top anyway. But the world could be wrong.

At the very peak, behind a barricade of flat stones, two men were peering through an ancient brass telescope at the sailboat that had just dropped anchor off their island. The sun had burned them brown, but they weren't like the other islanders at all. Their hair was light and their eyes combinations of blue and brown, their manner of speech not at all like that of anyone else in the world.

"What do you see, Jon?"

The man with the telescope extended it for a better focus, studied the boat a minute, then said, "Two boys, Georg. No one else."

"What could they want?"

Jon shrugged. "Who knows what any boys want? At least they are alone."

"That could be bad."

"Why, Georg?"

"Because there is no grown person there to control them. They might want to explore."

"Nonsense. Even boys would know it is too dangerous to try to climb up here."

"Jon ... they *could* find the way. It wouldn't be hard if they really looked."

"Why should they?" his friend asked. "There is nothing here for them to look for."

Georg was quiet a few moments, thinking. "Possibly Vali..."

"Vali is dead, my friend. He was an old man. He never could have survived out there alone. We tried to tell him, but he wouldn't listen. For too many years he had been dreaming about returning to put Tila on the throne of Grandau and it was too much for him."

"We should have stopped him."

Jon laid his hand on Georg's shoulder and shook his head. "We never even knew he left. Oh, sure, he talked about looking for the secret place hidden here on Halu where our ancestors were supposed to have provided a way for us, but we know such a place is only a story that old men tell children by the fires at night. There never was such a place, Georg. Old Vali must have roped those logs together that we saw on the beach and floated away on them."

"He took the king's papers and the Great Ring,"

Georg remarked sadly. "They can never be replaced. Now we have no proof any longer. The throne is not Tila's now."

"You worry too much, Georg. The proof will be found. Somewhere, somehow, we will find it."

Jon picked up the telescope and centered it on the anchored boat again. For a moment he watched the boys, then said, "They are blowing air into one of those funny soft boats like we found on the beach that time."

"A very poor boat. When I touched a knife to it the wind whistled out and it went flat. Whoever heard of making a boat out of cloth like that?"

"It is the ways of these water people, Georg. Remember, we are from Grandau; we must make ourselves remember that. Our place is far across this ocean."

"Too many generations have passed, Jon. There is no memory, only words and stories. The only land we really know is right here. There was a time when we almost did leave this island because we had to. There were just too many of us... then the earth shook and half the people died. When that terrible storm covered this place, even more went. I remember that ... I was just a child then, but I remember that. Now we are just a few."

But Jon was hardly listening. His eye was glued to the telescope and he said, "They are paddling this way." A few minutes later he folded the telescope shut and stood up. "They've landed on the beach. I think we should go tell the others. In case they decide to look around this island, we must be

ready to discourage their efforts."

IT WOULD NEVER CHANGE, Tila thought, *whenever an Outsider appeared near their Island, you could see the fear on their faces.* They protected her like a girl ... in fact, a young lady ... and except for the few boys and girls on the island, she had never seen anyone else her own age.

And now there were two of them below on the beach and neither Jon nor Georg would let her go near the rim. Even Helena and Margo were firm about it, their hands trembling, eyes darting about like a bird when a cat was near. It was a little annoying to be protected from *everything*. Why, when she was little they wouldn't even let her pick up a bug, and she was nine before they allowed her to feel the sand under her toes and the sea licking at her legs. Oh, they didn't just *let* her do those things ... she had to insist upon it, and then she didn't realize that she was a princess, heir to the vacant throne of Grandau. Sometimes she wondered where Grandau was. As far as she was concerned, the island they called Halu *was* the world. From the topmost part of it, all that could be seen was the deep blue-green of the sea.

The blood of that ancient King Tynere that flowed through her veins suddenly stiffened and Tila stood there flat-footed, legs spread apart, her hands on her hips. "You ... Helena and Margo," she demanded. "Am I your princess?"

"Oh, yes!"

"Tila ... of course you are!" Both women spoke as one.

"Very well. In that case I insist on being shown those who have come to our shore!"

"But, Tila..."

She didn't flinch. She simply stood her ground and looked at them sternly. It was the first time since her parents had died that this royal tone had been used, and once again they understood why the old ones had been so careful in marrying and having children to inherit the crown of a nation.

A word was spoken to the men, and while the others

stayed back, Jon and Georg escorted Tila to the viewing place. Jon opened the telescope and handed it to her.

Tila's hands were shaking so hard she had to draw a deep breath, then let it out slowly so she could see through the glass. For the first time in her life, she was about to see someone she hadn't known since she had been born.

When they finished eating, Josh raked dead ashes over the glowing coals to bank the fire and have it ready for later. Larry had cleaned up the metal utensils, stacked them away in the box, and now he was surveying the sloping face of the cliff behind the beach.

The area they were on was as long as three football fields, the sand littered with dried driftwood. White ghost crabs poked their eyes out of their sand holes, made sure they were safe, then hurled a claw-full of dirt into a ring around their nests. The birds that had flown off when they first landed had come back to dig tiny coquina clams out of the sand, then chased the waves back and forth, picking at the bottom for other minute sea creatures.

Josh came over and stood by his friend. "See anything?"

"Just rock."

"You must learn to see more when you look," Josh said.

"Oh?"

"It is rock that has been used, Larry." He pointed to a dark streak to his left. "See there, the line that goes up between the two boulders?"

When his eyes found it, Larry nodded.

"That is an old path."

"You've got eyes like a hawk," Larry said. "I would never have known that. How do you know it's an old one?"

"The color." Josh showed him. "If it were used more often it would be lighter."

"Who would use it?"

Josh didn't say anything. He tilted his head back and half closed his eyes. Larry saw his nostrils move gently and he knew what Josh was doing. Finally Josh asked, "Do you smell it?"

"Pal, all I smell is the ocean and some smoke from our fire. What are you talking about?"

"There is a smell of green things, Larry. It is more than the sea smells. It is like the garden behind my cousin's house when everything is almost ripe enough to pick."

"Where can there be any green things, Josh? Good golly, this place is all rock."

Josh pointed at the motion on top of a flat area partway up the slope. "What do you call that?"

"Birds," Larry said.

"There is something special about them. Just look close."

Then Larry let out a long, low whistle, and envied Josh's knowledge of the things of the wild. They were birds, all right, but they weren't seabirds at all. They were what the natives called *dekkies* and were only native to land areas where they could feed on seeds and nuts.

"You're right, Josh. There's green foliage around here and most likely on top ... and if there is green vegetation, that means there is water too ... so there could very well be people."

"I'm quite sure of it," Josh stated emphatically.

When Larry looked, Josh was smiling gently. "Why?"

"If you look at the top of the rim very carefully, you may see something."

Larry raised his eyes and searched the rocky lip above him. He had to scan the entire area twice, then he saw it. Up there a pinpoint of light reflected brightly off polished metal, and when he raised his head to study it more closely, it disappeared.

"You see it?"

Larry bobbed his head: "Somebody is watching us through a spyglass!"

"Exactly, and we don't want to disturb them."

"You're right, Josh. Tonight we'll just sack out by the fire here, and tomorrow, after they see that we're friendly, we'll find the way up there."

They should never have worried about that. Whatever went around their faces, whatever unguent was in that cloth held to their noses made everything dreamlike, and when they awoke their hands and feet were tightly bound, their heads a throbbing ball of pain. And when they looked up, framed in the only light they could see was the black shadow of some monstrous creature that babbled wild sounds, and both the boys moaned in total despair.

Jon stared down at the two figures at his feet and said to Georg, "Now we have stooped to capturing children."

"Those *children,* as you call them, have sailed a ship to our shores."

"I don't think they were trying to destroy us."

"You saw them watching us up here."

"That was an accident."

"Our princess's life was at stake!"

"My friend," Jon said, "always I have been accused of being the hotheaded one, always ready to do the foolish thing. Now you have led us to this mad act. What are we to do now?"

Georg simply looked at him, not knowing what to answer.

"Had we let them alone," Jon told him, "they might have left and never have come back."

"We don't know that. Ever since Vali Steptur fled we don't know what is going to happen!"

"Still, Georg, we don't make war with young boys, and when Tila hears of this she is going to be very angry."

"Tila is still a young girl," Georg said.

"Tila is our princess," Jon said. "Whether you like it or not, she is, for now, the titular head of the nation of Grandau and you and I are her subjects."

"Never forget, Jon, we are her advisors."

"But all decisions are hers. Never forget that, Georg ... and I will make sure you don't."

After a moment, Georg nodded. "What do we do with them?"

"Tila will decide. If she thinks they are a threat ... well, there is always the cliff, we cut their boat loose, and that will end it."

There was little need for the two men aboard the *Dragonfish* to fake a breakdown. Their lack of sailing skill did it for them. By the time they managed to get a line around the dock piling on Peolle, the three small boys fishing from one end were laughing so hard they almost went overboard.

Neither Aktur nor Embor liked to be laughed at, especially by kids. In their country they would have lashed out with vicious blows and those laughs would have turned to screams of pain and terror, but right now they had a job to do and couldn't afford to make enemies of anyone.

Faking a laugh, they asked the youngsters the way to the house of Vincent Damar. The boys showed them quickly enough. It was the only house on this section of the island, sitting just below the crown of the knoll.

On the way, Aktur Cilon said, "I would like to fix those kids for good. In our country they would be out working hard in the fields, not playing in the sun. They would be beaten for their attitude."

Embor nodded, agreeing with his partner. "They will be there later. We will take care of them then. We want no one alive who can recognize us anyway." He hefted the plastic suitcase he carried and pointed toward the house on the hill. "Let us hurry."

When they reached the edge of the crest they put on their prepared smiles as though they were friendly neighbors and followed the pathway to the door of Vincent Damar's home. Embor knocked, and when there was no answer, knocked again.

"There is no one here," Aktur said.

"I can see that, fool."

"Do we break in?"

Without answering, Embor tried the knob. It turned under his hand and the door swung open. "These peasants are too trusting. That is what kills them."

It only took them a minute to be sure the house was empty, and the way Embor muttered under his breath Aktur knew he was being eaten up by rage.

They had expected to find their victims at home and helpless and the pleasure of "eliminating" them would have made Embor especially happy and much easier to live with.

"What do you think?" Aktur asked.

His partner pointed to several framed pictures. They showed Vincent and Larry on the new *Blue Tuna II,* tied to the dock where the two men had left the *Dragonfish.* "That is his boat. Do you see anything familiar about it?"

Aktur looked at it closely, studying the detail. "If I'm not mistaken ... that's the cruiser that passed us when we were coming down here."

"You're not mistaken," Embor said. "There is no doubting those lines. We are still in luck. They were going north, and between here and Miami are all known islands, not one of which would be hiding the people we look for."

"Then they'll be coming back here!"

"Probably. My guess is that they are having their boat serviced and supplied."

"Then we wait for them," Aktur said impulsively. "We can hide..."

"Idiot," Embor snarled, "we have no *time* to hide. We have to be the first to reach that strange island and eliminate every last one of that bunch."

"But the old man ... the one on the tape. He is with this Vincent person."

Embor laid the plastic case on the tabletop and opened it. He took out six sticks of dynamite, their primer caps, and all the equipment to arrange a booby trap inside the house. "Here, comrade. You are the explosive expert. Put your bomb together so that it will destroy this house and everyone in it so completely there will be nothing left but dust."

A minute later Aktur had found the place. He pointed to the rocking chair beside the table. "A well-used piece of furniture, comrade. I place the charge beneath it and on the second or third rock the dynamite blows and there will be no trace of anything."

Embor was looking at a partially opened chart on the table. It was the top one of many and his eyes were going over every detail of it.

"Comrade ... do you approve of where I put..."

"Yes, yes, it is fine," Embor told him impatiently. Then he began to smile. He had spotted the circle that had been drawn and retraced in an excited manner around the tiny dot of an island in the Cardiff Chain, the last speck that marked the cluster of islands. He snapped his fingers, halting his partner in his work, and waved him over. "This is where they are." He tapped the map. "A place called Montique Island."

"But ... the old man called it Halu on the tape."

"That was *their* name for it. Now finish your job. It is time to leave."

From their place in the bushes, the three boys watched the men come down the path and search the dock area quickly. One boy said, "They are looking for us!"

"I told you they were not good men. You saw their eyes?"

"Quiet! The wind is toward them ... they could hear us."

On the dock the men looked as if they were about to probe through all the grounds, but they seemed too much in a hurry to do something else, so with a sharp kick at an empty gas can, they got back on the *Dragonfish,* turned the engine over, flipped off their rope, and backed away from the dock.

When they were sure they were out of sight, the boys stood up. "What do you think they wanted at Mr. Damar's house?"

"They weren't there long," one of the other boys said.

The smallest boy shrugged and added, "Well, they didn't take anything. They even left something there ... that bag they carried."

"Yeah," the other boy agreed. "They're probably Mr. Damar's friends."

"With faces like that?"

"Aw, come on. All mainlanders look like that at first." The first boy laughed.

Many thousands of miles northeast of the Caribbean, in a great fieldstone manor outside of London, England, Sir Harry Arnold was in a serious discussion with two people, one a high-ranking member of Parliament, the other an elderly man with the fine features of a scholar, but whose face for the moment bore an almost unbelieving expression. He was looking with controlled excitement at the picture Sir Harry had drawn of the ring old Vali Steptur had let them see, and his hands were trembling with passion.

"There is no doubt at all, Sir Harry. You have drawn an exact likeness of the ring seal of King Tynere! Do you know what this means?"

"From what Mr. Benson here has told me, I'm beginning to."

"When the people of my country first heard of this," he went on, "a change came over them that is hard to believe. They became a ... a *united* country again. It was hard to suppress some of the young ones ... they were all for throwing off the yoke of the oppressor at once."

"We still aren't certain, Mr. Milos."

"I know," Henri Milos said, "but even a rumor was enough. Now, with this . . ."

Mr. Teddy Benson, the member of Parliament from the southlands, held up his hand for attention. "Gentlemen ... one thing we must be certain of, and that is no violence. Any outward show of force in a revolt against the neighboring country and there will be a police action that will stop any attempt at independence."

"When my people see their own chosen royal family returning," Henri Milos stated, "they will be hard to restrain. For too many years they have existed almost as slaves to their conquerors."

"Nevertheless," Mr. Benson insisted, "it will be up to the more mature men to control the situation."

Henri Milos nodded, then his eyes clouded. "There is a problem."

"What's that?"

"Our ... enemy, as I shall call them now, knows about the existence of the Grandau royal family too. In fact, it was our informants inside their Organization who brought the news to us first."

"Have they taken action yet?" Sir Harry demanded. "Apparently so. Two of their men have been assigned to the project. They flew to Miami the same day they received the call about the tapes." He paused for a few seconds, looking at each of his friends. "These two men who were sent ... they are bad men ... killers. They do those terrible things their government finds necessary to stay in power."

A silence fell over the trio, then Sir Harry said, "I'll notify Vincent Damar at once." He looked at Teddy Benson and asked, "Have we any military ships in the area?"

Sadly, Teddy Benson shook his head. "Not any more. Britain no longer rules the sea."

"I'll try to radio him directly."

Benson smiled and nodded. "I'd even settle if we had the old ship of the line there now ... the one you told me about."

"The *Tiger*," Sir Harry said. "I'm afraid there is no *Tiger* around to help those people out now."

CHAPTER FIVE

RIGHT THEN TILA wasn't feeling like the ruling princess at all. Where before she had been insistent upon seeing the newcomers through the telescope, now she was hesitant upon viewing them in person. Her hands shook and her feet dragged as Helena and Margo led her to the low wooden building where the two boys were being held captive.

She paused at the door, hoping the older ones would call off this affair, but when she saw the expression on their faces, she knew that since she had chosen to act as a princess earlier, there was no way she could give up the role now. Whether she wanted to or not, she was their royal ruler and there was no turning back. But, princess or not, she was still only twelve years old, and having to stand face to face with a pair of those horrible Outsiders, the very ones she had always been told were the enemy, was going to take every ounce of her strength.

Tila swallowed hard, took a deep breath, and stepped inside. While she still had the courage, she said as fast and as regally as she could, "I am Tila of the House of Tynere, princess of the Kingdom and of all my people and you are my prisoners!"

Larry and Josh looked at each other in puzzlement and Josh shook his head. "What did she say?"

"Beats me, but she sure is pretty."

"She looks mean, pal."

"Come on, she's only a little girl."

"Phooey," Josh grunted. "She's our age and they can get pretty mean about then."

A small grin played around Larry's mouth. "You wouldn't say that about Mary Verne, would you?"

Josh blushed and grinned back. Mary was the sister of a friend of his and lately he had been taking an interest in her since they shared the same hobbies.

It was just too much talk for Tila, however. She put her hands on her hips, stamped her foot, and turned to her friends. "*What* are they talking about? How dare they smile like that! Don't they realize that this is my kingdom and they are my prisoners?"

Helena and Margo didn't answer her. They simply smiled back and Margo said, "You'd better pay attention to your captives then, Tila. I think they're trying to tell you something."

She turned quickly, and there was Larry, holding his hand out in a gesture that even she knew. It was one of friendship, and when she looked at his face she knew he really meant it. At first she was going to ignore it, but girlish curiosity was just too much and she giggled and took his hand in hers, shook it, and reached for Josh's.

Larry realized she couldn't understand him, but he made a few motions with his hands, indicating the room, pointing to outside, and showing how he didn't know what had happened. Then he said, "It's kind of a funny way of meeting, but we're sure happy to see you." He patted his stomach and made signs of eating. "Now, if you could only find us some breakfast..."

"They're hungry!" Tila exclaimed.

"All boys are hungry," Helena reminded her. "But they are your prisoners, remember?" She smiled gently, waiting.

"Well, we can still feed them, can't we?"

Testing her, Helena asked, "Suppose they escape?"

"Oh, nonsense," Tila replied. "They're only boys and we have plenty of men." Besides, where could they go? Their boat is well guarded."

"And you are not afraid of these ... wild Outsiders?"

Tila couldn't help it. She looked at Larry and Josh and giggled again. The thought of them being her captives made it seem even funnier. Here they had come from far away, sailing here themselves, totally unafraid, while she had never even been off this island.

With a forefinger, Tila tapped herself, said "Tila," then turned toward her companions and indicated, "Margo ... Helena."

The boys understood immediately and introduced themselves. Then, like any young lady, Tila un-self-consciously reached out, took their hands, and led them out into the sunlight.

"I think our princess has found two good friends," Margo remarked.

And friends they were, right from the beginning. Everyone gathered around to meet the boys, and almost instantly they were exchanging ideas with simple sign language and identifying and naming objects about them. Larry's watch amazed them, for they told time by the sun and stars, and the tricks he did with the magnet from the toolbox astounded them. It was a day of wonderful companionship, of learning and teaching, and as the sun was beginning to set on the horizon, Larry held up his hand for everyone's attention.

When all eyes were on him, he took a stick, and in the packed earth sketched a well-remembered design. As the men crowded in to inspect it there were sudden sharp gasps and Jon said, "That is a picture of the royal seal of Tynere!"

Georg's face was a mask of astonishment. "But where ... could they have ..."

Understanding came to Jon at once. *"They have found Vali Steptur!"*

Josh grinned and poked Larry's arm excitedly. "They know. Hear that ... Vali Steptur was one of them, all right!"

It took a while for everyone to quiet down, then with sand pictures and body motions, the boys described their rescue of the old man. They realized that the group was completely unfamiliar with modern living, so couldn't give them certain details, but they made it plain that old Vali was safe and soon there would be others here at the island with all the help they needed.

That night was one they would long remember, sitting there in the brilliant moonlight, the dying embers of the fire throwing a reddish glow over everyone's face. With the excitement of youth, Tila managed to convey to the boys all of their past history, the escape from Grandau in the old leaky boat that was sinking under the party, and the rescue by a mysterious ship that came out of the fog and carried them to safety.

"The *Tiger,*" Josh said softly. "The story was true after all."

Larry nodded and posed the question as best he could. He drew pictures, he acted out his thoughts, did everything he could to see if they knew whatever became of that mysterious ship that appeared so abruptly. But when they realized what he was asking, they all shook their heads and went through a pantomime of their own.

When they finished Josh said, "It was too long ago, I guess."

"Somehow," Larry told him, "I get the feeling that the ship got lost somewhere."

"But where? This isn't much of an island and from what they said, they hardly ever leave the top of it except to fish off the beach we landed on."

"That longboat came from someplace," Larry insisted.

"You drew a picture of it and nobody knew what it meant."

Larry glanced out over the shadowy faces and after a moment said, "Maybe it's a little too early to tell, Josh."

His friend wanted to know what he was getting at, but the hour was late and tomorrow was another day. Georg and Jon stood up and waved for them to follow, and with big smiles toward the assemblage and a handshake for Tila they went after the two men to the building that had been their jail earlier. This time there were comfortable beds, stools to sit on, and fresh water in a clay pitcher.

"Pretty neat," Josh observed. "Guess they sure are glad their trouble is all over."

This time it was Larry who couldn't escape a funny feeling. "Yeah," he said. "Let's hope so."

Night had closed in around the two men on board the *Dragonfish*. They had dropped anchor off a rocky little island that was one of many in the Cardiff Chain, secure in the knowledge that they were well hidden from any of the passing ships. They showed no lights and the silhouette of the *Dragonfish* blended in with the shadows of the trees on the island.

Aktur Cilon had been on the shortwave radio transmitter the past fifteen minutes, sending a detailed message as he consulted the sea charts of the area. He spoke in the native tongue of his country, but even so, the conversation was coded to keep its import from any listening ears.

When he shut down the power Embor asked brusquely, "Well?"

"Our submarine, the *Krolin,* is now five hundred miles west of our position. The captain will sail immediately for the island of Montique and wait for our signal." He paused, then added, "Now, how do you propose we proceed?"

Embor nodded thoughtfully. "It should be an easy matter. We make a landing, eliminate everyone on the island, retrieve whatever papers or information may be necessary, then leave."

"You are forgetting," Aktur frowned, "that the captain of our submarine will expect us to leave with him. How then do we make our escape?"

"Simple," Embor assured him. "We tell him we have to stay behind to be sure there has not been contact with the other island. As a matter of fact, we could deliver whoever it is of that royal family to his keeping to give him reason to get away quickly. The elimination of that one can be their problem."

"Excellent." His smile had an evil touch to it. "The best part is ... no one even suspects that we are here, and before any can, they will all be ... eliminated. The bomb in the house was a smart move."

Sir Harry had been on the radio for six hours straight without being able to raise Vincent Damar on Peolle Island. He knew that in his friend's different time zone they would be fast asleep with their radios shut down, but the situation was serious enough to try anything. A pair of deadly agents were aware of the information Vincent had and would be ready to do anything to keep that information from going any further. He glanced at the clock, scowled with impatience, and waited for the minute hand to make a full circle again.

Now, at Peolle Island, the sun would be coming up. He flipped the power switch of the radio to ON and picked up the microphone. At two-minute intervals he repeated Vincent Damar's call letters, then sat back and waited.

There was no answer.

A worried frown creased Sir Harry's forehead. There were killers loose and he hadn't been able to warn his friend. Desperately, he kept hoping that it wasn't too late. He picked up the microphone and tried again.

There still was no reply.

The *Blue Tuna II* was fifteen miles from Peolle when Tim came up from the galley with fresh coffee. Vincent was finishing his watch at the helm, listening to the morning news from the portable radio in the rack beside him. He took the coffee gratefully, turned the wheel over to Tim, and was about to take a break on the deck when he stopped short. He heard the news commentator mention the name "Mackley" and something made his skin crawl.

". . . apparently Mackley, the murdered man, had recently withdrawn a million dollars from his bank prior to his death. The Miami police have now definitely established the fact that the escaped convicts had nothing to do with the deceased except to discover the body minutes before they themselves were captured. At this time, there is no clue as to the whereabouts of the million dollars."

Tim gave Vincent a serious look. "Something is very bad, my friend."

"It ... may not have anything to do ... well, with Vali and that old boat."

"Do you really believe that?"

"I'm hoping," Vincent told him, "but we'd better not

take any chances just the same." He switched his radio on and gave the call letters for his friend Herman up on the Florida Keys. It was ten minutes before he answered and his voice was full of sleep when he came on.

"Yeah, Herman here. What's the trouble?"

"Vince Damar, Herm. I need some information."

"When?"

"As soon as possible. Look, get on your telephone and see who you can raise at the Miami Language Institute. See if Mackley left any record of getting a letter from me."

"That dead guy?"

"Right."

"You in trouble, Vince?"

"Not so far, but if it's coming I'd like to know what we're getting into. Rush it, will you? Get somebody to open the place up if you have to."

"Where do I contact you?" Herman asked.

"On Peolle Island. We ought to be at the dock in less than an hour."

He switched off and gave Tim a concerned glance. Up ahead, Peolle was looming up in the early morning sunlight, his dock a thin finger sticking out into the deep blue waters. On the top of the hill the sun glinted off the windows of his house as though there were a fire inside. Somehow it gave him a strange feeling in his stomach.

With his usual show of good seamanship, Tim edged the *Blue Tuna II* into its berth and cut the engines while Vincent was snubbing down the bow and aft lines. When he stepped onto the dock, Tim asked, "Did you expect visitors, my friend?"

"No, why?"

"There are marks where a red rub rail has brushed the pilings. They are fresh."

"Could have been an islander."

"None we know have red rub rails. It is a superstition they have."

Vincent inspected the spots, not liking what he saw. "Possibly a transient then. They could have gone around the other side of the island when they found us gone."

"Maybe. I will see." He nodded toward the up-turned gasoline can at the corner of the dock. "They are very careless with other people's property though." He picked up the can, looked at the scuff mark made by a boot, and set it back in its place. Then, together, they started toward the house.

Halfway up the hill they could see the gentle curve of the island and the ocean licking the opposite side. Fishing boats dotted the waves, out since dawn to catch the tide and avoid the heat of day. A few figures moved on the beach, but it was still too early for the kids, busy doing their chores, to be on the eastern side.

Vincent pushed the door open and they went inside, setting their gear on the floor. Then Vincent turned his radio on, unplugged the earphones and set it for loud-speaker, and turned around to find his friend looking at the ceiling with his eyes half closed. "What's the matter, Tim?"

Tim's head turned, then it became evident what he was doing. He was smelling the air, doing something the mainlanders had never been able to accomplish. "Someone has been here, Vincent."

"You sure?"

Tim nodded, still sniffing the air. "Don't move," he said. "There is more than a foreign man-smell here."

"Can you identify it?"

"Only that it is not a good smell, my friend. There is evil in it. Something hard and evil."

Vincent didn't dispute his friend. All too well he knew how keen Tim's sense of smell was and how perceptive his island intuition. He let his eyes roam around the room, remembering the details as they were when they left. At first, things seemed untouched, but then he saw his map. He had closed it after he had used it. Now it was open to the section showing the Cardiff Chain of islands, and with a sudden touch of fear he knew he had drawn a circle around the last one in the chain, Montique Island, where the boys should be right now ... and the remnants of a great nobility.

It was Tim that found it. His unerring sense of smell led him to the chair where Vince would have been sitting had he not stopped him in his tracks. He pointed it out and Vincent studied the booby trap until he was positive he could deactivate it, then disengaged the trigger mechanism and pulled the dynamite sticks out from under the chair. "You won't have to go looking on the other side of the island for visitors, Tim. They've been here and gone."

"Why would they do this, Vincent?"

Before he could answer, his call letters crackled from the Speaker and he said, "That should be Herman or the kids."

But it was neither. Sir Harry had finally reached him and his message was brief and to the point.

Everyone's lives were in total jeopardy. The agents of that European dictatorship were vicious, deadly men.

What made it even worse was that the two Sir Harry was warning him about already had a huge lead on them and there was nobody to stop them in their deadly game except two young boys who could hardly do a thing at all.

Tim said, "The International Patrol boat is still on the rails waiting for a new propeller. It will be three days before it's in the water again."

"I know. We'll have to go ourselves. If we're lucky we'll raise the boys on the radio before they get to them. Somebody must have seen the boat that was here, so let's get a description of it and let the kids know what to look for."

With a nod, Tim headed for the door. "I hope we're not too late."

"So am I, Tim, so am I."

CHAPTER SIX

THE BOYS WERE UP EVEN before the sun came over the horizon. Everyone worked on the island, even visitors, and theirs was the job of bringing in the water from the natural stone cistern carved into the rock by a million rainfalls.

Ordinarily, Tila would have had little to do, but this was one day she insisted on doing her complete share, personally making breakfast for her guests. She sat between the two of them, able to say a few of their words as they did hers, but it really didn't matter at all. Somehow they got their meanings across the way all kids can.

When they finished, the treasures of Grandau were brought out and laid in front of them to inspect, and Larry whistled in admiration at what they saw.

Josh looked at him curiously. The objects were new to him. "What are they?"

"This," Larry pointed out, "is a sceptre of office. The king or queen holds it while performing official duties."

"It looks like a club."

"At one time it was, only now it's a jewel-covered symbol."

"Wonder what it's worth?"

"Millions of dollars, Josh."

"That's too rich for my blood," Josh said. "What are those other things?"

"All the trappings of royalty."

"Friend, I wouldn't want to be a king then. That sword may be pretty, but it would never cut the head off a mako shark and I sure wouldn't want to be caught out in the rain in that fancy coat."

"That's an ermine robe," Larry told him, "or rather, what's left of it. Looks like the moths had plenty of meals on the fur."

They went over all the relics that were brought out, nodding in approval as they inspected the gold and silver Ornaments and when they had seen them all, Larry said to his friend, "There isn't much doubt about all this being real. I sure wish Dad were here to see this. No kidding, he'd really flip!"

At the mention of Larry's father, the boys looked at each other with stricken expressions. "We forgot to call them!" Josh gasped.

"They must be worried sick. Look, let's do it right now or they'll never let us go off on our own again."

It would be impossible to describe a radio to their new friends, so the boys simply indicated that they'd like them to go down and see their boat. When their intentions became clear, most of the people stopped smiling and a touch of fear clouded their eyes.

In his own tongue, Georg said, "Only a few have been to the waters. It is a place they are afraid of, a place where strangers might be ..." he smiled gently, "like you." He pointed to Jon and himself. "We will go with you."

But he had forgotten about his princess. Tila pushed herself forward and stood in front of the man who towered over her, shaking her finger at him. "Shame on you, Georg, shame! You want to have all this pleasure for yourself!"

"But, princess ... it can be dangerous ..."

"Nonsense! Margo and Helena have both been there and if they can go so can I."

"But..." Georg started again.

"No 'buts,'" Tina said proudly. "I am going."

The two men looked at each other and spread their hands helplessly. She certainly *was* the princess and now she was letting them know it again. "Very well," Georg agreed, "but we take Helena and Margo with us just in case."

It wasn't quite as easy as all that, however. The rest of the group had to be assured there was absolutely no danger at all to their princess, and even then, the entire population followed them to the descending path and watched every step they took until the little band was safe at the bottom.

From the excitement everyone was showing, the boys knew that their boat was what they wanted to see. The *Sea Eagle* was still anchored where they had left it, none of the guards having the nerve to try to go aboard.

Josh said, "Why don't we take them out on the inflatable raft? Tila ought to like that."

"Good idea. Watching that thing pop open ought to give them a thrill. Let's swim out and get it."

Thrill was hardly the word for it. When Larry yanked the lanyard on the CO^2 bottle and the two-man life raft came alive like a big fat sausage, the girls let out a concerted scream and Jon would have stuck his knife in it if Josh hadn't grabbed his arm.

Laughing, the boys pointed out that it was all right, pushing it into the water to show them what it was for. Then, one by one, they took them all to their boat, helped them over the side, and listened to the sounds of approval as their new friends looked over this strange marvel.

Larry went into the cabin and flipped his radio on, Jon standing right behind him, watching every move with amazement. He ran the collapsible antennae up to full height, then tuned the set to receive. He didn't have long to wait at all.

There were no call letters, no identification. It was just his father's voice, thick with fear; and he must have been yelling into the microphone. "Larry... Josh, wherever you are, stay away from Montique. Two men ..."

A roar blotted out the next words and Jon's great fist came down on the set. The one word ... *kill* ... seemed to come through, but the next blow of the fist demolished the set completely and Jon reeled back against the cabin looking at his bleeding fist, his eyes bulging with a wild fear of the unknown.

Josh came running in, saw the wreckage, and turned to Larry. "What happened? Good golly, look at our radio!"

Larry calmed Jon down and said quietly, "It isn't his fault, Josh. I should have known better. He probably thought the radio was an enemy or something. Anyway, he reacted out of sheer terror."

By now Jon was feeling foolish about the whole thing and was glad to follow Larry's motion and go back outside again. When he was gone Josh asked, "You reach your dad?"

"Yeah."

Josh saw the expression on Larry's face and a chill went through him. "What's wrong?"

"I don't know for sure. Besides, it didn't seem to make sense. All I heard was him saying for us not to come here."

"Why would he do that?"

"Beats me, Josh. His voice sounded like he was scared to death. He mentioned something about two men, then

Jon hit the set." He paused a moment, frowning with his lip between his teeth, then: "I thought he said one other word. It sounded like *kill.*"

"Larry..."

"What?"

"Your dad sure wouldn't want us to have anything to do with killing, would he?"

"Of course not."

"Then that message must have meant something else."

Larry saw what he was getting to and nodded. "Two men are out to kill us. That's why he wants us away from Montique Island."

"And if they want to kill us," Josh added, "they'll want to kill everyone else that's here."

Larry looked at the clock on the rack, then ran topside and searched the sea in all directions. At that moment the ocean was empty, but he knew how fast a boat could travel, even one under sail. Quickly, he sketched out a plan to Josh. Trying to make a run for it at this point might expose them to enemy action, so the best bet would be to stay on the island where there was some help, at least. Meanwhile, they removed the rotor from the engine's ignition, hid it in a safe place, then stripped the sails and put them in the rubber raft along with a small tool kit; then they jumped in and paddled the raft to shore, where they unloaded it. A few more trips and all the passengers were back on the beach, their eyes asking the question of what was happening.

It didn't take much pantomime to explain that someone who wanted to kill them was somewhere out there on that peaceful-looking ocean.

The submarine *Krolin* made contact with the *Dragonfish* forty-two miles northeast of Montique. The captain of the submarine watched with disgust at the sloppy way the trim ketch was being handled and said to his first mate,

"They are clowns, they never should have been allowed out of the bathtub."

"Captain," the mate reminded him, "they have completed many very dangerous assignments."

"Bah! They do things under cover of night. They are like snakes, doing sneaky things to people who are not aware of what is happening. They may have great reputations in the dark places of our government, but that does not mean I have to like them too."

"It is our job ..."

"Yes, yes, I know," the captain said irritably. "Unfortunately, we were the closest ship so we will assist them if necessary, but for the life of me I cannot see why a U-boat like the *Krolin* should be called for in a place like this. There can't possibly be anything more than an island war canoe to oppose us."

After two attempts, Aktur managed to get the *Dragonfish* close enough to the submarine so that a seaman could get a line aboard, then they stepped to the wet steel deck and nodded at the captain and his mate. While they were at sea, Aktur and Embor had gone over the details of their trickery until they were sure that when this affair was over they could disappear without anyone ever being the wiser. Those back home would not have firsthand knowledge, so would be easy to deceive, but the captain of the U-boat would be a wary and intelligent man and the last one to ever see them, so with him the act must be perfect.

Not really being men of the sea was a big help. They both saw the captain's scorn over their inferior boat handling and knew that as far as he was concerned, their being lost in the vastness of the ocean was something that could have been predicted.

So, for an hour, they went over the fine points of their plan to assault Montique; then when the captain gave his reluctant approval, they clambered over the side, almost falling into the ocean despite the steadying hands of the seamen, and managed, somehow, to get their engines going and pull away without crashing against the steel hull of the submarine.

"Such clods," the captain muttered, watching them slowly recede. "There must be idiots in the homeland."

"Well, sir, they managed to get here," the mate said.

"Only because the weather was clear, the sea calm, and we were able to give them a compass course to steer by. And they were lucky," he added. "They had better stay lucky if they want to stay alive. They wouldn't last long in a storm."

"Quite right, sir."

"Come, let us submerge and get to the rendezvous point. This is no place to be intercepted by any strange vessels."

Now a good mile away, Aktur Cilon and Embor Linero watched the gray cigar-shaped hull of the *Krolin* slowly sink beneath the surface until there was no sign of it at all.

"I think the good captain will now be able to write a report on the stupidity of our seamanship." Aktur laughed.

"He wouldn't be far wrong, you know," Embor replied seriously.

Disgustedly, Aktur shook his head. "Even an idiot could sail a compass course back to the Florida mainland. There are thousands of places in the islands along the way for us to hide in and we'll have all the time in the world to do it. The game is almost over, anyway. Who can stop us now?"

Aside from the jeweled ceremonial sword, there were no weapons on Montique Island. Their eating utensils and farming tools were all totally inadequate for defensive purposes and their only safety lay in being able to skill-fully disguise the path to the top, and in case of an invasion, hope that a barrage of rocks might deter any enemy until help arrived.

"But aside from our dads," Josh asked, "who could come?"

Larry thought for a moment, then said, "Your dad told us no natives ever come here, right?"

Josh nodded. "There's nothing here for them, and besides, they have some silly superstition about the place."

"Well, they're not dumb, that's for sure, so if we set off a good smoky fire in the middle of this place they'll see it from the other islands and *somebody* will come looking."

There was hesitancy in Josh's voice. "I don't know. These islanders down here are pretty far away from civilization."

"It takes a man to start a fire though."

"What's wrong with lightning?"

"Nothing ... it just doesn't make smoke signals too." Larry laughed.

"Okay, you win."

They waved Tila over and showed her what they needed and she ran to the group of men, talking excitedly. "They want a fire ... a big one when the time comes. We'll pile up the logs and get ready to make a lot of smoke. They're sure it will attract attention."

"Nobody has ever come before."

"We've never made a lot of smoke before."

"There is a problem." Jon looked concernedly at Tila. "Yes?"

"The lighting of it from our embers. The driftwood we will gather is so dry there is hardly any smoke. How can all this happen?"

The expression on Tila's face was so downcast that the boys had to laugh. At first she got angry and stamped her foot irritably, but Larry calmed her down and said, "All right, let's hear your problem. It can't be all that bad."

But it was to her, and with many motions imitating the billowing of smoke and showing them a piece of dry wood and a burned-out ash, she got her point across.

The boys still smiled, nodding. This time she didn't get mad a bit. Somehow she knew they had that all figured out too. When the party went down to the beach to collect the driftwood that had piled up along the shore, Larry and Josh went back to the boat, loaded a five-gallon can of gasoline and a couple quarts of oil in the life raft, and brought it back to land. When everything had been lugged to the top, Larry spilled a little of a gasoline-oil mixture on a bit of wood, then touched a match to it. The instant flame from that small stick made the group draw back in amazement, but when they saw the thick black smoke that came up from the ground, they knew the problem was ended.

Now Georg was sent to the highest part of the island with the ship's old brass spyglass. If any ship or boat came into view, the word would be passed. If it was one sailed by two men, then the island would be ready for defense.

While the boys were instructing Jon how the matches worked and where to pour the gasoline mixture when the time came, Tila walked to the edge of their encampment. Three of the men were still down below gathering the last of the wood, while behind her everyone else was busy at some assigned task.

Tila felt herself getting angry again. Here she was, their own princess, the ruler over every one of them, and she didn't have a single thing to do. Well, she thought, she could show them that she was useful as any of them and quite capable of getting about without a lot of people to help her.

She took a deep breath, stepped over the rim to the steep and dangerous path that wound its way down the side of the mountain to the beach. She got to the first cutback without slipping or sliding at all and suddenly felt very sure of herself.

Why, there's nothing to it, she thought. She didn't need anyone at all to help her! Now, wouldn't Margo and Helena be proud when she told them how she got all the way down the mountainside with no trouble whatsoever.

She was so wrapped up in her thoughts that she didn't see the loose rock in front of her. Her foot slipped on the loose shale, twisted, and she went down in a sprawling dive, going giddily headfirst into open space. Before she could scream, she crashed against solid earth and felt her consciousness leaving her.

The *Blue Tuna II* was in trouble. Two hours ago the port engine had begun to overheat and had to be shut down before it seized up entirely. Now the starboard engine was running irregularly and losing RPMs fast. "Can you find the trouble?" Vincent yelled.

Down in the bilge, Tim shook his head. "I found the break in the lines, but this is the best I can do. We won't get any more power from this engine until we get back to Peolle or find some spare parts."

"We're running out of time!"

Tim finished the repairs, wiped the grease off his arms, and went topside. "How about the International Patrol?"

"They're sending the old boat out of Miami, but you know how slow *that* tub is."

"And still nothing from the boys?"

Vincent wiped his hands across his eyes. "Not a thing. All I can hope for is that they picked up one of our transmissions."

"Maybe Sir Harry could do something through his government."

"Tim ... you don't deal with governments anymore. You deal with bureaucracies that check everything out before they move at all. If any government acted hastily it could blow up into an international incident, and *that* nobody wants."

"Things do not look good, do they? Even our engines are against us. But we can always run the port engine for fifteen-minute periods, my friend. It takes that long to get to overheating."

"Okay," Vincent said, "let's push them to the limit. We can't let time run out on us."

Embor Linero took the binoculars out of the case and raised them to his eyes to scan the horizon. According to his calculations, Montique Island should be dead ahead. He focused slowly, then he saw what he was looking for. He climbed down from the top of the cabin and stood beside Aktur. "Give us full speed, comrade."

Reluctantly, Aktur pushed the throttle forward. "Do you really think we should charge in like this?"

Embor shrugged. "Why not? We know we eliminated the others back on the island so there would be no alert, and besides, surprise would only be in our favor."

"I don't mean that," Aktur said. He indicated the fuel gauge. "We are low on gasoline."

"We do not know enough about sails to try and maneuver in close. We will use our engine until this is over, and then, very leisurely, we can sail off to our pleasures, learning how to work that silly canvas as we go."

An hour later the *Dragonfish* lay a quarter mile off the rocky mountain that was Montique Island. From his position in the bow, Embor surveyed the rugged terrain, then picked up the *Sea Eagle* anchored off the tiny beach. "Ah, yes," he said, "they are all there, waiting like a nest of ants to be eliminated."

"But where?" Aktur asked. "I can see no one at all!"

Embor raised the glasses until the rim of the mountaintop came into view. "Where else could they be, Aktur?" Suddenly he caught the barest glimpse of something moving in the rocks. "They are up there, of course." He put the glasses back in his case and stowed them away in the rack. From the overhead he took down a rifle, checking the ammunition in the clip, and put it back on its hooks.

"Drop the anchor," he said. "The time has come."

CHAPTER SEVEN

THEY HAD BEEN WATCHING the progress of the *Dragonfish* since it first appeared on the horizon, then Larry took over the spyglass and extended it to full power. He let Josh look at the boat and the two aboard and asked, "What do you think, Josh?"

"I have seen many tourists in these waters, but not quite like these. Their faces are not like ... well, Americanos. Their clothes are not right, either."

Larry took the glass back and peered through it. "Notice the way they've dropped the sails?"

"Yes ... like someone who never saw a sail before. They're running under power."

He could see the one called Embor scanning the island through his glasses too, saw him put them up and take down the gun from its rack. A minute later the anchor went over the side.

Jon tapped him on the shoulder and pointed toward the piled logs in the background. Larry shook his head. The sun was sinking below the horizon now, and before they could get the smoke up it would be too dark to see it. All that would be visible would be light from the fire, and on the mountaintop in the dark of night, that might only add to native superstition and keep them further away than ever.

"Everything ready, Josh?"

"The men are in their places," he answered.

"The trail covered up?"

"If they find it at all, it will take plenty of time. And if they do, they'll still have to climb it. We have enough throwing stones to drive them back."

"Josh ... they have guns, and these people have never seen what one can do."

For a moment Josh had a faraway look on his face. "It's almost like it was before, when they had to run from the same enemy in Grandau."

"Yeah, only this time there's no *Tiger* coming in under full sail to rescue them."

"Who knows, Larry? We did see its longboat."

Larry shot him a curious look. "Remember," he finally said, "how no one recognized the sketch we made of the longboat ... or the letters of its name we drew in the sand?"

"Yes. It was very odd."

"Yet the longboat was very real and Vali Steptur knew where it was."

"Then why wouldn't he have used it sooner, or at least told someone else about it?"

"I'm guessing on this," Larry told him, "but I think he put more faith in the old story than the others did. To them it was a legend ... to him something real. He was getting old and knew they'd laugh at him, so he set out to locate it and he did."

"But this island is barely a mile across!"

"You can lose track of a lot of things in a mile," Larry said.

Overhead the last of the fading light went into the darkness of night. From the west came the low rumble of thunder, and the faint glow of sheet lightning made billowing clouds glow yellow momentarily. There was a coolness in the air now, along with the smell of rain.

For those standing guard along the rim, woven palm-leaf poncho like hoods were handed out. Larry and Josh took theirs from Margo and thanked her. She still had one left in her arms and asked, "Tila?"

The boys looked at each other and shook their heads. They hadn't seen Tila since they'd taken up their posts and assumed she was safe in one of the houses. Margo gave them an anxious nod and went off, calling for her princess.

Once again, Larry aimed the spyglass at the beach and peered through the eyepiece.

"See anything?"

"Nothing." He collapsed the glass down into the big section and folded the brass cap over the lens. "This antique was made for daylight only. Now I appreciate the refinements of modern night glasses."

"Too bad we didn't think to bring ours."

"Well," Larry said, "it's too late now."

They were interrupted again as the first drops of rain reached them. Margo's face was frightened, her voice hoarse when she asked, "Tila ... Tila?" then went off into a flurry of her own language. Right behind her Georg came up and waited for their answer. When the boys shook their heads the frozen look that crossed Georg's eyes told them everything.

Tila had disappeared from the island.

It was the rain that awakened her. It was slashing with windswept fury across her face and a cold shudder racked her body. She moaned softly and opened her eyes, wondering where she was and why somebody wasn't taking care of her the way they always had.

A jagged streak of lightning split the night apart and

for a brief second she saw where she was, caught in the rocks halfway down the side of the mountain, and she knew she was there because she didn't want anyone taking care of her. Tears welled into her eyes, but she fought them back and tried to get her foot out of the crevice of rock that trapped her.

She had to give up. Her strength was giving out and her foot was still wedged in too tightly for her to get loose alone. For a while she lay there, breathing deeply, the cool rain making her alert again, then she began to yell for help as loud as she could. Twice there was a flash of lightning and the almost immediate burst of thunder drowned her out, then she yelled again. She knew her voice was getting hoarser every time she cried out, yet she dared not stop. All too often she had seen these heavy rains cut into the weathered sides of the mountain and break loose the flat shale that tore even bigger chunks out of the rock until there was another avalanche of sharp, deadly rubble sweeping down the steepness and piling into the ocean at the base with a roar that got lost in the spray it generated.

Tila pushed herself partially erect, looking toward the top of her mountain. There was nothing but blackness there and the rain tore at her face. She felt the first bite of stone particles hit her too and knew some of the aged facing stone was beginning to loosen.

Once more, she thought. I can yell for help just once more. If there is no answer, then I will go down the rock-slide and the House of Tynere will have come to an end.

She took a deep breath and screamed as hard as she could.

The voice that answered said, "Well, well, what have we here?"

But it wasn't in her language or the one the boys used either, and the tone of it was hard and flat.

Then, when the lightning came again, she saw the

face of the two men, recognized the deadly menace in their expressions, and knew then who they were and once more she screamed until there was no voice left in her at all.

High up above, Josh stiffened and turned his head ever so slightly. The strange ways of the storm had made the wind twist back on itself, and his ears, so finely tuned to nature, had caught something that should not have been there.

"What is it, Josh?" Larry had seen his friend being suddenly alerted.

"It sounded like ... a scream."

"You sure?"

He listened intently, every nerve on edge, ready to catch even the faintest note of that same sound. But there was none. He looked at Larry a few seconds, then nodded. "I'm sure. It was a scream, all right."

Softly, Larry asked, "An animal, perhaps?"

"No. It was a person."

And they both were thinking the same thing. The only person missing was Tila.

Larry knew how perceptive his friend's trained senses were and he was almost afraid to ask, but he had to. "Could you identify the voice?"

Josh confirmed his fears. "It was a girl's."

In back of them the search was still going on in the area and they knew there wasn't time to get help. Tila was someplace down the mountain, stranded in the storm and possibly hurt, and what counted right then was speed. Only Margo, who was still looking for Tila around the rim, saw them motion to her that they were going down the side, but she didn't have the faintest idea why because she was certain Tila never would have gone down there anyway.

Two minutes after they had stepped onto the sheer

slippery wet path the boys knew they had trouble. The rain had turned their footing into a mucky, slippery chute that could whip their feet out from under them and send them crashing to their death. Luckily, the roots of the bushes that lined the path were still holding fast, so that when they slipped they were able to regain their footing. At one turn Larry went down, his fingers barely hanging onto the stub of a dead bush until Josh gave him a hand, and before he could stand up his canvas shoes kicked loose a ridge of shale and sent it bouncing down into the darkness.

That same shale sprayed itself over Embor and Aktur as they yanked at Tila's arms. She beat at them, but they held her wrists until she stopped and Aktur said, "Why not leave her be? She won't last long here in this storm. Who could she tell about us then?"

Embor agreed and gave her arms another wrench. "She's only a stupid girl anyway."

The pain in her arms brought life back to Tila. In her most commanding voice she shouted at them hoarsely, "How dare you touch me like that, you beasts! Take your hands off me. I am the Princess Tila of the House of Tynere, the ruler of the Kingdom of Grandau. For this insult ..."

Aktur raised his hand to slap her, but Embor stopped him short.

"What is it?" Aktur asked impatiently. "We can't afford to waste time and ..."

"Silence, you clod. It's too bad you don't use your ears for listening to other people." He grinned and twisted those small arms again and heard her voice lash out at him again. He looked up at Aktur and said, "Did you hear it then, comrade?"

A frown of puzzlement was on Aktur's face. "I heard *Tynere* and *Grandau*, but . . ."

"It's such a pity you didn't go further in the study of languages," Embor told him. "She said something else ... *princess* ... and *Tila*. What we have right here, comrade, is the precious jewel in this whole search of ours. She is the last of the royal line of Tynere and when we deliver her to our people, who will get the story from her before her ... er ... elimination, our job is done."

"There are those up there that must be taken care of too," Aktur said.

"Certainly." Embor grinned evilly. "But why should we risk our necks on this mountain when our submarine can simply fire in high-explosive shells from its deck gun. I am certain the good captain would be happy to have a piece of the action knowing a medal and promotion would await him in the motherland."

The other man returned the evil grin and nodded. "Embor, you are right. Let us get her out of these rocks and back to our boat. I can almost taste those wonderful things our money is going to buy us in the United States."

"First we must get there."

"Of course." Aktur laughed. "And what could be easier?"

It was the glaring brightness of the lightning that made them see it. Right in front of their faces, snagged on the broken end of a twisted, half-uprooted bush was a piece of old fabric. The swirling gusts had almost ripped it away when Larry grabbed it. They both looked at it and knew what it was. The last time they had seen it, it was part of a dress Tila wore.

They waited for another sharp flash of lightning, and this time they knew what to look for. They saw the path of broken bushes that had partially cushioned the falling body of their new friend. Without waiting, they stepped off the time-traveled narrow road down and slipped and fought a muddy battle following the trail of bent foliage and a few more pieces of fabric until they slid into a rock pile gasping for breath.

"She's got ... to be here," Josh gasped. "There are ... no more bushes. All rocks now."

"Suppose she isn't?"

"Then...she went into the ocean. It's all over."

They had to wait for another flash from the night sky before they could be sure and they looked up, worried. The storm was drifting past quickly and the rain was beginning to diminish. Then it came, and they were able to look into the cluster of rocks beside them.

Another piece of fabric was caught on a shale outcropping, but there was no young girl there at all. The total shock of it broke over the boys like an icy wave and they could taste the bitter disappointment in their mouths. "We're too late," Larry barely whispered.

Josh would have agreed with him, but the final flash of lightning showed him something so startling he scarcely believed it. In that tiny moment of time when everything was daylight, bright with intense electrical energy, he had seen the imprint of booted feet in the wet earth and they were leading down-ward toward the beach!

There was no time for disappointment now. At least Tila was still alive. If she weren't they would have left her there. It was evident now what the two men had planned. They were going to stage their attack at night with the storm as cover, but they had heard Tila scream and had gone to investigate. Knowing how she would have reacted to her capture, the boys were sure it wouldn't take those men long to realize what a prize they had taken!

"How long has it been since we started?"

Larry checked his watch. "Forty-five minutes."

"They have a good start."

"She won't make it easy for them to carry her. We could still catch up."

"Then what, Larry? How do we get past their guns?"

"I don't know. We're just going to have to find out."

With the strange suddenness so typical in tropical lands, the storm above broke and the rolling clouds drifted by to let the soft glow of moonlight spill down. In a few minutes their eyes adjusted to it and they were able to position themselves. To one side the old path cut by and they'd be able to follow it down to the shoreline.

Pointing downward, Josh said, "Look."

The men's forms were indistinct, but they were visible, two blobs struggling with something between them. They could hear guttural sounds now and occasionally Tila's biting voice until it was sharply cut off.

As quickly as they could, the boys scrambled downward, the rushing water still coursing down the mountainside covering any noise they made. When they reached the sand, breathing heavily from their exertion, they saw what had happened.

Tila *had* been a heavy bundle for them. She must have been kicking and twisting every minute of the time and now they had tied her up and tossed her on the sand while they sprawled out to get their wind back. They were only a few feet from the water and the dinghy from their boat was at the now quiet surf's edge ready for launching. Plainly, they could see the rifles the men held and the holstered pistols on their belts.

Neither boy wasted time discussing the impossibility of the situation. Their own life raft was too far away and too well hidden to go for at this point and they both realized it. "There is one thing we can do, Josh."

"You name it, friend."

"I'm going to swim out to their boat. If I can get there ahead of them maybe I can disable it."

Josh's mouth dropped open. "In *these* waters at night? There are sharks out there and this is their feeding time!"

"You have a better idea?"

Slowly, Josh shook his head.

"Then I'm going," Larry told him. "What you do is run interference for me. When those men get ready to move, get in the shadows and throw rocks or shells or anything at them. Keep moving around so they'll think there's more than just one person, but keep them stirred up so I can get a jump on them."

Josh's concern was intense. "Look, you're risking your life when ..."

But Larry cut him off. "Buddy, this isn't the islands. These are city people and I know how the city people are. You don't think they're going to let her live, do you?"

"They can't just kill her!"

"Why not? Power and money is more important to their kind than life. No, if they get away with her, she is dead. Now go ahead and keep your eyes on those two."

Before Josh could stop him, Larry was wading silently into the water. He scarcely made a ripple, and Josh turned and went back into the darkness of the shadow of the mountain. Above him the moon was a huge white face beaming down and at any other time it would have been a beautiful sight. Now it was a danger. He searched around, gathered some good-sized rocks, and picked out his first position.

In the water, Larry breast-stroked slowly. He was well aware of the fact that sharks were there and *did* feed at night, and he knew any noise or vibration that resembled that of an injured or dying fish would attract them long before his scent reached them. Inwardly, he wanted to flail away at the sea with a racing stroke to get there as fast as possible, and it took all of his concentration not to.

He passed the point where the *Sea Eagle* was still riding at anchor, wondering what else the two men had done to disable it. A few hundred yards ahead, in the glow of the moonlight, he could see the men's ketch where it was moored in deeper water. He could feel his heart thudding now, because this was the critical time, swimming in the area where the sharks could be cruising. Behind him he heard a sudden yell in a strange language, then another and another, and he knew that Josh was creating a diversion. He began swimming again, still quietly, but with stronger arm movements.

Something caught his eye to one side. Was it real, or did he imagine he had spotted the outline of a triangular fin cutting a swath through the water?

He looked again, but there was nothing there. He could feel the panic creeping up on him because he knew the first attack, if it came, would probably be from beneath. He forced himself to stop and take several deep breaths to calm himself down; then he looked back toward the beach. There was something else back there and he knew what it was.

The men had gotten their dinghy into the water.

He couldn't waste another second. He had to take the chance now or risk losing the whole game. Sharks or no sharks, he broke into a speed stroke, arms digging into the water, feet beating in tempo as he churned his way to the boat ahead.

The moon threw a broad swath of rippled light across the water and he saw the fin cross it and disappear. It came back again, the direction reversed and nearer this time. Fear gave Larry a new burst of energy, and he put everything he had into the last few strokes that took him to the side of the *Dragonfish*.

And right behind him now was a fin angling toward him.

The men had left the ladder over the side for their return and Larry grabbed the rungs and hauled himself out of the water just as that huge gray body slid by beneath him. When he rolled onto the deck he had to lie there a few seconds just to get his breath back. They were a few seconds he could scarcely afford.

Ten yards away one man was pulling hard on the dinghy's oars while the other was tightly holding an enraged young girl to keep her from struggling. Larry only allowed himself that one look, then he crawled to the cabin, staying low and out of sight. He fumbled for the hatch cover over the engine, ran his hands around the edges feeling for the latch, but there was none, and he realized it was a remote-opening lock ... he wasn't going to be able to disable the engine after all.

One thing he did see ... and that was the key in the ignition lock. He yanked it out, dropping it into his pocket as the dinghy bumped the hull of the boat. He heard the key clink against the magnet in his pocket and grinned. There still was something he could do. He fingered the small magnet loose, stuck it behind the boom. Canvas was flopping loosely all over the place, and whenever he felt a rope he slashed his knife through it. He saw the men come over the side, pulling Tila with them. There was little he could do now, but as for those men, even if they could manage to hot-wire the engine and get it started, they'd follow a wild course with the magnet scrambling their compass, and there was no way at all they were going to be able to raise any canvas without a major repair job.

Larry watched while the men dragged the girl forward and tied her down. Next to him he could hear the gentle rub of the dinghy against the ketch, and while the others' heads were turned he dropped over the side silently, got into the dinghy, detached the line, and shoved it away from the boat. He was well in the dark when he heard the muffled voices of the men. Then there was silence a moment, the cabin door slammed, and a muted nasty remark was passed before the engine turned over, caught, then idled while the men pulled up the anchor.

Someplace, they had had a spare key.

Now it was all up to that little piece of magnetic metal, Larry thought.

CHAPTER EIGHT

"WHAT WILL BE OUR HEADING, EMBOR?"

"Eighty degrees at twelve hundred RPMs for one hour ten minutes. That will put us within range of the *Krolin's* radar and they can contact us."

Aktur Cilon turned the wheel and let the compass settle on the slightly northeast heading. He looked up, but there was cloud cover over the moon again and another rumble of thunder in the west.

Dratted tropical weather, he thought. There was no way you could rely upon it to remain stable. Now there were no stars visible, no moon to go by, and he had a very peculiar feeling about the direction they were taking. Finally he said, "Embor, are you certain we are headed properly?"

"What is your compass course?" Embor replied tartly.

"Exactly eighty degrees."

"In that case, you idiot, you are going correctly. Now pay attention to your steering while I attend to the girl."

"What will they think when they find the dinghy gone, Larry?"

"Nothing, most likely. I left the rope dangling from their rail so they'll figure it just came loose."

The two boys were standing on the deck of the *Sea Eagle,* Larry looking eastward through their night glasses. "Still see them?"

"Barely," Larry answered. "They seem to be swinging in a wide circle to the south."

"But ... that's empty ocean for five hundred miles."

"They don't know that. Right now they're following a compass course."

"Wouldn't that magnet keep it steady?"

Larry lowered the glasses and shook his head. "It's probably sliding around with the motion of the boat. I never figured on that." He peered through the eyepieces again. The dim spot of light from the cabin of the *Dragonfish* was still visible. It stayed within the scope of the glasses another few minutes then was blanked out. The edge of the cliffs of Montique Island had cut them off.

Now they had to play a waiting game. Somewhere out there would be their father, but he too was strangely late. If it got there in time the *Blue Tuna II* would certainly be more than a match for the *Dragonfish,* but the time they had left had reached zero. Tila was gone, the men were out of sight, and the boys were alone.

More to keep their spirits up than anything else, they lowered the rest of their supplies, including all the spare gasoline, medicines, and foodstuffs, into the dinghy and rowed it ashore to be hidden with the other load. They wanted to leave nothing of any value to the enemy if they came back again.

By Larry's watch it was almost midnight, but there was no thought of sleeping yet. Josh had come back from his scouting trip and led Larry to the edge of the water. The tide had receded a good ten feet from the rocks and he said, "There's a natural sand strip all the way around at low tide. Once we're on the other side there has to be some way we can get up on the cliff and keep that ketch in sight."

"That's good enough. Let's try it," Larry said.

They went single file with Josh in the lead, his feet feeling out all the sure places and staying clear of the soft, water-filled traps that could suck them under. They wound in and out of the irregularities in the face of the cliff, realizing they were in an area never explored by the inhabitants of the top of the mountain island. Twice Josh spotted the dot of light at sea and Larry picked it up in his glasses. It was the *Dragonfish,* all right, and the second time it seemed to be closer.

They were both so engrossed with trying to keep the ketch in sight that they didn't notice the strange sound that seemed to come to them through the rocks themselves. When they finally sensed it they came to a stop, listening intently. The sound had a surging quality and there was an odd smell in the air, different from the salty tang of the ocean.

Larry said, "That sounds like wave action."

"But the ocean has quieted. There is hardly any surf at all."

"I know ... but do you hear how muffled it is, yet how it seems to beat like a giant drum?"

Josh's eyes narrowed and his head tilted back. It was a common gesture and Larry knew he was smelling the air again. "That's a freshwater smell, friend."

"Here ... on the edge of the ocean?" Larry queried.

"There's a cave nearby," Josh said simply.

"What!"

"A big cave, Larry, and it is acting like a drum, making the sound of the water bigger as it runs out with the tide." He paused, listening again. "It is someplace ahead ... the way we must go anyway."

Carefully, they made their way around a projecting spur of rock just as the cloud cover thinned out and let the full moon throw a feeble glow around them. Josh stopped suddenly, his finger pointing. "There's their boat!"

The *Dragonfish* had changed course again, veering a good twenty degrees to the east. It was evident that the magnet Larry had left behind the compass had thrown the men into following an erratic heading, but now it could lead the ketch out of sight.

"We're going to have to get up the cliff face, Josh."

"I know. Well follow this shoreline a little longer and if there is any kind of cave ahead, there might be a way we can climb around it."

Once again the cloud pattern broke and let the moonlight through. For the moment the sand, the sea, and the side of Montique were visible in muted detail and they took advantage of it and worked their way ahead as quickly as possible. The sandy area had widened as the tide reached its peak ebb, and the dull roaring was louder with every step they took.

When they cut around the angular column of rock that swept like a crescent from the mountain, they stopped in sheer amazement and saw something so incredible that the hair stood up on the back of their necks and made their flesh crawl all over.

It was a huge stone mouth in the solid rock, with deep black water running out of it like a living tongue and a voice of thunder coming from the depths of its throat. The overhanging brow of the cliff kept it from being seen from above and the sheltering cheek of the great crescent and its natural camouflaging color made it invisible from the sea.

The wild mystery of this phenomenon drew them closer. There was no way they could resist standing in front of that gigantic cavern, and when they felt the winds trying to suck them into the opening they realized what caused the booming sounds like invisible waves.

On either side of the wide stream that passed back and forth from the ocean to the cave were the white sands of the beach that reflected the moonlight into the monstrous hole. When they had taken only two steps inside they were frozen in their tracks by the huge form that looked like a great bat about to sweep down and devour them alive.

Both the boys were gripping each other so hard they let out grunts of pain, and Josh said, "What ... what is it?"

Larry knew what it was, all right. It was absolutely unbelievable, but there it was, and absolutely real. It was there where the vagaries of the wind and tide had selected to put it and nature had chosen to preserve it. It was there, wet and slimy, with wings spread over the black fighting body that had iron teeth projecting from each side.

"It's the *Tiger*," Larry said.

"What?"

"Now we know what happened to it, Josh. She followed the push of the winds and the pull of the currents across the ocean until she was sucked into this cave, where she could go no further."

"But ..."

"You smelled it earlier," Larry reminded him. He reached down, dipped his hand in the water, and tasted it. "Fresh water, Josh. Someplace there must be a mighty spring of fresh water feeding itself into this basin."

"Larry ... even fresh water can rot wood."

"Not always."

"Back on Peolle ..."

"That's surface water there, Josh. Apparently this water has a mineral content that preserves wood and metal long past normal expectations."

"Look at those sails," Josh insisted. "They still wave in the wind. You'd think they'd be the first to go.

"That same chemical preservative must be part of the atmosphere here. There isn't any other explanation."

Without being aware of what they were doing, they had walked around the edge of the tremendous underground pool, staying on the rock shelf that acted as a natural pier. Beyond where they were the darkness was too dense and they dared go no further.

"Vali Steptur must have found this place too," Josh said.

"There probably were old stories and legends that he remembered. At least he believed them enough to try to prove that they were true."

"Larry ... do you think ... we ought to go aboard?"

"Do you remember what Sir Harry told us about the *Tiger* ... how they fitted her out for a complete cruise before they turned her loose?"

Josh nodded, wondering what his friend was getting at.

"That means the *Tiger* would have full stores of powder and cannonballs aboard. *Black powder,*" he emphasized.

Josh wasn't very familiar with explosives and said, "But black powder isn't nearly as strong as the modern stuff."

"Right," Larry agreed, "but the longer it sits, the more unstable it gets. After a long while, even the slightest disturbance could set it off, and with all the barrels of it on this ship, if that happened this island would be blown to smithereens."

"Good golly! And those people have been living with this beneath them all these years." He thought of something else and said, "What about the hurricanes and the earthquake they had here?"

"Back then the powder wasn't as unstable as it is now."

"Maybe we ought to get out of here," Josh suggested uneasily.

"I know," Larry replied. "There's something even more important than the *Tiger*."

"Tila."

Without another word they started picking their way back to the opening of the cave. Outside, the faintest gray lay on the eastern horizon. It was what was known as false dawn, the early light that goes ahead of the sunrise.

But that wasn't what worried the boys. The tide was coming back in and had already closed off the pathway in their original direction. The only thing they could do now was go back, and go back quickly. Had it been darker, they both would have certainly been caught in the treacherous sand traps or had their feet washed out from under them. But fear gave them wings and made them step carefully, hands scrabbling for holds in the rock, their breath whistling through parched throats.

It seemed as if hours had passed, but they made the final turn around the bleak stone and collapsed on the edge of the beach just as the sun began its ascent over the ocean, bathing the world in an eerie early red light.

And that strange morning glow illuminated a sight that filled the boys with a new source of strength because out there, wedged on the rocks where the falling sea had stranded it, was the *Dragonfish!*

From behind the protection of mussel-covered rocks, the boys scanned the ketch through the binoculars. It was perched there like a model ship on its stand, but apparently it was undamaged and the two men in the cabin were waiting for the tide to rise and float it off. Up on the forward deck, still tied down, was Tila. She wasn't yelling or squirming now. She was motionless, her face pale white and haggard-looking. For a moment Larry thought she was dead, but her head turned slightly and he knew she was only unconscious.

The two men came out of the cabin and peered over the listing port side, and again their voices could be heard in heated argument. Larry asked, "Think they can get her off?"

Josh nodded toward the watermarks on the side of the cliff. "There's a five-foot tide here. If she didn't get jammed in with too much force, they could make it."

"How long before the tide's in far enough?"

"Two hours."

"We have that long to get Tila back then."

"Maybe we should get some help," Josh suggested.

"No way. They'd spot us on the sand and pick us off with their rifles. Besides, we could never get up that cliff and back in time."

"What do we do then?"

Larry looked through the glasses again. "We're going to outthink those guys on the boat, that's what."

"Oh, great. How are we going to know what *they're* thinking?"

With a little grin twisting his mouth, Larry said, "We know what they're going to *have* to think. Right now what's in their minds is getting that boat free. They can't trust the sea to come in high enough, so they're going to have to help it when it does. So . . ."

"So they lighten the load and get ready to haul it off,'" Josh finished for him.

"You got it," Larry said.

"I have an idiot for a partner," Embor said harshly. He studied the rocks surrounding the *Dragonfish* and grimaced in disgust. "How could you have steered right back from where you started?"

"I tell you, I followed your instructions. The compass course you gave me . . ."

"Bah! Then why are we here?"

"Didn't you check the compass three times yourself?" Aktur demanded. "Was I not right on eighty degrees?"

Sourly, Embor said, "True, but what course were you on when I was *not* looking?"

"I'm telling you . . ."

"Forget it, Aktur. It is too late for excuses. What we must do is get this boat afloat. Then, with our naked eyes and without you following a compass course, we will get away from this accursed place. Let us hope the submarine is still waiting for us."

Aktur Cilon was too tired to bother arguing back. He simply asked, "What is your plan?"

"The book describes an activity called kedging. We carry the anchor out, sink it in the bottom, then pulling on the line together, we can haul this boat off."

"It is too bad the dinghy broke loose. We could have carried the anchor in that."

"Stupid," Embor hissed. "It didn't *break* loose. You didn't tie it tightly enough. Now go up there and get the girl off the deck and put her in the stern. Because of your stupidity we'll have to walk that anchor out there while the tide is still below our heads."

There are times when thinking and waiting must stop and action come into play, even when the odds against success are ten to one. The boys knew that this was their last chance to get to Tila, a slim, final chance that could well wind up with all of them facing a bleak end.

Out there the men were doing exactly as Larry and Josh thought they would, even to removing Tila from the forward deck to make room to lay out the anchor and as much rope as they had in the locker below. The men stripped down to their shorts. Then with much arguing they went over the side, dragging the anchor with them. They distributed the weight between them, then started to plod forward. From what Larry could see, there was at least three hundred feet of line on the deck and the men would probably use at least half of it.

He tapped Josh on the shoulder and said, "Let's go."

Together, they lowered themselves into the water, not daring to wade at all. With matching breast-strokes they went directly toward the ketch, keeping the hull between them and the men's line of vision. There was no holding back now and every stroke was strong and sure, taking them right under the stern of the boat.

Propping themselves on the rocks, they hoisted themselves aboard and slithered toward the bound figure of Tila. Josh grabbed her and pulled her toward the transom, then unbound her hands and started to take the gag out of her mouth. For a second her eyes opened and she started to scream, then Josh's hand closed over her mouth until she recognized him and became still. He lowered her to Larry, went in after her, and the two of them swam back with Tila floating face up, their arms under hers and their hands locked behind her back.

When they reached the shore they stumbled up the sand to the relative safety of the low brush and trees and kept going to get as far away from the *Dragonfish* as possible. They stopped when they were out of breath and eased themselves, gasping, down onto the cool earth. And as tired as she was, Tila gave them both the warmest smile of gratitude they had ever seen and reached for their hands.

Right then Larry and Josh knew that they weren't just two friends anymore ... they were *three*.

And as they all acknowledged the new friendship with big grins, they heard the bullets whine overhead and smack into the trees, with the delayed slam of the rifle shot a moment later.

Fury had turned Embor Linero's face a mottled red and he fired round after round into the foliage on the shore. He looked at his partner, who stood there with a rifle hanging from his arms, and yelled, "Shoot, you fool, shoot!"

"But I see no one!"

"Where else can they be? They are hiding in the brush. Cover the area now!"

Not wanting to arouse Embor's anger any further, Aktur raised the rifle and fired aimlessly into the trees, spacing his shots about ten feet apart. He kept one eye discreetly on Embor, knowing his temper. Ever since they had come back on board to find the girl gone and signs of those who had freed her on the transom, Embor had been like a madman. They couldn't leave the *Dragonfish* now lest it float free and follow the offshore breeze out to the end of the anchor line in the deeper water where the sharks were. If only Embor hadn't been in such a hurry...

"There ... shoot there!" Embor hollered. He fired a single shot to mark the place where he saw the motion in the treeline, and then both men opened up with rapid fire, reloaded, and fired another magazine into the area. Embor grabbed his binoculars and focused them on the beach. At first, he saw nothing and hope was beginning to rise that the intense firepower had gotten all of them, then he saw another flash of movement and muttered under his breath and put his rifle back to his shoulder. Aktur watched where the shots were hitting, then sprayed bullets on one end of the section.

A falling branch loosened by the second burst of gunfire had cut Tila's shoulder, and sand from a whining ricochet stung the boy's bodies. They knew the men had pinpointed their position when they made their last move toward new cover, and only the small sand mound they crouched behind kept them from being killed ... and even now bullets were eating into their scanty protection. "We can't stay here much longer, Larry." "I know. We can't stay grouped together in one target either. Somehow, we have to break up their fire."

"We have to get *rid* of it, Larry."

A couple of hundred yards away the *Dragonfish* had righted herself on the incoming tide and the men had a level platform to shoot from. "They could haul her off now if they wanted to," Josh said.

"What for? We have their prize and they have us pinned down."

"Somehow we've got to get them out of here."

Larry started grinning again. "You've got it, Josh, and I think I have the answer."

"Fine, just fine," Josh grunted. "I can see kids like us running off two grown men with high-powered guns and plenty of ammunition." He paused, then started grinning himself. "How do you figure to do it?"

"Think you can manage to get back down the beach a ways and draw their fire while you stay covered?"

"Sure."

"Good. Get to it then while I make Tila understand she's to stay right here with her head down."

"And what are you going to do?" Josh asked.

"Use a little firepower of our own," Larry told him.

They had to wait another five minutes before there was a lull in the shooting, then Larry nodded and said, "Go!" and all three went into action. While Tila burrowed into the sand, the boys went from tree to tree in opposite directions, and when the gunfire started again it was separated, no longer after a single grouped target.

Every tree became his fortress and Larry darted from one to another. Fifty feet more and he could lose himself in the thick undergrowth, and from there to the hidden cache of supplies would only take a few minutes. It seemed an eternity, but he finally made it and pulled himself to the spot he wanted. Right in front of him were the spare five-gallon cans of gasoline.

Luckily, the wind was right and his cover was excellent. The gentle morning breeze didn't leave a ripple on the water's surface, and when he unscrewed the cap and tipped the can, the gasoline burbled out to float in a multi-colored slick away from the shore directly toward the *Dragonfish,* already bobbing gently in the rising tide. The last two cans of gasoline were added to the first, then it was done. Larry ripped open the waterproofed packet of matches from the supplies, lit one, and tossed it out on the volatile slick. Almost instantaneously, the whole ocean seemed to erupt in flame.

On board the *Dragonfish,* Embor Linero and Aktur Cilon saw the smoking destruction being blown toward them and dropped their rifles. Gone was the idea of reclaiming their former captive. Right now, they had to save their own necks. With one accord they ran to the prow, grabbed the anchor line, and screamed at each other to pull, pull! They leaned into the taut rope with fear giving them strength, and just before the flames got to them the *Dragonfish* floated free, with the keel rasping against the rocks. The two men cut the line, got into the cabin, and started the engine.

Montique Island and its inhabitants had been too much for them. Now the submarine *Krolin* could stand off and blast that chunk of rock and its people to bits with its deck gun.

The boys were too hurried to cheer their victory. They grabbed Tila and got to the path that led to the top. They were bedraggled and tired and suddenly every step was an effort. That plateau on top was a long way off, an almost impossible climb in their condition, and they wondered how they were ever going to make it.

But then they heard the faint shouts and saw the men snaking their way down the path to meet them, and they knew they were safe. At least for now. Help was on its way and the fire barrier kept the *Dragonfish* off. Most of the flame was gone now, but the men were taking no chances any longer. The ketch was sailing about eighty degrees, a course that took it away from Montique. What they didn't know was that it took it closer to the submarine.

CHAPTER NINE

THE THREE OF them slept around the clock without awakening once. The people from Grandau, grateful to have their princess back safely, looked after them, made sure they were comfortable, and waited for nature to wipe out their fatigue and bring back their youthful exuberance.

Most likely, it was the smell of breakfast that aroused them. The three of them were famished and ate heartily while Jon and Georg told how they were torn with the grief of their princess's disappearance, then bewildered when the boys were gone too. But from their mountaintop they had been able to witness what was going on. They saw the *Dragonfish* on the rocks and the boys' rescue of Tila, but they didn't dare interfere because something was happening there they didn't understand but the boys did. Then, when they saw the flames and the ketch retreating, they knew they could come down to complete the rescue.

Festivities were called for then. The old costumes were brought out, the cookfires kindled, and musical instruments from another age all transformed the top of

Montique Island into the old and royal courtyard of Grandau. And Princess Tila of the House of Tynere and her two escorts were the chief guests of honor.

So great was the fun that hardly a person noticed the passing of the day until Helena, who was intrigued by Larry's binoculars and had been studying the terrain most of the time, came to the boys and pointed eastward across the ocean. She handed Larry the glasses and he adjusted the focus and looked out where she was pointing.

There, on the horizon, was the ketch. It was returning to Montique ... and following behind it was the long cylindrical shape of a submarine, its conning tower jutting skyward. He handed the glasses to Josh, and when he did the entire assembly went quiet.

"How much water does that submarine draw, Larry?"

"I doubt if they'll want to pass the fifty- or sixty-foot mark."

"Then they will have to stay at least two miles out there."

Larry's face looked glum. "We're well within range of their deck gun then. They can sit out there and pick us off like tin cans on the back fence."

Behind the mountain the sun had set and late dusk was about to give way to night. "Well," Josh said heavily, "at least we have tonight. There's not going to be much to shoot at until they get some light." He paused and shook his head sadly. "Boy, we don't have any luck at all. We think we've almost gotten them, then kerplooie! It all goes down the drain."

"Maybe not, Josh. Maybe not."

"How can you keep saying that, Larry?"

"There's still the *Tiger.*"

"Come on ... we agreed not to tell these great people about sitting on top of a bomb like that."

"Not *tell* them," Larry said. "We're going to *show* them."

Josh was completely puzzled now. "Larry ..."

"They all said it was a jinx ship, remember? But maybe it wasn't. Maybe it just was a ship that had a purpose. It saved the people from Grandau and later its longboat was there to get one of them out to tell the world the House of Tynere was ready to come home."

"But this is *now,* Larry!"

Larry wore a faint, faraway smile. He nodded in agreement with his friend's statement and said, "And *now* the *Tiger* is ready to finish her chosen assignment."

At first Josh thought his buddy had gotten a little too much excitement, but when Larry explained what he had in mind, the possibility of success dawned in his mind and he said, "It could work, Larry."

"It's all we have left."

"Let's get to it then!"

With the ever-present language barrier, the boys couldn't explain what they were going to do, but they were able to convey their excitement to the men, and while the women stayed on the mountaintop to protect their princess and light the smoke signal at the first light of dawn, the rest made torches to light their way down the path to the beach.

No longer did it matter if their lights were seen. They were trapped anyway, with no means of escape, and the enemy knew it so they could attack when they chose to. So the group went down the steep incline, the glare of the torches lighting their way. When they reached the beach they went toward the southern tip of it and Josh walked ahead. He called back, "The tide's going out, Larry. We'll have plenty of room."

Having already gone the route, the boys knew the way and the pitfalls to avoid, and this time they reached the cave entrance in a fraction of the time it had taken them earlier. There was one thing they had to do, however, and that was prepare the group for what they were about to see. The boys were so serious, their diagrams so complete, and the past events so vivid, that every man took them at their word and not one gave an unbelieving look.

But even so, when they stepped into that enormous chamber with the flaring torches shooting out yellow fingers of light, the sight they beheld froze them motionless, while their minds raced back over the stories that had come from their fathers and grandfathers.

Even after all these years, there was something majestic about that old square-rigged British ship of the line. She was an old lady, but she was still in her prime, her planking solid, her three masts tall and firm, with sails ready to billow out at the first touch of a breeze.

"This time we're going to have to go on board, Josh."

His friend said, "I know. We have to get the bowlines down to the men."

"If they're not rotted."

Josh's face creased in an optimistic grin. "I don't think the old girl would do that to us. Let's get up there,"

The boys stood on the shoulders of Georg and Jon, were hoisted up to the open gunport, where they got a handhold on the cannon and a foot in the frame. From there they could reach the rail and they hauled themselves onto a deck that hadn't felt the feet of a human for two hundred years.

From where they stood the eerie sensation was greater than ever. It was as though the *Tiger* herself was watching every move they made and was making certain they made the right one. Something unspoken said that this was the hour of the *Tiger* ... the very day it was built for. A long time ago she was commissioned to do something great. Not right then, but in the distant future, and for that event she had held herself in battle readiness until the true foe appeared; then she could go forward in her proud charge and do what she had to do.

Walking softly, not wanting to disturb the dignity of the moment, the boys tested the ropes coiled on the belaying pins, feeling the still-resilient tar woven into the fiber itself. "They're like new," Josh said.

"Toss them over, then. Make sure they're well secured on those forward bitts."

While Josh was at it Larry looked alive. There were two things he had to do. The first one took him to a small locker. Never before had he been near a ship like this, but it was as if he was being led. His fingers found the catch, opened the mahogany door, and reached in for the folded oblong canvas. He closed and latched the door, then went back to the mainmast. Unerringly, his fingers found the right line, unwound it from the cleat on the mainmast, and to the rings he attached the brightly colored canvas from the locker.

Every eye was watching him as he ran up the *Tiger's* battle flag to the very tip of the mainmast and fastened the line on the cleat. From deep in the bowels of the ship there seemed to be a rumble of satisfaction. Josh had the lines over the side now and the men were holding them as they were instructed to.

Then Larry did the final thing he knew he had to do. He walked to that spot where the *Tiger's* handsome engraved ship's bell was mounted and sounded it until the echoes reverberated from the walls of the great port that had hosted the guest ship all these years. Then he detached it, handed it over the side to Josh, clambered over the railing to the cannon mouth, and jumped to the ledge where the others were standing.

With the outgoing tide to help them, the men hoisted the lines on their shoulders and leaned into them. The initial motion was so slow they barely noticed it, then step by step the *Tiger* began to move toward the vaulted cave mouth, back to the sea she had left so long ago.

Once again, the false dawn greeted them as the ship of the line moved past them from the momentum they had given it. There was no way she could be stopped now, and they shook the lines loose and watched her go by.

"Larry ... we never set the sails. We didn't even know how to!"

"I don't think they have to be set, Josh. I think the *Tiger* knows exactly what she's doing. She managed a trip across the ocean all by herself and even found a safe harbor until she was needed. Now she's going out to do what she was designed for ... fight and beat the enemy."

"That's a modern submarine out there, Larry, and the *Tiger's* only an old wooden ship!"

As if to answer his statement, a morning breeze curled down from the mountain and filled the vast sail area, and the *Tiger* came alive with a glorious leap ahead that held for a minute; then, slowly, she turned and headed in a new direction slightly northeast of the island.

Josh could only stare, amazed. "Larry ... she's sailing in the direction of the submarine!"

"I know," Larry said. He picked up the *Tiger's* brass bell and waved everybody back on the path. As fast as they could, they made their way back to the beach. Just as they got there they heard the first high-pitched whine of a cannon shell go over the island, then a second that landed a hundred yards out in the ocean, throwing up a geyser of spray.

"They've got the island bracketed! The next one will come right in on it," Larry yelled. Nobody had to be told to dive for cover. The awesome noise of the shells and the explosion in the water told them what was happening. Now they had to wait for the final one.

The captain of the *Krolin* could hardly believe his eyes. The early low-hanging mist lifted just as he was about to give the command to fire the deck gun. From now on all the shells would be high explosive and he had figured that a dozen rounds would completely eliminate all signs of life from the island. But then this ... this thing ...

"What is it?" the mate asked anxiously.

"If I didn't know better I'd say it was an old British naval ship. Look, look." He pointed. "She's flying her colors and her battle flag!"

"Why would she do that?"

For a few minutes it didn't dawn on the captain. He stood there mute, watching a ship so antique she shouldn't be floating bearing down on them. And even that crazy island was doing something strange too. Now a thick tendril of smoke was going straight up into the fresh morning sky, a signal that would be visible for miles to ships and planes and could bring the wrath of nations down on his back if they were found here.

And the ship kept coming. Now he knew, all right. "She's going to attack us," he told his mate.

The mate had the *Tiger* in his field glasses. "An impossibility, Captain. She isn't even manned. Her decks are empty!"

"You fool, she's on a collision course and we can't maneuver!" He cupped his hand around his mouth and shouted to the gun crew. "There, *point-blank fire!* Stop that hulk ... sink it!"

With empty eyes, Aktur Cilon and Embor Linero watched the fierce action as the crew swung the gun and aimed it. They could have told them it was no use, no use at all. The whole thing had been a jinx Operation and now fate was laughing at them, and they knew that all the evil they had done had finally caught up with them.

The deck gun blasted that high-explosive shell at the hull of the *Tiger* rearing up above the highest point of the *Krolin's* conning tower, and all Embor and Aktur could think of was, *How can you fight a ship that really isn't there?*

The tremendous blast as the tons of unstable black powder in the hold of the *Tiger* exploded shook the island of Montique. From the shores they could see the mighty tongues of flame spit from the eruption of the fireball that boiled on the ocean's surface long seconds before gusting upward in a great draft of acrid black smoke.

When it was quiet again and the sky and water were clear, no one spoke a word. Out there the sea was serene, just as though nothing had ever happened at all. There was no ketch, no submarine, and no ship of the line with its battle flag snapping in the breeze.

Larry hefted the weight of the brass bell in his hand.

But there *had* been a *Tiger*.

From the top of the mountain they heard the warning horn, and in his glasses Larry saw Helena pointing out to sea. He turned his glasses in that direction and grinned.

"It's the *Blue Tuna*" he told Josh. "Just like our dads to get here after the action is over."

Two months later the helicopter landed at Peolle Island and a real princess stepped out with her guards, Georg and Jon, and her ladies-in-waiting, Margo and Helena. They had been two grueling months for the people of Grandau, coming back from the past to a renewed kingdom where they were eagerly awaited. Sir Harry had arranged for no mention of Embor and Aktur or the submarine to be made if Grandau was to be given complete freedom again. The dictatorship that held it considered it their best move and signed the papers of release.

Now they were going back, but before they left, it was

the desire (and command) of Princess Tila that they see their old friends once again. It was supposed to be very special and very formal, but the three friends were filled with too much youth and vitality and they just grabbed at each other, jigging with happiness and trying to talk all at once.

And the boys were certainly surprised when they found that Tila had learned their language in those two months. Then the day was over and the party had to leave for Miami and the trip overseas.

Tila shook each boy's hand and said, "We're still friends, aren't we?"

"You bet," they agreed unanimously.

"Then I want you two to visit me in Grandau next summer. Will you do that?"

"Even if we have to swim," Josh said.

Behind them, Vincent whispered to his friend Tim, "They'd probably try it too. Maybe we'd better buy them tickets."

"I'm going to expect you, now. You two seem to know all about boats and the Caribbean and big cities on the mainland, but I want to show you where I live."

"But you don't even know what it's like," Larry said.

Tila smiled and drew herself erect. "Don't worry, I'll make it what I like," she told him.

"Just like a girl," Josh muttered playfully.

Then Larry brought up his package. He held it out and let Tila fold back the wrapping until the brass shone in the sunlight. "For you," he told her, "so you'll never forget us."

Slowly she pulled the cover all the way down and her eyes glistened with tears. It was the ship's bell from the *Tiger,* a secret that could never be told. Not that it mattered; it would never have been believed anyway. But the bell cemented a friendship among three people that could never be broken, and they all knew it well.

But it was a great story and for them it really had happened, even if it was a story about *the ship that never was*.

THE SHRINKING ISLAND

CHAPTER ONE

IT HAD BEEN a full year since Larry Demar had been to Miami, and for his friend Josh, the very first time he had ever been away from that little group of Caribbean Islands where he had been raised. The fantastic white skyline of that great Florida beach had made Josh go speechless when he saw it from the air, and now, strolling among the enormous hotels and beautiful homes made him shake his head in wonder.

"Larry", he said with an Island lilt, "It is hard to believe."

"Pretty, isn't it?"

"How could men with their bare hands build such a place?"

"They had mighty big tools, Josh" He pointed to a French crane on the roof of a partially completed building. "Like that one".

Josh could hardly believe his eyes. "How did they get it up there?"

Laughing, Larry gave his friend a nudge. "Take one step at a time, pal. When I first went to Peolle Island I couldn't see how you could toss those fishing nets or stay upright in the dugout canoes."

Josh nodded and shrugged. "I'll never learn all this."

"Forget it. All this stuff is what we have at home, except bigger. Besides, what they're going to test us on isn't the layout of Miami. It's simple 'readin', ritin' and 'rithmatic, like they said in the old days."

"Why do we have to do this, Larry?"

"Because the law says we have to. Anyway, dad's a great teacher, he's licensed to do it and as long as we pass the government tests, we can stay on the island and learn there."

"Crazy laws."

"We need them, though."

"Maybe here, but not on our island," Josh said.

"Well, there are only a couple of old slow trucks on Peolle and no roads, so we don't need traffic laws...."

"Nobody steals," Josh added, "And if they did, we take care of them ourselves."

"And we don't dirty up the place, so we don't need pollution inspectors."

"True," Josh told him, "and if our house burns, we just build a new one that afternoon, so we don't have much use for a fire department, so why do we need all this government."

Larry couldn't answer that so he simply said, "Let's just say we got it anyway and if we're lucky, maybe it will come in handy someday." He put his arm around his younger friend's shoulders. "We have a whole day to ourselves. What would you like to do?"

"Eating sounds pretty good to me."

"And afterwards?"

"Remember...you were telling me about the place where all the books..."

"The library?"

"Yes. That's right. And you said there was much history made around our islands...that's what I want to see. Those stories...the pictures..."

"Okay, Josh, Miami's the right place to find those things. But first, let's get some of the native food up here. You're never tasted anything like it before."

There was grim expression on Josh's face. "I don't want to eat a dog, Larry."

"Hey, buddy, how many times do I have to tell you a hot dog isn't really a dog?"

"Then what is it?"

"It's a .... oh, come on and let me show you."

AT FOUR O'CLOCK that afternoon the both of them sat at a table in a restricted section of the library poring over books and manuscripts so old they weren't in general use. The head librarian, sensing their sincerity and having been told where they lived, took charge of their library expedition, and got them all the information they needed. Not that he minded since the history of those days of exploration and piracy on the high seas were his favorite subject.

One leather-bound account he let the boys see was only to show them the fine illustrations they did back then, it was written entirely in Spanish. Suddenly, Josh's eyes lit on something and he said, "Larry, look. Here is mentioned the island of *Landau*, southeast of Peolle."

"Let's see." He glanced at it a moment and nodded. "The captions about this ship here...the *El Capitan Uno*."

"What does it say?"

"I don't know. I can't read Spanish."

"Here, let me take a look at it," the librarian said. After glancing over the paragraph, he told the boys, "This is quite a famous ship, you know. It was a Spanish galleon loaded with gold from the Vera Cruz mint and was en route to Spain with the treasure."

"What happened to it?" Larry asked.

"Nobody seems to know. One minute it was there, then it was gone."

Josh looked puzzled. "How could that be?"

"Seems like they put into a place called the great sandy lagoon at Landau Island. The ship's master and the crew were out looking for food and water and when a terrible storm came up, they were caught on the other side of the island. None of them worried about the ship because it was well anchored. There were no enemies in the area, and it was in a protected place. But when they went back, the *El Capitan Uno* was gone."

"They didn't find a trace of it?"

"Nope. And no signs that any other ship was there either."

"It had to go someplace," Larry suggested hopefully.

"All they could assume was that the tide rose her above her anchors, and she drifted out to sea during the storm and was lost there. The crew waited ashore and two weeks later were picked up by another ship from their fleet who saw their smoke."

"Strange," Josh mused.

"What is?" the librarian asked him.

"I've been to *Landau Island*. My father has a friend there...old Poki George. And Great Sandy isn't a lagoon... it's just a big hollowed out sandy place that has water in it sometime. Poki George remembers when it opened to the sea a little bit when he was a boy, but you sure couldn't anchor a big ship in there at all."

The librarian nodded. "Sometimes these old reports were more fiction than fact. And sometimes they didn't know where they were. That great sandy lagoon they mentioned in the ship's log could have been somewhere else."

Josh shook his head stubbornly. "Not in the Caribbean. There is only one *Great Sandy* and it's on *Landau*, right where they say it was."

"And one other thing," Larry asked, "You said it was in the ship's log."

"Exactly," the librarian said. "The Spanish would never leave a ship without taking the log with them."

"Wouldn't they leave somebody on watch?"

"You might think so...but the island *was* deserted and it's quite possible they needed all hands to collect the necessary supplies."

"The island *wasn't* deserted," Josh said quietly.

Both of them looked at him.

"Poki George's big grandfather lived there then. When he saw the ship, he was scared, and he and his wife got in the dugout and paddled over to *Gamu*. He didn't come back until after the other ship came by."

"Now where did you get this from?" Larry asked.

"Old Poki told me. I thought it was just one of those wild island stories until now."

"What got him started telling you that?"

"I asked him about the model ship he's got in his house. It's the one that looks like this one here in the book."

"And what did he say?"

Josh shrugged. "He just told me another crazy story about his big grandfather. Said the old man found it and kept it, that's all."

The librarian laid his hand on Josh's shoulder. "Excuse me, but what's a 'big grandfather'?"

Larry tapped his hand. "It's island talk. He means a *great* grandfather but not how far back."

"Wise guy," Josh grinned, "Just because you showed me what a hot dog was..."

But the librarian wasn't listening. "Odd," he said. When he caught the boy's eyes watching him, he explained, "A month ago somebody else was in here looking for information on the *El Capitan Uno*, a big tough-looking man who got mad when we couldn't let him remove the old manuscripts."

"What would he want with all this?"

"I got the impression," the librarian told him, "That he wanted to find that ship. It carried quite a few millions of dollars in gold bullion."

"But it's been lost for over three hundred years."

"I think he had some information that told him where it was," The librarian said, "And the way he was talking he'd destroy anything to get it."

The grade instructor who had given the boys their examinations shook their hands and congratulated them on their high scores. Josh had even surprised himself with the knowledge he had gained from Larry's father over the past year, but when they were outside something seemed to disturb him.

Larry said, "Okay, spill it. What's the matter?"

"I was thinking of Poki George."

"So?"

"He's an old man. He's my father's good friend." He paused a moment they looked at Larry, his eyes serious. "I have a feeling he could be in trouble."

"You mean...what the librarian mentioned?"

Josh nodded.

"You know," Larry said, "you get the darndest feelings. The trouble is, they're usually right."

"That's island feeling, Larry."

"Yeah, I know. Now tell me what you're thinking."

"I'm thinking of how I'd like to see old Poki George."

"*Landau Island* is fourteen hours by sail, Josh."

"We could use your boat," Josh suggested.

"Hey...what's this we business?"

"You wouldn't want me to have all that fun alone, would you?"

"Josh," Larry said with bewilderment, "sometimes you amaze me."

"Why?"

"You think my father and your father will let us take an eighteen-foot skiff out of the sight of land for half a day?"

There was a silence for a long minute while both the boys thought of the same thing. "They said if we got good grades on our tests..."

Larry let out an amused grunt. "Well, we've done pretty well so far. I guess it wouldn't hurt to ask. After that day when the sea rolled back...they were pleased with us then."

"Let's go get on that airplane," Josh said. "I am tired of eating those hot dogs. I want a nice fresh caught fish wrapped up in banana leaves and buried with the hot coals and..."

Larry gave him a playful poke. "Shut up and move. Now you have me hungry too."

VINCENT DEMAR STARED at his son, marveling at how boys grow up without anybody noticing. Josh's father had an amused smile on his face and Vincent said, "Timothy, where do our kids find these crazy ideas?"

"From us," Timothy said.

"You?" Amazement was in Vincent's tone.

"I took a dugout to Landau when I was his age."

Timothy knew what his friend was going to say and

smiled. "The sun was our compass in those days. It was the way we traveled. Now the people who live in the States can go nowhere unless they have a car or a fancy boat with a big captain. The islanders...we went because we had to, and we wanted to. A dugout was the way."

"And Larry's skiff is even better, I suppose."

"Quite, Vincent. He even has a radio. There's plenty of room for extra food and water."

"What did you take in the dugout?" Vincent asked him.

"One dried fish and a gourd of water. It was enough."

"Dad, can we go?" Larry asked.

Vincent ignored him and looked at Timothy. "Supposing the dugout swamped...you were tossed into the sea. What then?"

Timothy shrugged. "It would have been a long swim, I think." His smile became gentle and he added, "The skiff is no dugout. The boys...they are growing, my friend. There are things they must do."

Vincent looked at Larry. A grin flickered at the corners of his mouth, but his eyes were stern. "Okay, kiddo, you got yourself a trip, but if there's any trouble, you're going to get grounded...like flat out. Good enough?"

"Sure, dad."

"One more thing."

"What's that?"

"I don't care what Tim took in his dugout...you guys load up on plenty of canned goods. You might want to stay a while."

CHAPTER TWO

THE BELINDA WAS an ex-Navy mine sweeper, converted for salvage use, but Henry Blackstone and Stoney Marks had let the hull and equipment run down until it barely got by the Coast Guard test of seaworthiness.

Neither of the partners cared much for outward appearances or even safety. Their entire life was tied up with the desire to accumulate a fortune and spend it any place they wanted to, and to get riches like that, there was nothing they wouldn't do.

Until now, their search for money and had been a losing battle. Everything they touched had turned sour, and no matter how badly they had treated everyone else, their situation had gotten even worse.

Then they had grounded on a sandbar off Gamu Island and had come ashore to get help to float them loose, and that's when they heard about the *El Capitan Uno*. It had only been an off-chance remark by one of the natives, but Henry Blackstone had remembered the story of that ancient ship and had asked a few discreet questions, and the friendly natives were only too happy to tell them everything they knew.

Even though Henry and Stoney knew stories could be distorted by time, they realized that most of the native legends had a great deal of truth in them when looked at from a modern viewpoint. What really caught their attention was the familiarity in all the stories.

It was the big grandfathers who had been there, and they all had seen the wondrous sight of the *El Capitan Uno* with its great white sails and bearded men who yelled and bellowed in a strange language. It had gone into the lagoon on Landau and they had even seen the campfires of those foreign people, but after the mighty storm that night, the huge canoe with the white wings was never seen again, and Landau became a haunted island never visited by the natives even though the ancestors of Poki George had made their home there.

And now Henry Blackstone and Stoney Marks were poring over an aerial photograph of Landau Island and Stoney was tapping the area that marked the eastern side of it. "That's it right there, see?"

"It's sand, that's for sure, and plenty of it. Trouble is, where's the lagoon?"

"A few hundred years changes the landscape, remember? It's only sand and even a stiff wind could alter its contours."

"So?"

"Look, Henry, right now it seems to be a big bowl of sand with the low part in the middle, right?"

"Right."

"See that section directly in the center?"

"Yeah. It looks wet."

"The topographical reports said there's a small water pool there. Looks like it's maybe a hundred feet around."

"Stoney...that's no lagoon."

"Cut one end out and let the sea water in and what have you got?"

"A lagoon."

"Easy, isn't it?"

"You're nuts."

"Why?"

"Because that's ten thousand yards of sand there, that's why. You know what it'd take to move it?"

"How about a hurricane?"

"You gonna arrange for a hurricane?"

"No, but maybe one happened all those years ago."

"Sure," Henry said sarcastically, "and it blew the '*El Capitan Uno*' out to sea and sank it."

Very carefully, Stoney Marks rolled the photo into a tube and slid it back into its cardboard holder. "Suppose it didn't blow it out at all. Suppose that hurricane came in from the sea and kept that ship right where it was anchored."

"Then what happened to it?"

"The storm buried it under thousands of tons of sand. It's still there, the ship, the treasure and everything we've been looking for all our lives."

Both of them were silent for a long moment, considering the grandeur of the situation, then Henry's eyes narrowed and he said, "There's only one problem."

"Like what."

"Those old stories tell of a storm, like an overnight storm. Nobody said anything about a hurricane. Nothing we found in that library mentioned it."

"That's right," Stoney told him. "Nobody has any imagination. They take everything the way it was written down. That's why nobody ever really looked for the *El Capitan Uno*."

"But supposing somebody else..."

"Come on dummy. We have all the information available except for that one book in the library and the logbook in the archives in Madrid. Who else is going to bother looking for her?"

"Yeah...guess you're right, Stoney."

"I know I'm right. I can feel it. All that gold is right there waiting for us."

"That's an awful lot of sand to move around."

"Not with a bulldozer and a power shovel."

The expectant look on Henry Blackstone's face suddenly faded. "Stoney...those two pieces of equipment would cost fifty thousand bucks apiece. Where are we going to get loot like that?"

"We're not."

"Great, so how do we get the dozer and shovel?"

"Easy. We steal them."

"Oh," Henry said. "Now I understand. Only one thing I don't understand. How we gonna get them on our boat?"

"Simple. We don't. They're already on a barge ready to be towed down to Panama. We just go in, hook up first and be two hundred miles away before anybody knows they're gone."

"You ever heard of air searches, Stoney?"

"Sure, but in this case, it won't do them any good. We'll already be there and believe me, nobody's gonna believe that kind of equipment would go to a little no-account island like Landau."

"Except the people, maybe."

"And those," Stoney said savagely, "we take care of if they get in our way."

MILES AWAY TO THE SOUTHEAST, the island of Landau faced the rising sun, the bright rays glistening from the white sands of the huge embankment that lay like a giant teacup on its seaward side.

Every morning old Poki George had walked from his palmetto house until he reached the lip of Great Sandy, then followed the rim until he could see the sun come up, a bright read arc that grew and grew until it seemed to fill the hole horizon.

Poki George was a small man, but his shoulders and arms showed the marks of having seen heavy labor at the fisheries and in helping build the island to where it was a happy place and self-sufficient. He was old now, his hair snow white, and to the islanders he was a very special person who had taught them and taken care of them. Now they were taking care of Poki George, repaying for what they had been taught.

When the entire orb of the sun was above the sea, Poki George turned and walked back to his house. In another hour, the dozen children would be there for their lessons and for a few hours the old man would be happy in his work.

The only thing that bothered him was the lack of supplies. There was little money on Landau and what they had went for food, boat parts and fishing supplies. At one time, there was a pearl bed that had brought them enough to pay for the boats and the radios and a few other necessities, but the bed had petered out and only the fish made those few extra dollars.

Now, there was hardly a demand for the smoked fish from Landau. The islands closer to the mainland were able to supply those things faster and cheaper. And Poki George felt the pain in his mind because there was little anybody could give the young people that were growing up on the island.

What really made him sad was that Ben Westley had come to him with the early results of his experiments with oysters. He had developed a strain that could grow cultured pearls faster than any known species, but to do it at a degree large enough to make Landau beautiful, happy and an economically sound place for its people, would take more money than they could ever dream of.

So Poki George stared at the model of the old ship that sat on the mantelpiece of his fireplace and said softly, "Oh, if you were only real. If we could have the treasure you carried, the one you stole from people like us, we would be made well again."

He hadn't heard Billy Westley come in until he said, "Poki, what's *with* that ship?"

Poki George turned around, startled, then smiled. "It's only an old model."

"Papa said it's the best in the world. He told me some men offered you a lot of money to put it in the museum in Miami."

"That's true."

"Why?"

"Because it's perfect in detail, Billy. If you look at it closely you can see how every single plank, how the spars, the stays...everything, was made individually and to exact scale."

"Who made it?"

Poki George shrugged his shoulders. "No one knows for sure. My big grandfather didn't know, but the story is that his father found it floating in the water off Great Sandy."

"You don't float models," Billy said. "At least not when they're that good." He walked over and looked up at the galleon that sat there, its sails sagging because there was no wind to fill them. "Papa said everything worked on it."

"Well," Poki told him, "I haven't tried to fire the cannons, but as far as my big fingers could find out...everything moves and works like a ship should."

"Tell me something," Billy said. "Where do *you* think it came from?"

"That, my little friend, is something that always puzzled me, because when the *El Capitan Uno* was built, they didn't make models to work from, so all I could suppose was that one of the crew members had taken it on as a project, the way latter day sailors did making scrimshaw...know that that is?"

Billy looked puzzled and shook his head.

"That's drawing and carving on whalebone and walrus tusks. The sailors had plenty of time for it then... hours to use up when there was nothing to do at sea."

"Don't you think that ship would have taken a long time?"

Poki George nodded. "A very long time. I still can't figure out how the builder cast the iron cannon or made those tiny pieces of glass for the Captain's quarters."

"Guess the big grandfathers were right," Billy said.

"What do you mean?"

"About there being the real *El Capitan Uno*."

"Maybe there was only this model," Poki George told him. "Now go get the other kids and let's start school."

And over the horizon were other people who had the *El Capitan Uno* on their minds too, although neither knew about the other.

Larry and Josh had set sail long before first light. The Coast Guard weather reports had been favorable, the winds right for the trip and since there was no need for speed, they had decided to go well off shore to test their skills at navigation without really putting themselves in any position of jeopardy.

Every thirty minutes Larry had called his father on the radio, and now that the sun was well up, the sea calm, Larry said, "Suppose I call you when we get there, dad. This trip is a real milk run, like you used to say."

"Weather comes up fast, son."

"I know," Larry said, "But we can see it and if it looks bad, we can lower the sail and hook up the outboard motor."

Vincent Demar was still wary, but he knew his son pretty well, so told him, "Okay, you pirates, just stay in the sea lanes where we know where you are. I'll keep this frequency open if you want to call. But make sure to radio us when you reach Landau."

"Right, Dad. And look...your transmitter is bigger than ours, so how about telling Poki George we're on way and he can call you when we get in sight."

"Okay, kids, you're on your own."

Larry hung up the microphone. "Hear that?"

"Yeah, but I don't like it."

"Josh...it's a great day. What's bothering you?"

For a second, Josh stared forward, then pointed. "That, for sure." Straight ahead was a small shape on the horizon, it's outlines blurred by the heat rays dancing off the water. "There were no reports of anything in this area," he said.

"Hey, friend, we're not the only ship in the sea."

"When's the last tine any ship that size has been out here?"

"About a year," Larry said, "and everybody knew about it."

"It's heading the same way we are."

"That doesn't mean anything."

"I told you, I have a funny feeling about this whole thing." Josh said.

"Well, we'll find out just what it is in about an hour. We're going faster than it is and since it's your turn to make the sandwiches; I figure we'll know her name by the time we've eaten."

ON THE DECK of the *Belinda*, Henry handed the binoculars to Stoney. "What do you make of it?"

He made an adjustment to the glasses, studying the sea behind them. "Looks like a skiff under sail. Two persons in the stern."

"Nobody's supposed to be out here," Henry said.

"THOSE NATIVES GO ANYWHERE."

"Not in that kind of a boat. You see how they're coming up on us?"

"So what?"

"All they have to do is spot this tow. We got a barge with a bulldozer and a shovel back there. When would they ever see something like that?"

"Okay, okay, who could they tell anyway?"

"You'd better take a look at that mast Stoney. You see that radio antenna sticking up there?"

When he picked it out, Stoney nodded. "Go check the frequencies. They could think we're just another ship and before they call anybody, they'll check with us first."

But there was no radio exchanged at all. Henry Blackstone ran a check on all his channels, but aside from the normal sea traffic, there was no communication from the boat behind him. He left the set on ship-to-ship channel, switched on the deck speaker, and went back to Stoney. "Anything?"

"No. They're having lunch. Looks like two kids."

"Then what are we worrying about?"

Stoney put down the glasses and looked at his partner. "Man, do you know how much trouble two kids can be?"

"Come on," Henry said with a disgusted glance. "What could they do anyway?"

WHAT LARRY and Josh *were* doing was being pushed by a fresh wind so that before they expected it, they could see the ship and its tow ahead of them.

At first Josh couldn't make out the outlines, not being familiar with the big yellow pieces of equipment, then Larry said, "That's a Caterpillar bulldozer and shovel they have there!"

"You mean...earthmovers?"

"Exactly."

"But there's no place to use something like that out here. They must be lost!"

"Maybe not...the government does a lot of things we don't know about."

"Putting a bulldozer out here?" Josh asked incredulously. "Why?"

Larry grinned at him. "Since you're so inquisitive, let's get up closer and ask them. I'm sure they'd be glad to tell us. There's nothing secret about the government, is there?"

With the wind behind them, it didn't take long to draw alongside the *Belinda*. They stayed wide, out of the wake, waving at the two figures on deck, then Larry picked up his glasses, found the name of the ship on his stern and said into the microphone, "*Belinda* from the Seahawk, do you read me?"

He put down the mike and looked at the ship on his port side. One of the figures went into the cabin and Larry waited for an answer. He never saw the ugly snout of a telescopic rifle come out of the window on the bridge, then suddenly the radio beside him exploded into fragments of metal and in the shock of the impact Larry's arm hit the wheel so that the Seahawk veered abruptly, and the next shot went over his head.

Luckily, they had turned into the wind and their boat

was dead in the water, the speed of the *Belinda* separating them so that another shot would be difficult. Just to make sure the wind wouldn't catch them, Josh eased to the starboard side and loosened the lines so that their sail dropped to the deck. "And your dad called *us* pirates." He said. "What do we do now?"

Ahead of them, the Belinda was pulling away, Larry said, "We hook up the outboard and get in close to shore. I don't know where they're going, but wherever it is, I sure don't want to be there."

Josh looked at the remains of the radio. "Your dad's going to be pretty sore about that."

"Not as long as the bullet didn't hit us," Larry said. "Now plug in the gas tank and I'll get the motor going. Those guys can stay as far out to sea as they want. We're going right in off shore."

"Like the '*El Capitan Uno*'?"

"Exactly!"

CHAPTER THREE

POKI GEORGE HAD BEEN WAITING for the sight of the sail and when it came into view he hurried back to his set and called his friend Timothy who was sitting at Vincent Demar's radio. "They are here," he said. "About two miles out and doing like boys do."

"Oh?" Timothy didn't quite understand. "And how do boys do?"

"They are coming in under sail and motor both," Poki told him.

"Both? Are they sinking?"

"No, just having a good time."

"That doesn't sound like Josh or Larry."

"If you want, I'll speak to them about it."

"Please, my friend. Make sure they are all right."

"Do not worry. I can see them from here. The evening is beautiful, the sea is like glass and my friends are already going to the beach to meet them. Young people sometimes get excited and have to hurry when there is no need for hurry. I will call you later."

"Thank you, my friend."

Poke flipped the switch that turned his power off and

looked back out to sea. The sail had been furled on the boy's boat so that they were coming into the shore gently under power. Josh was in the prow, jumped out when the water was knee deep, and in the stern Larry cut the engine and hoisted it up, disengaging the gas hose and the power connections.

———

VERY NICE, *he thought,* after many years, the son of his friend, and *his* friend, were coming for a visit. It had been a long, long time since anyone had visited Landau Island and new faces would be welcome. There would be new things to learn and to teach so that one day the people of Landau could have some of the things other people had.

Poki George took a cold drink of water, put the glass down and went to meet the crew of the Seahawk. He never noticed the glass tip over and the water swirl into the battery circuit and he was gone before he could smell the acrid smoke that swirled up from the casing. It sparked and sputtered, stunk without anyone noticing it, then plopped into a slow death.

Before he got there, all the young people were hearing about the contact with the strange tow ship and looking at the bullet riddled radio. Then Poki George said, "Are you sure this was deliberate?"

"All we did was call them," Larry added.

"Then they shot at us," Josh added.

"You could have been killed."

"We weren't."

With cautious eye, Poki George looked at Larry. "For a young man, you don't seem worried."

"Should I be?"

"I would be." He held up his hand to stop the sudden

talk. "People who shoot at people *need* to be worried about."

"Well," Josh told him, "We got out of there."

"But you didn't know why they shot at you."

Soberly, Larry looked at the old man. "That tow they had was something special."

Poki took Larry's arm. "Let's go up to the house and you can tell me about it."

But there was too much excitement when they got there to relate the details of what might have been an accidental gunshot. The radio was out, the battery destroyed, and Landau Island was cut off from the rest of the world. Not that it mattered, since a ship rarely called at their shores, but there was no news and no way to transmit news until the damage to the equipment was repaired.

However, how could it ever get repaired when nobody even knew it was broken.

Josh nudged Larry and said, "See...I told you I had a funny feeling."

"Baloney. It was an accident. Things like that don't happen for real."

"Is that real?" Josh was looking at the ship model on the mantel.

Larry let out a long, low whistle. "Beautiful," he said.

"That's the *El Capitan Uno*," Poke George told him. "You like it?"

"It looks exactly like those pictures in the book."

"That's what I have been told. It is supposed to be one of the finest ship models in the world."

Larry nodded appreciatively. "That kind of work isn't done anymore." He walked up closer and stared at it intently. "It looks real, doesn't it? Almost like you expected somebody to walk the decks."

The old man came over and put his arm around Larry's shoulders. "Yes, I know. I have found out it is not too good to look at too long. Now, you've had a busy day, and your beds are ready."

———

OFFSHORE, the *Belinda* waited, two pairs of eyes watching the shore through night glasses. "That skiff's there," Henry Blackstone said.

"You're a nut you know that? You fire a shot at a stupid little sailboat and they head for shore like a scared rabbit. And where do they put in? Right where we want to go!"

"You said they were only some natives!"

"I'd like to rap you right in the chops."

"Oh yeah," Henry said belligerently.

"When I get time, I'll do it. Right now, you get on the fathometer and give me the depth soundings. This tow has got to be just right at low tide if we want the equipment to walk ashore on their treads."

"Then what do we do with the barge?"

"We let the sea swallow it up, you nut!"

"Who you calling a nut?"

"You, that's who! Wanna make somethin' of it?"

"Okay. No."

"So do what I told you, nut!"

The tide went out slowly, minute by minute, and when the sand dried around the barge Henry Blackstone and Stoney Marks fired up the bull dozer and the shovel. The diesel engines caught, coughed into life, and settled down into a throaty roar. Gently, they eased the power to the pair of mechanical giants and let their tracks take the weight onto the sand.

Both the bulldozer and the shovel were new, high powered with low sound and their progress was steady and almost quiet. The deep bite of the tracks took them out of the water onto the dry land and when they were away from the tidal edge and up on the beginning of the ridge of Great Sandy, Henry and Stoney cut the engines and went back to the barge. Several slices with the axe and the hawsers were cut through. The tide did the rest. The barge bucked a little, settled then slowly floated out to sea. Thirty minutes later the dull sound of the dynamite they had planted in its bottom echoed across the water and the two men looked at each other and grinned.

That part of their scheme had gone down to the bottom of the ocean. Now...if the rest would only go as well...

———

EVERY PERSON on Landau Island had gathered at Poki George's house. They had arrived at sunup to meet Larry and Josh, but what they saw made them stare unbelievingly. There anchored offshore was a big salvage ship and slowly climbing the slope of Great Sandy were two bright yellow steel monsters the like of which they had never seen.

It didn't take long for the boys to tell them what they were, but the islanders didn't seem to believe the power they had. "Listen to me," Larry said, "that equipment can just plain chew up this island if it wants to. What one can't do, the other can. They can take down every tree and level every hill."

"But why would they want to do that?" Ben Wesley asked.

"Well, maybe that's not what they're planning," Larry said.

"They're not here for anything good," Josh reminded him. "Don't forget...they're the ones who shot at us."

Poki George was looking at the men at the controls of

the machines through an old pair of field glasses. When he put them down his face looked worried.

"Recognize them?" Ben asked.

"The one in the front. I think he is the person they call Stoney. I have heard many bad stories about that one and his partner."

Larry was feeling pretty uneasy too. "You sure you know him?"

'I saw him twice on the big island. The second time the police tried to arrest him, but he fought his way free and got out to sea. Last year Henri Beth and his cousin floated in here on the wreckage of their fishing boat. They had been deliberately rammed and the description of the boat that hit them matched that one out there."

"Poki," Larry said, "who owns this island?"

"Now, son," the old man said, "a thing like that never came up before."

"Somebody has to."

"It was here before we were born and it will be here after we're gone," Poki George told him. "We just use it and try to keep it nice for those behind us."

"Sure, I know that," Larry stated, "but there has to be deeds of some sort around."

"Paper?"

"Yeah, paper. But it's important paper."

Poki nodded solemnly. "Yes, there is a paper some-where. It is called a...a gift."

Larry thought a moment and suggested. "You mean grant? A land grant?"

With a broad smile, Poki George nodded. "Yes, that is it, a land grant. I remember my father telling me about it. It has been passed down in our family since it was given to a big grandfather from a king far across the ocean."

"This was originally Spanish territory," Larry said. "Nobody ever sold or traded any of it off, have they?"

"Who would want our land, Larry? It is poor enough as it is."

Larry looked out at the machines. They had reached the lip and had stopped, Their engines quiet. Two men were standing together, looking down inside Great Sandy. "Somebody obviously wants it," Larry said.

Josh moved up and stood beside him. "Can they *really* take it?"

With a motion of his hand, Larry indicated the small group of people. "They have machines and guns over there, Josh. All you have here are a few peace-loving natives. Think that's a match for them?"

Josh shook his head, "Guess not, but we have to do something." He glanced at Larry for any answer.

"First we ought to find out what they're looking for," Larry told him.

"What's second?"

"Getting Poki to find that land grant."

"What good will that do?"

"It gives him a reason to get them off the island."

"Sure...if we could call in the Coast Guard or some-body. Only we don't have any power for the radio." When Larry started to grin, Josh frowned. "What's so funny?"

"Oh, there's power to be had, all right."

"Where?"

"On those machines and out there on their ship. All we have to do is figure a way to get to it."

"You know what they'll do to us if they catch us, don't you?"

"Yeah," Larry said, "I know. There's just one thing we have to do, that's all."

"What's that?"

"Don't get caught."

"Oh, great," Josh said, but his voice sounded weak.

"What do you think, Stoney?"

They had walked around half the rim of the area and were studying the bright sandy surface, looking for any irregularities that might give them a clue to their prize. "I don't see nothing, that's what." He wiped the sweat from his face with a bandanna, grimacing from the heat. "That's funny looking sand."

"What's funny about it."

"The color, that's what."

"White is funny?"

"Look at it away from the sun...over there where the shadow is.

Henry Blackstone followed his nod and squinted in that direction. "Looks purple like. Never saw that before, even in a shadow. You figure it's the way the light hits it?"

"I've seen sunlight on white sand before, but it never got that color."

"So, what difference does it make?" He reached down and sifted a handful through his fingers. "It'll clear away as easy as any other color. When do we get started?"

"Unless you feel like spending a month out there searching, we'd better get a good idea of where to look." His eyes ran around the landscape. Here and there he saw movement of the few islanders, all seemingly intent on their business. "And if anybody'd gonna know about what's under all this sand, it'll be one of them."

"You said they were only dumb islanders, Stoney. What would they know?"

"They remember stories, dumb head. They haven't got newspapers so they hand down stories and even if they get all turned around, maybe we can make sense out of them."

"Suppose they're scared to talk. Suppose after what those two in the skiff told them..."

"Come on, Henry," Stoney said impatiently, "they didn't know for sure we was shooting *at* them. Could have been an accident and you're just dumb enough to make an accident happen."

"What about the barge. They knew we had that."

Stoney looked at his partner like he was with a stupid child. "Did you ever hear of a tow breaking away?"

"Sure, but..."

"Forget the buts...that's what happened to us if anybody asks. We got the equipment on shore and during the night the line parted and the barge went out to sea. It sank because it was a leaky old wreck, that's why."

But Henry still wouldn't let up. He wanted to know some more answers to questions that were gnawing at him. "Okay, okay. Then if we find the El Captain Uno under all this sand and we do get all the gold it was carrying; you're going to get people around who want to see the wreck and all that stuff."

"Simple, Henry, we just bury it back up again Isn't that easy?"

"But...these natives will know about it and..."

"From under all that sand, what could they say?"

Henry looked at the evil smile around his partner's mouth and swallowed nervously. Stoney Marks has done some pretty terrible things in the past but what he was contemplating was the worst ever.

"Let's get moving," Stoney finally said. "We have a camp to set up, we have to get the gas and oil off the Belinda and arrange some traps around the dozer and the shovel to keep any nosey islanders away."

AFTER SUPPER, Poki George and the boys went through the old sea chest that had been wedged in the attic rafters for a couple of generations. The papers were old, yellow, and brittle, mostly business accounts from the sale of smoked fish or beautiful pearls from the oysters that had once been plentiful in the ocean around Landau Island. There were several letters that mentioned the *El Capitan Uno*, but each reference was to the model and how it was an important inheritance.

Poki told them about the first time an outsider had seen the ship model, and how he had mentioned it to a historian at the museum in Miami. He gave such a glowing account of the ancient replica that the curator had to see it himself. Even he couldn't believe his eyes, because the model was so exact, so detailed, yet with every part in complete working order, it was hard to understand why any artist could have put so much effort into something that was never going to be seen by the public.

The offer he had made to Poki George was far more than the old man had ever seen...or would ever hope to see, but since the model of the *El Capitan Uno* had belonged to his father, and *his* father's father before that, there wasn't enough money in the world to buy it from him.

"There is only one sad part, my young friends," Poki said.

Both boys looked at each other.

"I have no one to leave it to. Many years ago, my wife died and we had no children. Now, the only thing that all my fathers' thought was so great we should always keep in our family...it goes to no one."

"You could still sell it," Larry suggested. "The money could go to all your friends on the Island."

"I have thought of that," Poki smiled, "but I'm afraid there really wouldn't be much money. You see...no one knows who made it, nor if it is a model of the *real El Capitan Uno*."

"Still, it's a beautiful piece of work," Larry said. "Who

ever thought of carving tiny spots that look like barnacles on the bottom."

With an impish grin, Poki said, "You had better look again. They are not carved there. They are separate things that was put there. That is why we never handle the model...it is too old now and all those little pieces are aged. Like me. Soon it will all fall apart."

"Poki," Larry said seriously, "you got a long time to go."

"Let's hope so. But when the ship falls apart, so will I. Only then will the gold come out?"

"What gold?" Josh demanded.

"Oh, the artist was even better than you suspected," Poki smiled. "In the captain's cabin...and you can see it in the light, there is a pile of gold bricks in a wood crate, with the lid off and lying right there on the floor as if someone had been examining it."

"*Real* gold?"

"Oh, yea," Poki assured him. "It was what amazed the man from the museum. I opened the glass ports on the cabin and he took a tiny sample of it. Yes, it was real gold, all right. Of course, as it is, it wouldn't be worth more than a few hundred dollars."

"Boy," Josh exclaimed, "If it *was* full size, imagine how much it would be worth?"

"Many millions of dollars," the old man said, "but just remember, this is a just a model. There may never have been a real one."

"History says there was," Larry said.

"I know. But maybe the *El Capitan Uno* is like the Flying Dutchman...just a story."

"There are pictures of the Capitan?"

"Josh," Poki said gently, "there are pictures of the Flying Dutchman too."

Larry's fingers tapped the table. "There are two men

out there who are after something, and the only something around here that was ever connected with Great Sandy was the *El Capitan Uno*."

"Big Sandy has never been a lagoon. There is no place a ship could put in there."

"Maybe not now," Larry said.

"Even great hurricanes don't change the shape of the island that much."

"You have any early maps of this place?"

"No. There was never any need of one. From here you can almost see the whole island." He looked disturbed and shook his head. "I can't understand what those men want to do."

"It isn't hard to figure out," Larry said. "They had earth moving equipment out there and that's what they intend to do...move earth. They're going to start digging into Big Sandy."

"But why, Larry?"

"Because they think the *El Capitan Uno* is buried under there."

CHAPTER FOUR

BEN WESTERLY'S boy had come back the next morning with the news of the two men's progress. So far, they had used the winch cable on the shovel to drag ten fifty-five-gallon drums of fuel and oil to the shore where it was stacked well above the tide limit inside a barbed wire enclosure. A fire had been kept going all night, and that morning the dozer had gone to work knocking down trees until there was enough firewood to last them a month. They had a lean-to erected and a couple of rifles could be seen propped against the opening.

Ben said, "These men are dangerous and there is nothing we can do."

"Why can't we take one of the boats and get to the nearest island for help?" Josh asked.

"Because there is no boat here that can outrun the *Belinda*," Ben reminded him. "They will not let anybody leave."

"But from the west side of the island..."

"Have you been to the west side yet?"

Josh shook his head.

"There is no way you can put a boat in from that side."

"Maybe," Larry mused, "there *was* a lagoon where Great Sandy is now."

"That is only a story, my young friend. It was long gone like the oysters that once made this a happy island when the pearls were ours to trade."

"Your way of developing cultured pearls isn't a story through, is it?"

"Larry, for me it is only a story." Ben said patiently. "For the area to be built to do such a thing, for the jetties to be laid up, the protecting groins to be built...it is impossible. There is no money so it is only a story."

"But you *could* do it," Larry insisted.

"Only if there was the money. Then the island would be happy again. Poki George would have his new school, we could hire a teacher, have boats, we would...well, there is no use wishing for what is impossible. Is that not so?"

"Come on, Ben," Larry said. "That's when you *do* wish."

"Let me show you something." Ben left the room and came back with a soft leather pouch. He tugged at the drawstrings, opened the mouth of it and let four marble-sized pearls roll out into his palm. They were beautiful things, dully lustrous in the light, seeming to glimmer as though something were burning at their core. "See...this is what we *could* produce."

Larry and Josh let out low whistles. They both had seen pearls before and realized what they were looking at. "You know how much they are worth, Ben?"

"Very well, I do. But these are only four. There isn't nearly enough to lay in the beds. You see, to get these few, I had to work over ten years."

"Now you'd be another ten years to get more?" Josh asked.

Ben looked a little wistful, "No, not now. See, I have learned how to speed up the oyster's progress in growing such fine pearls. In one year and a half I could have hundreds just like these."

"Surely you could get money from the outside and ..."

Ben held his hand up to stop Larry's talking. "Friend, there is no such way. If the outside world knew of it, they would find a way to take it all. They would destroy us and our island for such riches." He nodded toward the far side of the island. "Look at what two men are doing for something they only think is here. What if they knew I had these pearls and could get many more like them?"

"Couldn't they grow those cultured pearls too?"

Ben Westerly studied the perfectly round pearls in his hand. Finally he said, "I have told my cousins on two other islands about these beauties from the oyster. They did exactly as I did, but nothing happened. They got pearls, all right, but small crooked ones, like you sometime find in clams. They had no color and were worthless."

"What was special about your way, Ben?"

"Nothing. It was not me at all, I am sure of that. It has to be the water. For some reason, everything is perfect around this island for the growth of pearls of enormous size and beauty. Unfortunately, we lack the money to do it." He stopped and grinned. "However, maybe we're better off. We wouldn't have any place to spend it anyway."

"Except on a school and boats," Larry suggested. "Just enough to make everything better than it was without causing any trouble."

An hour later another one of the boys came in to tell them that the two men were very busy around their supply area. The way it looked; they'd be a couple of days getting their base camp ready before they went into operation.

"Might be a good time to take a look at Great Sandy," Josh suggested.

"Never better. Let's go."

It was an eerie feeling, standing there on the lip of that enormous sandy crater. Below them the pool was glimmering, deceptively small looking, but both the boys realized it was pretty large and could be deep.

"What keeps the water in there, Larry?"

"Seepage, most likely. You can see tidal marks around the pool from where it's gone up and down."

"It's low tide in the ocean now. How come the water's way up in the pool then?"

"That sand is like a thick strainer. It's slow getting in and slow getting out. Want to go down and take a look?"

"You want to?"

"I can think of better things I'd like to do."

"Me too," Josh said. "So I guess we go anyway."

Together, they started down the side of the slope, their feet kicking up the sand. Halfway down they stopped and Larry said, "You notice anything strange, Josh?"

"Yeah." He looked back at the tracks they had left. "It doesn't feel like sand at all. It's just too firm."

"How about the color."

"That's another thing, Larry, it doesn't look white at all from down here."

"Well, it's only plain sand, that's for sure. Ben's kid and the others play in it all the time. They see it so much they never saw anything special about it."

"Larry..."

"Yeah?"

"I got that funny feeling again."

Larry let out a laugh, said, "Come on," and yanked at his arm. Both of them went down at full speed, their bare feet racing until they reached the pool, then they stopped out of breath and dropped face down alongside a half dozen vine-wound palm logs that had come down from the land overhead during some distant windstorm. When their panting stopped, they waded into the pool, cooling themselves off. They were only about six feet from the shoreline, but the water was up to their waists and Larry glanced at Josh who was right behind him. "Some drop-off here."

"The bottom's pretty solid."

"You'd think there'd be more of a sand spill into here, wouldn't you?"

Josh shrugged gently. "The earth is a strange place, my friend. It does what it wants to do whether we like it or not. My people on Peolle Island tell many stories and people laugh, but there is truth there. Remember what we saw when the sea rolled back?

"How could I forget it?" Larry said, thinking back to last year.

"So whatever the earth want to do shouldn't be strange. If we love her, she will love us. If we do not enjoy her, watch out."

"Well," Larry said, "since we both love her, let's take a look at what's in the middle of this pool. The water is so clear we can see right to the bottom."

The idea made Josh break out into a big grin. "Hey, fine...but let's make a raft and take our time. We can push those logs in and tie them together with the vines the way my father used to tell me about."

"You and Robinson Caruso," Larry said.

"Who?"

"Never mind. You would have thought he had it easy. Let's go make that raft."

They spent a good hour rolling the logs into the water, then tying them side by side until they had a platform that would support them. It wasn't anything special as rafts went; but then again, they were in a clear area with nothing especially dangerous to worry about. All they wanted to do was lay flat on their stomachs, paddle their raft around and peer through the clear waters to the bottom that was shimmering in the sun beneath them.

It took them a half-hour to cross to the other side and a little longer to go the length of the watery basin and when they were back in the middle, Josh said, "You see anything funny?"

"Nope."

"There's no fish."

"How could they get in here?"

"Beats me, but they always do get into places like this."

Larry studied the bottom. There was nothing down there at all that seemed of any consequence. "You know... there might be a reason."

"Like what?"

"The water that comes in here might lose so much salt going through the sand that ocean fish couldn't stay alive. Taste it...notice how light the salt content is?"

Josh scooped some up and tried it on his tongue. "You're right. It's real brackish like that pool near the spring on Peolle Island." He flipped his hand in the water and sent ripples rolling out from the raft. "I wonder if the *El Capitan Uno* is down there someplace."

"What are you thinking about, Josh?"

"Well, if this was a lagoon then, and it was this deep, it sure could have held that galleon."

"Now where would they anchor a ship like that?" He paused and they both looked around for the answer. "It wouldn't be too close to shore because of the depth, but it would be far enough into the lagoon to get away from bad weather. In fact, if this had been a lagoon, it would have been a perfect spot for a Spanish galleon carrying a cargo of gold bullion to drop anchor. Why, the sand hills on either side would even rise above the tips of the masts."

"There's one little thing wrong with that, Josh."

"What's that?"

"If she went down, the hulk would be right under us... and we've dived on enough wrecks to know they leave some good-sized traces. There's not a sign of cannon or ballast rock down there."

"My friend," Josh said slowly, "Who is to know if we are over the middle of that old lagoon or not. You know how sand shifts."

"You're right, Josh...but if you take a look around, there's only so much sand here. When you get over the rim it's coral and coquina rock and that's been there for thousands of years, so if there was a lagoon at all, it was right here and if there was an *El Capitan Uno* that sunk here, we're right around it and if we don't find it, those men with the machines are sure going to."

"Unless," Josh reminded Larry.

"Unless the storm did blow the galleon out to sea and sunk it."

"I hope you're wrong."

"So am I," Josh said.

"Let's get this raft back and go see Poki George then. Somehow, we have to get that radio of his repowered and contact our dads. They're probably thinking we're having so much fun we forgot all about them."

"Not your dad," Josh said.

"Why?"

"Because he knows we had good equipment and just to be sure, he's going to call the Coast Guard and have them check up on us. And let me tell you, I'll sure be glad to see them when they come."

"So will I," Larry said, "so will I."

BUT THAT WASN'T what had happened at all. After the last transmission from Larry, there was a loud hiss and a small explosion in Vincent Demar's radio receiver. He took the back off his set and muttered to himself, annoyed at what he found.

There wouldn't be any way he could receive short wave frequency communications until he got a few parts from the mainland, unless he wanted to go to Timothy's house, and the way the rain was coming down he decided that no harm would be done if he simply waited for the rain to stop and called in to have the supply ship drop off the equipment.

The kids, he was sure, would be fine. Where they were the weather had been beautifully calm and by now, they were enjoying the hospitality of old Poki George and Larry would understand that the receiver on Peolle was temporarily out of order. Meanwhile, there was nothing at all that could bother them.

"You sure? You're real sure, Stoney?"

Angrily, his partner glared across the campfire. "Yeah, I'm sure."

"You said they were natives."

"In the boat they looked like natives. One was a native, all right. The other was so tanned he looked like one and they were the same pair I spotted down on that raft."

"Stoney...you said they were kids. What would kids be looking for down there? All they was doing was swimming, that's all."

"How do you know, dumbhead?"

"What else would kids do? You don't think they're smart enough to think like us, do you?"

"Not like you, anyway," Stoney said sourly. "I just don't like anybody prowling around here."

"What difference does it make. I saw their boat. That shot of mine took their radio out and when I hear them talking up there it was how the main radio was cut too, so nobody but us can talk to anybody outside."

"You'd better be right, Henry."

"I'm tellin' you what I know."

"Then tell me what you heard on the weather report."

"Nothing special. Light showers over most of the islands like there usually is and in some places a few thunderstorms lasting an hour or so. Every year it's the same thing down here, you know that."

"No I don't because I've never been here before and neither have you."

"Well, that's what I heard on the report from the Miami station."

Changing the subject, Stoney said, "Suppose they come looking for those kids."

"Hey, partner, anybody who would let their kids go out to sea like that ain't gonna come looking for 'em. They ever come looking for us?"

"They sure did."

"I don't mean the cops or the Coast Guard," Henry said quickly.

"Partner, I hope you're right. If you are, it's the first time."

Henry ignored the insult and spit onto the sand. "What's our next move?"

"Number one for you is...make sure that old man's radio is out. I want it smashed, you hear?

"Sure, Stoney."

"Then you get the axe and stove in every boat on the beach. Gamu Island isn't all that far away and somebody might get brave enough to make a try for it."

"Why didn't they do it already?"

"They figure we can catch them with the *Belinda*, dopey!"

"Not at night."

"They don't know our radar's out. All they see is the antenna."

"Guess we lucked in, didn't we?"

"Just as long as they can't call out, we got it made."

"If the *El Capitan Uno* is under all that sand you mean."

"Don't worry," Stoney said, "It's there, all right." He looked at the sun disappearing behind the island. "Get moving. It'll be dark in another hour."

CHAPTER FIVE

HENRY BLACKSTONE MOVED like a shadow across the face of the island, one big hand clutched around the shaft of a fire axe. Already, he had uncovered three boats capable of longer than inter-island cruises and had smashed holes in the hulls big enough to keep them beached for weeks. He didn't bother with the log outrigger canoes since they were too solid to attack and besides, they weren't designed for long trips at all.

Now there was only one other craft he had to put out of action and it was drawn up on the beach above the high tide mark and tied firmly to a giant palm tree. The moonlight glistened off the loamy earth enough to let him see clearly, and he was glad the natives didn't keep dogs on this island.

Twice, he disturbed nesting birds and they rose in a wild flurry of wings and raucous squawking before they settled back down again. Each time he remained motionless, his heart beating frantically, afraid that he might be heard.

Perhaps the people here were only island natives, but when they found their property ruined and themselves in danger, they could become deadly adversaries. When he was sure no one had been alerted, he made his way through to where the *Seahawk* was dragged up on the beach.

It was a pretty little skiff, well made with honest hands and had been taken well care of by the two boys. For a minute he felt a touch of remorse, because to him a boat was something special, then he remembered what Stoney would do to him if he didn't follow instructions and he raised the axe over his head and delt the hull a great cutting blow beneath its waterline.

He was about to hit it again, then shrugged. It wouldn't go out to sea now without a lot of work on it and there wasn't any sense tearing up such a nice little boat any more. He looked up at the light coming through the window of the old man's house. That was where they had the radio. On all the island, it was the only place with an antenna, and the lead wire ran right into the building.

Yet so far, there had been no calls for help, or inquiry about the two strangers with the earth moving equipment. New he was going to make sure nothing like that would happen at all.

———

"COME ON POKI GEORGE, finish the story," Josh insisted.

"Oh, it isn't much of a story. And besides, it was such a long time ago."

Larry said, "Let's hear it anyway."

The old man made himself comfortable in his chair and leaned back thoughtfully. "Remember now, this is what Ben Westerly told me, and he was only a young boy then."

Josh and Larry looked at each other and grinned. For

some reason, their trip was getting more exciting every minute.

"Ben was a boy like you, at that time, working for his father at the fisheries most of the time, but when he had off, he roamed around the island until he got to know every inch of it."

"One day, after a big offshore storm, he was walking the beach when he found the remains of an old campfire. Now, to a lot of people that wouldn't mean much, but Ben remembered the story of the *El Capitan Uno* and searched through all the area and he found the remains of the camp that the crew of the ship had left. Has he shown you the things he found?"

The boys shook their heads.

"But you do know the story?"

This time they nodded together.

"Apparently, when they saw the sails of the ship that was to rescue them, they forgot everything else and got away from this island as fast as they could. Maybe that other ship sent in a boat for them, or maybe they had a raft made like the one you boys built in the pool of Great Sandy, but everything was left behind."

"Valuable things?" Larry asked.

"Perhaps. If you consider cooking utensils and some rusted weapons valuable."

Josh was too excited to restrain himself. "Poki...tell us!"

"Well, it was just an old diary that one of the crewmen had started. When they left the ship, he took it with him and described how it was when they found the *El Captain Uno* completely gone after the big storm. One of the strange things he mentioned was the color of the lagoon area, the odd purple color of the sand."

"We saw that the other day," Larry blurted out.

Poki George smiled and nodded. "Oh, that's nothing

new. It always does that before certain storms." He looked toward the blackness outside his window. "Nobody wants to go near Great Sandy during that time, you know."

Larry seemed puzzled. "but why, Poki?"

"Superstition, maybe. Or it could be the way the air seems to tingle and the hairs on your arm stand on end."

"That's static electricity," Larry told him.

"Yes, that's what the books say, my young friend, but this has a very different feel and until it is gone, nobody wants to go near the place we call Great Sandy."

"Poki..."

"Yes, Larry?"

"You said it always does that *before* certain storms."

"True."

"Do you think..."

"Larry...I know. The season is here for those storms again, but do not worry, you will both be safe with us."

"I'm not worried," Larry said.

"Oh?"

"I'm thinking of something."

Before he could explain they all heard the strange sound and felt the chill of apprehension come over them. There was just that one dull smashing sound then the tinkling of glass and the brief flurry of feet on the wooden floor...then silence.

Larry was the first to move. He ran to the back of the house, looked out the window and saw a brief movement near the trees, a figure like that of a running man.

"What is it?"

"Somebody was here, Josh?"

"One of those men?"

"I don't know."

Poki George came in with the lamp and the yellow glow searched out the gloom. They saw what had happened immediately. The battery for the radio that they had been drying off in hope of repairing was smashed into a mass of plastic, lead and battery acid that was beginning to eat into the wooden top of the radio desk.

Neither of the boys had to be told what to look for next. They both ran to the edge of the hill, followed the path down to where they had left the Seahawk and when they found the gaping hole in the starboard side of the hull they almost wanted to kick something.

Overhead, there was gentle glow of lightning and the beach lit up with a soft light. A soft rain fell on their faces and Larry said, "Now we won't even be able to follow the footprints. The rain will wash them all out by morning."

"Larry..."

"Yeah?"

"We didn't think we could fix that battery to start with. Remember what you wanted to do?"

Larry grinned at his friend. "You got it, Josh. *They* have the power so all we have to do is go get it."

"Hey...you think that'll be easy?"

"Nope, but I bet we can do it."

VINCENT DEMAR WAS TOO impatient to wait any longer. Rain or no, he got in his Jeep and fought the road across the island to Timothy's house. Twice, he had gotten bogged down in a mudhole, and each time he had to hook the cable from the front-end winch of the Jeep to a tree alongside the road and pull himself free.

By the time he reached the old cypress board house overlooking the bay it was almost midnight, and hearing the roar of the engine, Timothy had come out to guide his friend into the shed with a flashlight.

Once inside, hot coffee beside him, Vincent said, "For

some reason I'm worried, Tim. Let's try the kids on your radio."

"My friend you think I have not?"

"Did they reply?"

Sadly, Timothy shook his head. "There was no answer at all. Old Poki George's radio was still."

"Is that unusual?"

"Very," Timothy said. "Landau Island does not get very much traffic, so they are always anxious to answer their calls. This time there is no response at all."

"What do you think?"

"A breakdown happened here." Timothy reminded him.

"Would it happen to the kids and to Poki George and us too?"

"With this weather, it doesn't sound reasonable. I checked the Coast Guard and at Landau there is only a small rain condition. It happens this time of the year and they are not worried."

"Timothy...we could take your boat and go after them."

"My friend, they are boys growing up. Would they respect us as fathers if we interfered with their adventure so soon?"

"But if there's trouble..."

"Vincent, there is always trouble. I'll tell you what we will do."

"Like what?"

"We will stay on guard and ready. At any moment we will go to Landau if they call or if there is no news from them after...how long?"

"One more day," Vincent Demar said.

Before Vincent could answer him, the radio static sharpened and Timothy went to the set to correct the interruption. The voice that came on was loud and clear. "Three Two R C," it said.

"Three Two RC here," Timothy answered.

"This is KL BG 4 in Miami," the other voice answered. "We've been trying to contact Vincent Demar on Peolle and apparently his radio is out."

"Quite right, sir," Timothy said. "However, he's right here."

"Great. Put him on, will you?"

Timothy held out the microphone to Vincent who took it and held down the transmit button. "Vincent Demar speaking."

"This is Monte Tucker in Miami. I'm with the Louden Museum and your boy and his friend were here a while back."

"Yes, I know. They were taking their State exams there."

"Did you know about their interest in the *El Capitan Uno*?"

"Well...that's a local legend in these parts. Yes, my boy and his friend were quite interested. Why?"

"I won't bother you with the details, but other people were interested too, and I've just found out that the Florida police have an interest in those persons. As long as they're not in the state, there's nothing that can be done, but from what the boys were talking about...looking into the history of the *El Capitan Uno* and all that...I think you should know."

"Mr. Tucker," Vincent said, "Those boys are already on Landau Island."

"Oh dear."

"What's wrong?"

After a pause, Monte Tucker said, "Quite possibly nothing, but the two men I mentioned, Stoney Marks and

Henry Blackstone, have made inquiries about Landau Island..."

"Who cares?" Vincent demanded impatiently.

"They have filed for possession of the island under International Law and if nobody can refute their claim...well..."

Vincent Demar was almost out of breath. "*Well what?*"

"They can destroy Landau Island." There was a break in the transmission, then Monte Tucker's voice came back on again. "If there really is an *El Capitan Uno* there, and they find it, the world will lose a tremendous treasure, even if it is just an old hulk."

"Mr. Tucker...there are plenty of old hulks around!"

"From what we overheard...these men seem to think it is buried there."

"But who would care?"

"Mr. Demar...have you heard of the Vasa?"

"The Swedish naval ship that was sunk on the maiden voyage over three hundred years ago?"

"Correct. It is now one of the biggest museum sites in Stockholm, Sweden today. It is living history, Mr. Demar."

Very calmly, Vincent said, "Listen here, you've had plenty of time to look into the remains of that old wreck. Why is it suddenly very important."

"It's been brought back to life, Mr. Demar. We here at the museum...which is associated with the library, are extremely concerned with any details of Caribbean history."

"Why now?" Vincent asked him.

"Because two people who could destroy an artifact like the *El Capitan Uno* were interested too."

"How about the kids?"

"That makes it even worse," Monte Tucker told him.

"They are only children and have no way of protecting themselves."

LARRY FINGERED the hole in the hull of their skiff and looked up at Josh. "He did a good job."

"How long will it take to fix it, do you think?"

"A week anyway, if we get the tools."

Josh looked toward the southern end of the island that was still framed in the moonlight. "they don't want anybody to get off here, do they?"

"Sure doesn't look that way."

"Larry...you think it's the *El Capitan Uno* they're after?"

"What else could there be, Josh?"

"Ben Westerly's pearls."

"Now, how would they know about that?" Larry asked him.

"It used to be the business here...and besides, you know how people talk about things."

"Not from Landau Island, Josh. It's further away than Peolle. Ben never told anybody about how he learned to develop those pearls in oysters. Until now, it was a specialty only the Japanese were great at. The big difference between the Japanese method and his was that he never had to dive for the oysters...they were all developing those cultured pearls in water a foot deep."

"And that is better, I guess."

"For money, yes. About a thousand percent better. But since nobody knows about Ben Westerly's system, let's keep him out of it. What we have to do is find a way to reach my dad or yours."

BEN WESTERLY LIKED to watch the moon sitting there in the night sky, a bright eye looking at the earth. For some reason, tonight the moon didn't look quite right, with the early tendrils of rain clouds drifting across its face. All his life had been spent on this island, and like the boy Josh, he too had "funny feelings."

He looked up into the night, watching the ominous swell of white that tried to wipe out the moon and knew that another night storm was on its way, the first of many that would come for the season.

Long ago the natives of Landau had learned to shelter themselves away from these strange storms with their savage lightning strokes that leapt from the sky to sear burning holes in the earth. As far as he could remember, nobody had ever been hit with those wild, hissing spears from the sky because they had always touched the ground around Great Sandy, but the ear-splitting waves of thunder that rolled across the island made everyone fear for their lives.

Nothing like this had ever happened on Gamu, that other island ten miles across the water. There they got the clouds and the lightning but never anything like that which happened over Landau. Maybe that was why the islanders of Gamu never enjoyed coming here, and why they had never settled here. It had taken a hardy family like old Poki George's to land on *this* island and make it home.

Overhead, the thunder rumbled like a sow's belly and Ben Westerly nodded. It was coming on. Maybe not tonight, but maybe tomorrow or the next, but surely by the end of the week, the first big storm would hit.

It was the start of the strange season, the one the big grandfather told them about...when it was better not to look outside because you would not like what you saw.

Or be very afraid.

The darkness was complete now, and Ben got up to walk back to his house. He was halfway there when the hands reached out and he tried to yell, but his voice was choked off and while he was still trying to squirm out of that grasp, he felt the blow on his head and slipped to his knees, his mind in total darkness.

CHAPTER SIX

NOBODY HAD SEEN Ben Westerly since last night when the rain had come down, but then, nobody was really worried since Ben had gone off many times looking for those odd places where he had found the oysters that could develop the pearls.

Young Ben didn't seem concerned at all and when Larry told him he was curious about the diary his father had found he said, "Oh, that's right here. Would you like to see it?"

"I sure would," Larry told him.

He rummaged on top of an old cabinet and brought down a small box. It was hand made of black oak from an old wreck that had drifted on the shore, the hinges of yellowed brass. He opened it, found the dried leather book, and handed it to Larry. "Be very careful. It is many years old."

Gently, Larry took it into his hands, then carefully, began turning the pages. They were coarse and brittle and most had been written onboard during the voyage, but shortly he found what he had been looking for, the section describing how the *El Capitan Uno* had anchored in the magnificent cove, surrounded, and protected by the great sandy hills, safe from the strange storms that were working on the horizon, coming closer to them each night. The captain and the crew seemed to realize that to stay at sea would be foolish, and since they needed food and water, and this perfect spot was at hand, how much better it would be to anchor in the safety of this strange cove.

There were not natives there, even although they thought they had spied a boatload going to that island called Gamu on the charts. It was funny and they all laughed, since the natives had never seen ships like theirs and were afraid, even without hearing the thunder of the cannons.

Oh, there was nothing to fear at all, so they left the ship and made a base camp to have a place to gather their supplies and that same night the wild storm came up and the next day the *El Capitan Uno* was no more.

There wasn't even the sign of a snapped anchor chain or the smallest bit of wreckage to be found on the shore! The *El Capitan Uno* had simply disappeared into thin air. They had stayed at their camp until the sails of the sister ship had showed on the horizon and...

At that point, the diary ended.

"You'd think he would have finished writing," Josh said.

"Not if what happened here scared them that much."

"So they lost their ship."

"Josh, that's what scared them. It was in a good landing, well anchored and just like that...poof! It was gone. All he says is about the funny color of the water and the sand."

"Storms always make things seem different," Josh said.

"Let's find Ben and see what he says, I'm getting as many funny feelings as you."

"Y'KNOW," Stoney said to his partner, "I send you out to do a couple of little jobs and you mess everything up again. Right now I'd like to pop you one right in the chops."

"Hey, you crazy, Stoney? I told you what I heard... then I run across the guy they was talking about right in front of me." He pointed to the figure he had trussed up on the ground.

"I have to tell you something, Henry."

"What's that, Stoney?"

"You're dumb. Real dumb. You do everything that can get us into trouble."

"He's only a native!"

"Suppose he got rights?"

"What rights can a native have?"

"Idiot." When his fingers clenched into a fist, Henry drew back a few feet. "You know we only got a few weeks to work this place out, don't you?"

"Who cares, Stoney? When we get to own it..."

"Right now we don't own it!"

"But it's only a stinking island in the middle of the ocean!"

"Henry, you're getting dumber!"

"Come on, Stoney..."

"We got our bid in to buy this place, okay?" Stoney said quietly, trying to keep his temper down. "As long as nobody has any claim to it, we can make it."

"Yeah, I know," Henry said. "First we need the dough."

"Right, stupid, so don't mess us up."

"All I did was grab this guy, Stoney. He was sitting right there and I remembered from when I saw him before."

"Beautiful...only now we have to make him talk about that thing he found."

"That should be easy," Henry said.

Actually, he didn't realize how easy it was going to be.

Ben Wesley was glad to tell them about the strange affliction that touched Landau at certain times. He was pleased to tell them about the diary he had found, and about the strange color the lagoon had been, along with the sand...if you wanted to believe there was a lagoon at all to start with.

Stoney Marks was about to turn him loose because he thought he was a dumb native, when he saw the soft leather pouch in his pocket and yanked it out. When he saw the pearls inside it, Stoney's eyes gleamed and he said, "Whether we find the *El Capitan Uno* or not, we got ourselves a treasure, partner."

In the gleam of the lamp, the pearls winked a pinkish glow, soft and expensive.

"Wow," Henry breathed softly.

"Look at the size of those babies," Henry said.

"Only one place he coulda gotten those from."

"Yeah, the wreck of the *El Capitan Uno*. Besides the gold, she was carrying jewels back to the ladies in Spain."

Ben Westerly's eyes were open now. He had heard their conversation and he knew what they were talking about. They had his pearls it had taken him ten years to develop, but all they thought was that they came from the old wreck everyone always talked about.

So when Stoney Marks said, "These come from the *El Capitan Uno* buddy?" Ben simply shrugged. To Stoney and Henry, that meant yes, and Stoney asked, "Where is it?"

Ben didn't even know what they were talking about, so he said, "Where else would it be?"

"You were right," Henry stated. "He means it's there... under the sand."

That evil grin touched Stoney Mark's face again. "Tie him up, Henry. This guy knows more than he's telling us now, but if we don't find what we're looking for, he'll tell us the rest, won't you?"

Ben Westerly didn't answer. He looked at him and there were daggers in his eyes. All he could think of was that these two men who wanted to destroy Landau Island and all the people on it were worse than all the pirates who had made the coves and inlets of this coral outcropping their old hideouts.

Stoney Marks and Henry Blackstone didn't scare him. Landau was a small island, and although there weren't many people on it, and no people at all with weapons, they wouldn't let him stay long in the clutches of these modern pirates.

For some reason, he kept thinking of the two boys who had come in their skiff to visit old Poki George. They weren't children and they weren't men yet, but there was something about them that showed they were growing into the stature of right people.

———

TWO YEARS AGO, Stoney had laid claim to an island he thought had mineral potential. Nothing had panned out, but he learned the ways to gain control of property that had lain unclaimed in the sea. A month later he did it again, and before they had instituted their attack on Landau, his claims were in. This little island was there, a place claimed by nobody, wanted by nobody, a coral atoll out in the middle of the Caribbean and when Stoney Mark's claim was recorded, he would own Landau Island

and all that was on it, including Great Sandy and the wreck of the *El Capitan Uno* beneath it.

A lightning stroke turned the night into day for a moment and Henry said, "I don't like this one bit."

"You don't like anything."

"The sky is all funny."

"It gets that way this time every year. You heard what this guy told us." He gave Ben's inert body a nudge with his foot.

"We got to get started soon, Stoney."

"Yeah, I know. Those machines roll at daybreak, so we get ready. I'm gonna hit the sack. You keep watch until I wake up."

"Hey Stoney, I did all the work. How come I can't get some sleep first?"

"You wanna rap in the mouth?"

"No, not really."

"Then do what I told you."

IT HAD TAKEN them the whole night to figure out what they had to do, and by the time they had it planned it was almost morning. Josh said, "We have to make sure they stay on the beach."

"If they have those machines going, they're *on* the beach."

"Larry...there's no way they can miss seeing us swimming out to that boat in the daytime..."

"I wasn't planning on doing it during daylight."

"My friend..."

"I know the sharks are night feeders," Larry told him.

"Then how can we get to their boat?"

"We'll find a way."

"All the canoes are smashed and the Seahawk is stove in."

Larry nodded. "I know. So we get that inflatable raft out of the locker in the skiff and paddle out. If we're lucky we can get a couple of twelve-volt batteries out of their shelves and once we make contact with Peolle and our dads, we got it made."

"Larry, you're out of your mind!"

"What makes you think so?"

"They won't leave the *Belinda* all alone out there!"

"I didn't think they would."

"So how are you going to get the batteries?"

"Josh, you just don't know how sneaky I can get."

"I hope you're right," Josh told him.

"We'll find out soon enough," Larry said. "Right now, let's get some sleep."

Josh grinned, his teeth gleaming in the moonlight. "My friend, you know you are a real islander, don't you?"

"Why sure," Larry said. "All us pirates are alike."

———

BEN WESTERLY HAD ALREADY CUT himself loose. Neither of the two men had bothered him at all, and the ropes they had put around his wrists and ankles were sliced open as soon as they had tossed him behind the compound area. All Ben could think of when he was rubbing his wrists was, "*Stupid flatland foreigners. They think anybody away from the mainland is a nothing, an islander, not to be considered.*" For a little while he thought about running for help, but when he considered it, he didn't know what kind of help to get.

Now, it might be better if he waited. Find out first what the enemy was planning, then act.

He lay back in his former position, as if he were still

bound. When Stoney Marks came in to look at him, Stoney thought he was asleep.

"ANYTHING?" Vincent Demar asked.

Timothy shook his head. "Some ships at sea, but they haven't seen the *Seahawk*."

"Then they're on Landau. There's no way they could have missed. Their last call put them right on course."

"Vincent..."

"What?"

"I told you before, don't worry so much."

"Great. You worried about Josh?"

"Absolutely."

"See what happens when you're a father?"

"You're right, Vincent, my friend. I think we had better make up our minds. Of course...there's that weather outside..."

"Timothy," Vincent said, "you sure want those kids to be on their own, don't you?"

"Have they asked for help?"

"Not yet. Suppose they want to?"

"They'll find a way," Timothy said.

"How?"

"Let's wait until they ask," Timothy told him.

IT HAD STARTED TO RAIN, a wild, lashing rain that came down so hard a person couldn't see further than he could reach. Three hours later the downpour had heightened to a fury greater than anyone had ever seen before.

Luckily, all the lightly built houses were on high ground, and since there was no wind, they were still standing. Long ago the fresh water cisterns had filled and over-flowed, and paths were being cut into the soil as the water drained off toward the ocean.

———

WHEN THERE WAS A LET-UP, Larry and Josh made a dash toward the high side of Great Sandy to make sure the broken boats were still tied up. Even if they had been damaged, it would be a lot easier repairing them than building new ones. They spotted all but one dugout, which they remembered having been left right where a small river was rushing down the slope.

Josh said, "Hey, our raft is still in the pool."

"For how long?" Larry pointed toward the sea side of Great Sandy. The driving rain had washed out a cleft into the oceanside of the sand embankment, and already the water from the pool was seeping out on the wet bench.

"You know, Larry, there may be a lagoon here yet."

"It'll take an awful lot of rain to wash out an opening for a ship to come in."

"Who knows? It could have happened that way. One hurricane can wipe an island right out of the sea...or it can build a new one."

"And it could even cover up a whole Spanish galleon in one night too?"

"Why not?"

"The masts, Josh. They were a hundred feet off the deck of the ship. The survivors would have seen those masts."

"Even if they snapped off and were covered up too?"

"Well...you could be right." He looked up at the sky. "This storm could go either way. Right now, it's quieting down. Want to try to get that raft from the *Seahawk*?"

"Yeah, we'd better before those two men might think we have such a thing aboard."

Overhead, the lightning crackled in the sky. The boys nodded, then ran through the sand to where it dropped off to the beach, and in great, flying strides made it to the bottom and stayed along the tree-line until they reached their battered skiff.

It didn't take them long to locate the rubberized canvas sack that held the life raft and they dragged it free and carried it to a safe spot among the palms. When it was tied down and hidden from view, they rose, struggled against the rain and made their way back to Poki George's house where he was waiting with bowls of hot clam soup for them.

Poki George nodded toward the horizon. "Look. The clouds are lifting. Soon the rain will stop."

"How long will it be afterwards before those machines can be used?" Larry asked.

"My son, the sand will breathe deeply and dry before noon tomorrow."

"Then we go tonight, Josh."

"Go?" Poki George said anxiously.

The boys grinned at him. "A little plan we have," Josh said.

CHAPTER SEVEN

STONEY MARKS FINGERED the smooth orbs he had taken from Ben Westerly and his eyes shined when he looked at them.

"How much do you think they're worth?" Henry asked him.

"What they're worth now is nothing to what they'll be worth later."

"How's that?"

"Nobody ever made a collection of just a *few* pearls like this, dopey. These are first rate, see? They're big...part of a collection."

"And that guy has the rest?" Ben queried hopefully.

"If he had, they would have been in that pouch."

"Guess you're right, Stoney." He frowned, thinking. "Then where are the rest?"

"Someplace around the same area he found these. They could have been scattered, but they didn't go far." He held the pearls out on his palm, pinkish white spheres as big as marbles. "A dozen more like this and we'd have a million dollars in our hands."

"Then we don't need the *El Capitan Uno*! We could..."

"Shut up, Henry!" Stoney closed his fist around the pearls, then took a deep breath and settled down. When he put the pearls back in the pouch he looked at his partner with a fierce frown and said, "A million bucks would never be enough for me, you got that?"

"Sure, Stoney, but I don't need that much and..."

"Unless you want to wind up feeding the sharks, you do exactly what I tell you. That clear?"

"Okay, okay, Stoney, I just thought..."

"That's your trouble, thinking. So what do we get with a million? If we can get the pearls and all the gold off the *El Capitan Uno* at the same time, why not take it?"

"But we got those pearls *now*," Henry reminded him.

"It'll only take a little while longer, you nut. We got the power equipment, we got the place...and that's even better we haven't got trouble at all. Who's to stop us from getting the entire haul?"

"Guess nobody is, Stoney." He gave him a funny glance and shrugged. "Unless somebody else owns this place."

Stony dropped the pouch in his pocket, straightened his belt and stood up. "Nobody owns little islands like this. We got our claim in and if nobody comes up with papers to prove otherwise, this here little hunk of coral belongs to us and we can do anything we want with it including throwing all the natives back into the sea."

"There's a bunch of 'em, Stoney."

"Yeah, but we got the guns," his partner said.

Ben Westerly inched back into the rear of the shed and huddled in the corner. Stoney Marks was sure about the way he had tied him up, so sure he didn't bother to investigate, but let Henry do the checking. The trouble was, Henry didn't like the dark all that much and as long as he could see a bundle in the corner shadows, he was satisfied and called out that everything was all right.

He didn't realize how mistaken he was. The bundle he thought was a prisoner was only a pile of burlap sacks formed into the shape of a man and unless someone looked very closely, there was no reason for them thinking otherwise.

And now Ben was outside, wanting to make his way back to the house of Poki George, but the rain had softened the sand enough to be dangerous and the water coursing down the hillside was cutting off any direct flight across the island. All Ben could do was wait until the storm drifted off and hope that neither Stoney Marks or Henry Blackstone found him gone. They had the flashlights and the guns and he wouldn't be too hard to locate out there in the open with only a tree or two to shelter him.

POKI GEORGE OPENED his hands helplessly. "What can I say? Never have I been asked for papers to the island...nor had my father. If they are here, I do not know where."

Josh made a gesture of impatience. "My father said you were careless about those things..."

"Son...nobody cared before. Who would want this place except us?"

"Those two guys with the machines," Larry said.

"Really *want* it?"

"Just enough to tear it up. Those two power movers can spread this island right back into the sea."

"What can I do?"

"Keep looking," Larry told him. "My dad always told me if you had it to start with you can always find it again."

"Your dad isn't here," Poki said.

"He will be. Tonight we call him."

"But...there is no battery for the radio."

"Tonight there will be. In another hour, that storm will be over."

Poki George looked at the two boys carefully. There was a sincere expression on their faces and a determined set to their shoulders. He smiled, remembering what he had thought before. They were young and they were boys, but they were growing and soon they would be men, and the men they would be, would be formed by the boys they were.

"If you will be careful tonight," he said, "then I will search for those papers that says we own the island. There are still some places I haven't looked." He walked to the model of the *El Capitan Uno* on the mantle of the fireplace. "The old ones used to talk about this ship. I should have listened more carefully."

At midnight the moon broke through the clouds and lighted up the sands enough so Larry and Josh could see what they were doing. The rain had stopped an hour ago and as they stood on the lip of Great Sandy they could look down at the cut on the seaside edge. It looked as if someone had taken a chip out of one side of a teacup. The pool was there with only a trickle of water fingering its way out to the ocean.

"I don't think you're going to get your lagoon, Josh."

"No, nothing bigger than a twig could float out of there now. I guess later all that sand will fill back into the bowl again."

"Most likely," Larry told him. "The way the winds and the tides work, another few days will see that gouge filled back in again."

"Larry..."

"Yeah?"

"Isn't it a funny color down there? All green like?"

"Sure is." He looked up at the sliver of a moon in the sky. "It could be that," He pointed, "or our imagination."

"Look again," Josh said. "You imagine that?"

"Nope, but that's the way it is so let's forget about it."

Josh grabbed his arm. "Remember what that diary said...about the strange color of the lagoon...when it *was* a lagoon?"

Larry nodded. "But right now there's no galleon anchored down there, is there?"

"No."

"Josh!"

"Well, I can't see it and there's enough light..."

"We left it in the weeds by the shore. Of course you can't see it now."

"The shadow of it should show. It would have made a big, dark square."

"Who cares, Josh. We aren't going to need it anyway."

Josh nodded. "Guess you're right. It's just those funny feelings I keep getting. My father would tell me it was because I was born on Peolle and I had sand between my toes."

"You don't see me wearing shoes, do you?" Larry asked.

"But we're not the same color..."

"Great...I spend all my time in the sun so I can look like you." Larry put his arms around Josh's shoulders and squeezed. "Buddy, we're people. Just don't you laugh any more when I get sunburned."

Josh stifled a laugh and said, "Maybe we'd better get to our rubber boat."

But they didn't make a move.

From behind them they heard the soft whispering of sand and were ready to bolt when a voice they recognized said, "It's me...Ben Westerly."

They both pivoted and took a deep breath of relief. "Ben!"

It only took a couple of minutes for Ben to tell them what had happened and when he had finished, Larry said, "Now we know we have to get help. Those men know about Ben's pearls and there will never be any way to stop them by ourselves."

"My pearls didn't come from the *El Capitan Uno*."

"We know that," Larry told him, "but *they* don't"

"They will find me gone in the morning...then what will happen?"

Larry let it run through his mind a moment, then said, "There are two of them and more of us...but they know there's no place for us to go...and they have plenty to do with those machines in the meantime. Frankly, I don't think they will really worry about us at all. If we even tried to attack them, all the guns are on their side."

"Then what do we do?"

"Nothing."

Ben's eyes narrowed. "Nothing?"

"As long as they think there's nothing we can do, then we can do everything."

"Larry..."

"What, Josh?"

"That doesn't make sense."

"Look...they'll forget about us. What can we do against their guns and machines anyway? On this island everybody is peace loving. Nobody fights and nobody makes trouble, so when it happens, what would we know to do?"

"My friend," Ben said, "They have my pearls, they know money is here and they expect to find more."

"And that," Larry told them, "is my point. Let them expect to find what they want. As long as they are expecting, we'll be free to do what we have to do. The minute they think there is nothing here for them they'll either start shooting or run for it."

Ben grabbed Larry's hand and turned him around. "Why would they start shooting?"

"Because they've already gotten themselves into so much trouble there's no way out," Larry reminded him. "And don't forget, they shot at us out at sea, so they're not worried about doing it."

"You said something else."

"Oh?"

"About running."

"That," Larry said, "is if we can get behind and push."

A dull flash half lit up the sky and Josh squinted upward. "I thought the storm was over."

Ben shook his head. "Strange things happen this time of the year."

As if to accentuate his statement a bolt of lightning hissed in the air and buried itself into the side of Great Sandy. For a few moments everyone was blinded, then the thunder rumbled heavily and receded into the distance.

And just as suddenly, the clouds broke and the moon came out, letting the faint yellow rays touch the island.

Larry said, "Ben, tell everyone on the island to stay quiet, then you go help Poki George find his papers of ownership."

"Are you boys..."

"We'll be all right," Josh said.

"Okay." Ben ran off in the semi-darkness toward Poki George's house and Larry asked, "Ready?"

Josh's grin was a broad-toothed smile in the moonlight. "You know, our dads would give us the dickens for this."

"What would they give us if we didn't?" Larry asked.

VINCENT DEMAR and Timothy sat together over a pot of coffee monitoring a set that still hadn't brought in a signal from Landau Island. When Timothy poured his friend another cup he said, "Please, do not worry about the boys...you know what the weather report was."

"A storm shouldn't cause all that much interference, Tim."

"Storms can do anything, Vincent."

"Perhaps...but it's those two men that are bothering me."

"Marks and Blackstone?"

"That's right."

"Vincent...you've already spoken to Miami. They only can claim the island if there is nobody else with papers to prove ownership."

"Poki George is *your* friend, Tim. You said he's careless about those things."

"Perhaps, but I can't see him being *that* careless."

"Tim, he's old and nobody's ever cared about Landau Island before. All of a sudden the Miami museum is interested, those men on the Belinda are interested...and our kids are interested. What can make it worse...we don't know what's happening."

"Can't we call the Coast Guard?"

"Landau is foreign territory, Tim."

"Would the Navy respond?"

"It isn't a war, my friend."

"Then who would look into it?" Timothy demanded.

After a few moments, Vincent said, "Here, we could call for help from the United States, but Landau Island is under a different protectorate. It's little and unimportant, so even the United Nations wouldn't be interested in it."

"Somebody has to be," Timothy said softly.

His friend nodded. "Only if there's real trouble. Then we can call them."

"Would they go out of their way?"

"You can bet on that," Vincent told him.

"Why?"

"Because we're American nationals," Vincent said.

ON THE HORIZON, the bulk of the *Belinda* was a dull smudge, a vague outline a quarter mile offshore. Ordinarily, it would have been an easy swim, but the boys realized they were in shark waters where a fifteen-foot monster could tear a human body in half with one twisting wrench of its jaws and the only way they could get to the ship laying offshore was with a craft of their own.

On top of that, they had another problem. They had to get a battery from the Belinda back to shore and that would be a sixty-pound piece of equipment to handle.

Softly, they eased their bundle down to the shoreline, then pulled it from the rubberized container. When they had it spread out Larry pulled the knob on the CO_2 container and the in-rushing gas filled the life raft within a few seconds.

The boys looked at each other and grinned, but their smiles came too soon. They picked the raft up, started carrying it to the shoreline, when Larry tripped and they both heard the hissing sound together.

A jagged chunk of coral they hadn't seen had snagged the raft and ripped a six-inch gash in its bottom.

The big yellow bulldozer roared into life and Henry Blackstone kept his eyes on the dials until he knew everything was ready to surge ahead, then he looked back at his partner in the shovel, raised his arm and the two machines started to climb the white mountain of sand in front of them.

Even though their prisoner had escaped by sawing his

bonds loose on jagged shells, they weren't worried. After all, what could he say, and who would hear it?

Nobody on Landau Island had a working radio, so who could call for help? And who was big enough to beat Henry Blackstone and Stoney Marks anyway? In the heavy machines, both men smiled to themselves, thinking of the riches that were about to become theirs. Ever since they had taken the pearls from Ben Westerly, there was no doubt about there being treasure. From now on, it was simply a case of how quickly they could get it.

It was a pretty day. The storm was over and the sky was cobalt blue with a southeast breeze that kept the dust down and their faces cool.

They had made a twenty-yard-wide cut in Great Sandy that ran all the way down to the trench the storm had gouged out when Stoney held up his hand to stop and cut the big diesel engine off.

He pointed down to the side of the sandy hollow and said, "See how all the storms came in from the North Side?"

Henry bobbed his head, noticing the ripples in the sand.

"It's got to be down beneath us...maybe fifty feet."

"That's a lot of sand to move, Stoney."

"You have something better to do?"

Henry shrugged. "Let's get moving then." He looked up at the sky. "If you think it's okay."

"What do you mean, if I think it's okay?"

"That storm isn't over yet," Henry protested.

"You nut, get that machine rolling! That storm is done, you hear? If you ever want to smell that gold get that sand shoveled outa there."

"Stoney..."

"Now what?"

"See that cloud?" He pointed toward the East, his face twisted into an uncertain expression.

"Yeah," Stoney said, "I see it."

"Looks like it's coming this way."

"So let it come, you nut! It's only a cloud. Now roll, hear me?"

"Sure, Stoney. Okay, okay."

ON THE BEACH, Larry and Josh were crouched out of sight, watching the two machines tear into the side of Great Sandy while they were trying to figure how to repair their raft.

Larry was disgusted. Even nature had gone against him, he thought. Out there he could see the surface of the ocean being sliced by the fins of the huge sharks that inhabited the area, the dorsal fin cutting the first swipe, followed by the lazy sweep of the tail.

Every once in a while there would be flurry on the surface and the water would boil with a crazy activity and the boys knew the sharks had found another victim to feed them.

Then they realized how safe the *Belinda* was, anchored out there with her guardian sharks. But sharks only went by sound and smell, and in the life raft, the sharks would have had neither.

They were so engrossed in their problems that they didn't hear Poki George say, "Trouble belong to all do they not?"

Larry drew back, then saw the old man and nodded. "What can we do, Poki?

The old man smiled gently and said, "It isn't all that bad. All you have to do is think about it."

"I have."

"And what did you think?"

"We have to fix it."

"Then fix it."

Larry looked stricken. "How, Poki, how?"

"There are those old wrecks on the north side, my son. In the seams of their timbers there is pitch...tar, you call it. And if properly used that strange boat of yours can be repaired."

"That will take another day, Poki."

"Everything takes time, son."

Larry and Josh looked up at the old man. There was something odd about the way he smiled and Josh said, "Poki George..."

And before he could ask the question, Poki said, "I found the papers. Landau Island belongs to us by right of the grant of the King of Spain."

"Poki!"

"It was underneath the model of the El Capitan Uno. I never even knew it was there. It was Ben who found it."

"Underneath?" Larry asked.

"That's what Ben told me," the old man informed him.

Josh looked at Larry and knotted his hands together. "My funny feelings are coming back."

"Let's go see those papers...and Ben."

"TELL ME EXACTLY WHAT HAPPENED," Larry said.

Ben nodded, took a deep breath, and walked back to the door. "I was all wet. I went to the fire to dry off and I looked up at the little ship...the model of the *El Capitan Uno*."

"Okay, go on."

"I was mad at the men who were searching for her. I

picked up the model and held it in my arms, looking at that beautiful ship, wondering what had ever become of her, then I heard Poki George coming into the room and I put it back on the mantle."

"What happened?"

Ben shook his head in total bewilderment. "I don't know, the papers were just sticking out of there all of a sudden."

"Just like that?" Larry asked.

"They were wet."

"Wet?"

"I don't know why," Ben said, "But they were wet."

"Did you get them wet, Ben?"

He looked at Larry for a long moment then shook his head. "I don't even know they were there. I put the model back on the mantel piece and the papers were in the way."

"Wet?"

"Yes. They were wet."

Larry looked at the two sheafs of papers Poki George had handed him. They were still damp, but there was no doubting their meaning nor their origin. The seal of the King of Spain attesting to their authenticity and Larry said, "You know what this is, don't you?"

Poki George smiled. "This island was here before the King of Spain."

"But you have title to it," Larry said. "This island belongs to you who have lived here and their descendants!"

"We have always lived here," Poki said gently.

"They're going to take it away from you!"

"How, my son?"

"I wish I knew, Poki, I sure wish I knew."

"Then don't worry. Tonight you go to sleep. Because you couldn't do what you had planned, think that tomorrow will be a better day."

CHAPTER EIGHT

BETWEEN THE BULLDOZER and the scoop shovel, an entire section of Great Sandy lay in ruins. What had been a beautiful white natural teacup had become a ragged slice of ground and in its bottom the pool had leaked out into the ocean through a little narrow pathway, and now Great Sandy was only part of where it had been.

The big yellow bulldozer and the scoop shovel had torn the heart out of the ground and now they needed a rest. Stoney put his machine down low so he could get a better bite of the sand when he was ready and his partner pulled to a halt directly behind and above him.

"There's nothing here, Stoney."

"We only got half the sand moved out."

"So something should be showing." He got down from the shovel and walked over to his partner. "Man," he said, "All we got is sand."

"How much do you want with one day's digging?"

"Stoney...in sand we should show *something*."

"We showed something without digging, you big stupid."

"You mean the pearls?"

"Right. And you let the guy get away!"

"Stoney...where can he go?"

"Buddy, for a change you're lucky, now get back on that shovel and let's get that area cleared out."

"Hey Stoney."

"Yeah?"

"Can I ask a question?"

"Just one and that's all."

"There's another storm coming up. What'll we do?"

But he had spoken too soon. With a terrible clash of thunder, the skies darkened and a great stroke of lightning hit the ground not a hundred feet from the bulldozer. Henry heard Stoney yell, and they both hit the sand and ran toward the shelter they had set up. By the time they were huddled together from the downpour, the blazing storm had struck their area a dozen times. They looked at each other with odd expressions, wondering what had brought them and this crazy weather together at the same time.

THE TAR POKI GEORGE had made them from the scrapings of the old ships on the north side had sealed the gash in the life raft and Larry and Josh were ready to put their boat out to sea. Josh said, "You sure?"

"As sure as I can get."

"Well, as long as you're going..."

It had taken another day and night, but now the darkness, surrounded them and the machines were silent on the other side of the beach. They could see the lights of their campfire and realized that this was the time to move.

Together they ran the raft out to their waist's depth, then jumped in and picked up their paddles. Without a sound, they began stroking toward the dark shadow of the *Belinda*, anchored a good quarter mile off shore.

It was a warm night, and the water was lit up with the fluorescence that made a long silvery streak of any fish that swam past in in a hurry, and a big swath of light when some unknown creature swept by with a massive cut of its tail in the constant search for food.

Josh said, "The sea lives, my friend."

"I hope it's not looking for us."

"Whatever it is will take anything in its path. Luckily, in the raft, we have no vibration of dying food or the smell of such."

"I hope you're right," Larry said.

"We'll find out soon enough."

"How?"

"If the sharks are hungry, they'll hit us from the bottom, flip the raft and we become shark bait."

"Buddy," Larry said, paddling furiously, "I sure hope you're wrong."

Then they both heard the weird sound and saw the bubbles coming up from alongside the raft. Josh said, "We're sinking!"

Larry saw the trail of bubbles and paddled even harder. "Keep at it, Josh. We can make the *Belinda* before we go down!"

POKI GEORGE and Ben Westerly were looking at the papers Poki had and Ben made a face of disdain. "What can be so important about these things?"

"They were never there before, Ben."

"Never where?"

"Anywhere. Until you found them."

"Poki," Ben said, "I came in here all tired and wet and

picked up your model to look and suddenly those papers were there. Right underneath that little ship of yours, like they were sticking out of the rack the ship was sitting on."

"Impossible," Poki George said.

"But it happened."

"Ben..."

"Yes...?"

"Remember how the boys had that funny feeling?"

"That...I remember."

"I'm getting it too."

"So am I, Poki, and I am afraid..."

"Ben, something very funny is happening."

JOSH GRABBED the anchor cable of the *Belinda* and swung the life raft around so that it snuggled up against the hull of the ship. The last of the air was going out of the rubberized compartment and by the time Larry and Josh had worked their way up the cable, their raft was a partially deflated thing already floating away on the tide.

On the bow of the *Belinda*, Larry held up his hand for silence and when there was no response he said to Josh, "We're alone. They've left their ship unguarded!"

Josh's voice was very sour. "Great." He looked around the bare deck of the ship. On the port side the radio antennae jotted up to make a cross against the sky. Inside, somebody had left a commercial station on and the dull throbs of drums backed up by a heavy bass resounded into the night.

"What do we do now?"

Larry checked out the area, then said, "We use their radio, pal."

"Beautiful."

For a full minute they stood there, making sure neither

Stoney nor Henry were aboard, then when they knew they were alone, they looked out at the dim spot of light that marked the campfire of the two men and Larry said, "This is our only chance, Josh."

His friend nodded, and they eased their way toward the cabin under the antenna. Larry tried the door and found it locked, but there was enough room in the framework to force the tongue of the lock mechanism back with a piece of metal and the door swung open.

The light from the moon danced across the metal, reflecting back at them from the glass faces of the dials. The radio sat there in the place, a beautiful piece of electronic equipment, but it was no connection to Peolle Island and their fathers for them now.

Both the boys knew what the smell was, the acrid odor of burned insulation and overheated metal. Josh turned, ran out and looked at the antennae on its mast and saw what they had missed the first time. "Lightning got the radio, Larry!"

Double-checking the switches, Larry nodded. The set was dead; there was no doubt about it. Even the four batteries under the desk were ruined. "At least it didn't destroy the ship."

"Would it make a difference? We don't know how to run this boat."

"Yeah, Josh, there's a difference. At least if we can't get away, maybe we can make those guys leave."

Josh was staring at something. He peered a little more intently into the far rear corner, then walked over and kicked at something. When he turned around he was grinning. "Maybe all is not lost, Larry."

"What's there?"

"A spare battery."

"Just one?"

"It takes four to run this set," Larry reminded him.

"But not the one at Poki George's house."

Larry was so disgusted all he could say was, "We going to swim back with it?"

"No, but there ought to be something on board here we can put together to get us back to Landau."

Josh's enthusiasm touched Larry and he grinned. "Why not pal? We got this far...we might as well go all the way. Come on, let's see what we can find."

Thirty minutes later they met at the starboard side with glum expressions on their faces. The *Belinda* certainly wouldn't meet with the safety standards of any country, including that of its registry. All they could dig up were six old and weathered life jackets, the cork inserts powdering in the torn fabric pockets.

"They don't even have a life ring on board," Josh stated hotly.

"How did that dinghy check out?" He was referring to the small boat lashed upside down on the aft deck.

"Forget it. The seams are half-inch apart. We wouldn't get ten feet in that. You find any timbers, Larry?"

"Just a handful of boards that would only make good paddles."

"Then we are stuck here, my friend, caught between the sharks and those two men."

"Well," Larry told him, "right now neither of them has us. What we have to do is attract attention from our friends on shore."

Sadly, Josh shook his head. "Even if they tried to get to us, those men would see them. From their position of Great Sandy they can cover all this area. No, my friend, I think this time our luck has run out."

A heavy tail beat the surface of the ocean and a spray of greenish tinged water covered them. The large form of some sea creature dove toward the bottom, the glow from its passage fading slowly.

Idly, Larry watched the quiet motion, then cocked his head to one side. Barely audible was the sound of a thumping against the hull of the *Belinda*. Curious, he grabbed the rail and looked over the side. A grin split his lips and he said, "Maybe our luck's still with us Josh. Look down there."

"What is it?" He leaned over and couldn't believe what he saw.

"Our log raft from the pool, buddy."

"But...how could it get out here?"

"Maybe those men opened the whole side of Great Sandy."

"They didn't Larry. We know where the gap was when they quit. A raft that big never floated out by itself."

After a moment's thinking Larry said, "Their shovel could have picked it up and heaved it over the lip to the beach."

"Larry...why would they bother to do that?"

"It got out here some way."

"Well, let's not wonder how tonight. Get a line down to it and I'll go drag that battery out here."

From the equipment locker, Larry pulled out a coil of half-inch hemp rope. After two tries he had the loop in one end snagged securely over the end log in the raft, then went back to help Josh with the battery. He let Josh slide down to the raft, then hitched the line around the battery case, tied it to the edge of the dock, and then with the line looped a few times around a stanchion, lowered it to the raft. As soon as it was solidly in place in the middle of their irregular decking, he slid down the line, climbed aboard and pushed away from the Belinda, the pieces of board he had found paddling them toward shore.

Stoney Marks was nervous. Sleep didn't come easily to him and twice that night he had gotten up to go check the dozer and the shovel. He was smart enough to realize that the old man whose radio battery was broken up would know where to find another, and so would those two kids. For some reason, the kids worried him the most.

Earlier, he had bolted down the steel battery compartments on the machines, even though he knew the batteries were too big for kids to remove, or to be extracted without the noise waking him up.

But he didn't feel right and looked up at the sky above. Maybe it was that storm moving in that bothered him, he thought. This crazy place had more freak storms than anywhere he had ever been. At least the two machines were safe from any washouts, sitting together on the flat section they had carved out of the hill. The keys to both switches were in his pocket, so there was no chance of anyone starting them.

Another flash of lightning brightened the sky and Stoney peered out at the dark area of the ocean. Did he just see something moving there? He kept watching seaward until another flash illuminated the water, but either he had missed the spot he was looking for or he had imagined it.

He figured that to be sure, he'd walk down to the shoreline and check it out. Quickly, he jacked a shell into the chamber of the rifle and started toward the lip of Great Sandy.

But then the rains started, a warm, hard driving rain and Stoney Marks shrugged, unloaded the gun, and forgot about it. Being caught out in the weather on Landau Island was something he didn't want to experience. Besides, it was probably only his imagination anyway. He wished he could do like his partner...put his head down anywhere and sleep until somebody kicked him awake.

Out on the water, the boys were taking the full beating from the storm. They paddled hard, hoping they were heading in the right direction but when they hadn't reached the beach after a certain lapse of time, Josh said, "Friend, I think we're lost."

"Stop paddling and listen."

The boards came out of the water and they sat motionless, ears alert to pick up the sound of the mild surf. The rain beating down was a noisy thing, but it flattened out the usual small chop of the waves and if any were rolling onto the beach they didn't hear it.

For another ten minutes they pushed themselves into the face of the storm, sat, rested and listened hard. "We could have gone around the north edge of the island," Larry said.

"Then we wait," Josh told him. "Until we are sure, we sit here and go no place."

It wasn't a pleasant prospect at all, but they had no choice...that is, until the sky lit up again and both boys saw the dark sweep of the trees that rose from the far end of the beach.

"There it is Larry!"

"Okay, paddle for all you're worth."

Both the boards went over the starboard side until the raft had changed direction, then each took his own side again and bent their backs into each stroke. It seemed like an hour, but actually it was only a few minutes before the bottom grated under their logs and they hopped out gleefully, pulled their raft as high up on the sand as they could get it, then pulled it to safety.

The first light of dawn was on the horizon and the rainstorm had drifted off to the south. One by one the night stars winked out as the day grew near. Just a little way off, Ben Westerly and his son came out of Poki George's house and turned their eyes toward the *Belinda,* which was just becoming visible in the east.

"Will they be all right?" the boy asked his father.

"Yes," Ben said, "I'm sure they will," though by the tone of his voice the boy knew he was worried.

Then his son pulled at his arm and pointed. "Look there!"

Even from where they were, Larry and Josh could hear Ben's shout of relief.

When he reached them Larry said, "Are we glad to see you...this battery has just about worn us down."

Everyone wanted to hear what had happened, but Poki George made them quiet down until the boys got their breath back. They finally got all of the story out and Larry added, "Let's hope that after this the battery is a hot one and not a dud."

It only took an opened pair of pliers touching each terminal to get a fat spark and everybody began smiling. Poki said, "Do not feel too glad too soon. There is still much work to be done. The wire leads to the set are torn and the connectors crushed. I hope we can find something to replace them."

"There *has* to be something," Larry said.

"I don't know, my son," Poki told him. "There was never a need for parts before."

"The skiff, Larry..."

"Remember where that bullet hit, Josh? It tore all that out of our set."

For a moment, the boys looked at each other, thinking the same thing. Oh, they could get the equipment, all right, but it meant another trip out to the *Belinda* and back, and this time they might not have the luck they had the last time.

Larry shook his head. "We'll keep that trip to the ship for last."

"What will we do, then?"

"If we have to, we'll snag wires from those earth moving machines out there."

Ben's son suddenly looked up, his face thoughtful. "Pop..."

"Yes?"

"It's that kind of heavy electric wire with the rubber on it...that's what you need?"

"There is no electricity on Landau Island, son."

"Wait a minute," Larry cut in. "what have you got in mind?"

"A long time ago one of those big wooden spools drifted in, remember that? Manuel made a table from it."

"Yes, I remember."

"And that heavy wire was wrapped around it and mom tied it to the trees to hang her clothes on."

"Ben," Larry said, "I think we have it made! Let's go get that wire."

"I sure hope ma didn't hang out any wash," Ben's boy said. "She can get pretty mad."

CHAPTER NINE

STONEY MARKS SAID, "You're crazy, Henry. You're absolutely outa your mind."

"Go take a look then!"

"What do you call these?" Stoney held his hand out under Henry's nose.

"So they're the keys to the machines!"

"Then how could anybody steal them, you nut?"

"I'm telling you," Henry insisted, "They're gone. They're not there anymore."

Stoney put the keys back in his pocket and balled up his fist. "All I told you to do was check those diesel engines for fuel. I didn't tell you to be a wise guy and make jokes. Now you go back and..."

"Go look, will ya, Stoney?"

"Henry," his partner said, "Sometimes I can't believe you. If those machines were moved we would have heard them. They roar like a hundred bulls."

"It was raining hard..."

"Not that hard!"

"Stoney..."

"And if they were stolen, where could anybody hide them? You ever think of that?"

"Well, the island..."

A wave of his hand cut Henry off. "The island isn't big enough to hide a bicycle far less than a bulldozer and a shovel."

"You'd better go look."

"Okay, I'm gonna look, and if there's something wrong with your eyes, I'm gonna make both of them black before I take you to get some glasses."

Henry Blackstone swallowed hard and nodded. He hoped there was nothing wrong with his vision, that was for sure. Stoney could get real mean when anybody played a joke on him.

THEY HAD BEEN TRYING for an hour, but they couldn't raise Peolle at all. Larry finally took the headset off and flipped the switch on the set to OFF. "Let's not work that battery too hard."

"You think they may not be at the radio?" Josh asked.

"It's pretty early. They could have been up late trying to get our signal."

"Can you raise Miami?"

Larry waited until Ben had drifted over to talk to Poki. "We haven't enough power. This is an old time set and I'm not quite sure how it works, but I've only been able to receive the inner islands so far." He rubbed the back of his neck and added, "You check that generator connection?"

"The windmill is working," Josh said, "But the driving gear isn't. Until it gets fixed, all we have is the battery."

"Well, a short rest will bring it back up some."

"Larry..."

"Yeah?"

"How do you think it *really* looks?"

"You got a funny feeling, Josh?"

"Funnier than ever before."

Larry nodded. "It doesn't look good, buddy, but we're sure going to keep trying."

IT WAS SO hard to believe that Stoney Marks just stood there wiping his eyes and staring at the spot where they had left the equipment. They had finished leveling off the area directly above where they figured the *El Capitan Uno* should have been, made sure there was no danger of any slides, then shut down the diesels for the night.

They had left thirty tons of bright yellow, earth-moving equipment sitting right there in that flat spot the bulldozer had carved out, a pair of mechanical monsters too big to budge without the masters at the controls, the ones with the keys to the ignition.

But no matter how long they looked, neither of those great, roaring brutes were there!

"This is as crazy as you are, Henry."

"Hey, I ain't crazy, Stoney! It's like I told ya..."

"I can see it, I can see it!"

"Then what happened to 'em?"

"How do I know?"

"You're the boss, Stoney. You're *supposed* to know everything."

Stoney Marks wiped the sweat off his forehead and nodded. That was right. He *was* the boss and the least he could do was know who had swiped two huge pieces of equipment.

His mind drifted to the contours of Landau Island, remembering how it was from the map and what he had seen for himself. Unlike other places, Landau had no secret coves or hidden caves. There were areas behind the tree line that could shelter the equipment, and that was the only place it could be.

One thing, it wouldn't take long to find out what had happened, and when he did, the people on this island would know about it. He'd use the shovel to scoop out one big hole and the bulldozer to push all of them in it.

He knew Henry was talking to him but he hadn't been listening. "What?" Stoney barked.

"The little kids. How about them?"

He remembered the little kids whose faces they saw in the bushes, kids so fascinated by the big machines that they had to watch what was happening. "*What* about them?"

"Well, maybe they…"

"You get dumber every minute. How can little kids mess with those machines. And what makes you think so anyway?"

"They left their toys over there where the dozer and shovel were, Stoney."

"Who cares?"

"Those toys were like our stuff."

Stoney Marks was so mad he could hardly see straight. "We're looking for two big pieces of machinery, remember, Henry? We ain't playing with toys!"

"But those kids don't play with toys like that…"

"Shut up and move!" Stoney snarled. "One more word about toys and I'm gonna play with your face!"

———

TIMOTHY SHOOK Vincent Demar out of sound sleep and pointed to the clock. "Have you heard?"

"Nothing since I shut down three hours ago. I had to close my eyes or I never would have made it."

"Try them again, my friend."

Vincent flipped the switches on his set, let it warm up, then squeezed the button on his microphone. "Landau Island from Peolle, this is Vincent Demar...over."

He repeated the message twice, then sat there listening intently.

Miles away Larry held the headset closer to his ear. When he was sure of what he heard he touched his mike button and said, "Dad, Dad?"

The voice from the speaker sounded faint and far away but Vincent recognized it immediately. "Larry...this is me. You all right?"

Knowing how low the battery was, Larry didn't bother with details. All he said was, "Dad, right now we're okay, but we need help as fast as you can get to us. There are two men here on a ship..."

"Yes, we know."

"Get somebody here quickly and ..."

Vincent Demar tapped his set impatiently. The voice of his son had faded out completely and all that he was getting was a low hum. "They've lost their power," he told his friend.

"What will we do now?" Timothy asked.

"Call the Coast Guard in Miami."

"That's a long way off," Timothy said.

"Yes, but with their authorization, the International Squadron can move and they're not far from there on Landau."

Vincent ran his fingers through his hair with impatience. "But whatever it is, the boys should be able to stay on top of it."

"They're only boys, my friend."

"Sure but isn't it better to think that they're young men."

Timothy smiled and nodded. "You're right. They are young men and they will survive."

On Landau Island, the boys heard nothing of their father's opinions or decisions. They looked at the radio set, the reading on the dial that indicated their power was almost gone and Larry threw the switch to *Off*. It had been a long and difficult struggle, but at least their message had gotten through.

"Maybe we can take it easy for a while," Larry said.

The small voice said, "I don't think so. Those men are not far away. Both of them have guns and they look very mad." Ben's son was watching them from the doorway.

"Why, what's up?"

"Somebody stole their big machines, I think. They are gone from where they left them."

"What?" Larry could hardly believe his ears.

Josh looked at him, stunned. "Who could take them? Where could anybody put them?"

"Something's wrong here, buddy." He got up and stepped away from the radio. "Let's go see what's going on."

But before they got out the door, Poki George and Ben came in from the side entrance and waved them over. "This way," Poki told them.

Without asking questions, the kids followed the men outside, stayed behind them until they were hidden in the thick shrubbery, then Poki pointed to the rear of his house.

Stoney Marks and Henry Blackstone were moving through the brush, their rifles at ready, looking for anything that moved.

Quietly, the small group moved out. Poki George wanted Larry and Josh to come with him, but the boys were too curious to want to hide. One thing they knew, the men would be easier to spot than they were and there was enough cover to keep them concealed.

They all agreed on a plan...the men would contact the others on the island and get them to a safe place, and Larry and Josh would keep tabs on Stoney and Henry. There was no doubt about what those outsiders intended and it had to be stopped.

When everything was working, Larry let his curiosity take over and said to Josh, "You know, we got to see where they left those machines."

"Of course. Who could steal such things?"

"Come on."

They had to skirt along the edges of the palms, sometimes flattening themselves out where the brush was low, because always in back of them, the guns deadly things in their hands, were Stoney and Henry.

For a little while they missed them, then they heard the smashing of glass and Stoney Marks bellowing voice shouting at Henry. "They got a battery! You said they didn't have one!"

"And they didn't!" Henry shouted back.

"Where did this one come from then?"

There was a pause and they heard Henry Blackstone say, "Look at it, Stoney. Look at this mark. You put it right there when we bought it."

His voice carried across the distance. *"They got it off the Belinda!"*

"Let's wreck this place," Henry said with utter finality.

But Stoney Marks was too mad to listen to him. "What we do is find the people on this crazy island and destroy them."

"Stoney..."

"Do what I tell ya, Henry, or you'll go first."

"Okay, Stoney," Henry said.

"They're coming out the front," Josh called over his shoulder.

"Good. Let's cut toward the beach and let them follow us. We can do better in this sand than they can."

Josh nodded his assent, then Larry stood up and let himself be seen by the men. One of them yelled and pointed, and when they were running toward them, the boys cut in another direction, swerved back, squirmed through the bushes and made a trail so difficult that if anyone tried to follow them, it would take a good two hours...and where they left their trail was only a hundred yards behind the wiggling figures of the two men who were trying to pick the thorns out of their pants and follow the footprints of the boys at the same time.

IT WAS QUIET, there on the slopes of Great Sandy. The boys picked their way down to the flat section where the machines had been and looked around them. All over were the gouges made by the treads of the dozer and shovel, and right where they ended they could see the indentions in the sand.

Josh said, "What's that over there?"

"Looks like a couple of toys."

"The kids here don't have toys, Larry."

"One way to find out," Larry said.

They slid down the slope a little further, then cut across to the site and Larry walked up to a pair of little toys sitting there in the sand. One was a bulldozer and the other a scoop shovel and they were all made in beautiful detail, exactly as the model of the *El Capitan Uno* had been.

The expression on Larry's face was too peculiar to describe. His eyes were deep and thoughtful and he scanned the irregular lip of Great Sandy, following the slopes and contours where the machines had bit into it.

The pool was still at the bottom of it, smaller now, with the opening to the sea still the same.

"Josh..." He pointed down to the trickle of water still seeping out to the ocean. "Remember when our raft was here?"

"Very well."

"It couldn't have floated out, do you think?"

"I don't know how, Larry. There isn't that much water for anything nearly as big as that raft. It was made out of full logs."

"Now *I'm* getting that funny feeling," Larry said.

"You'd better."

"Look up there."

On the top of the rim of Great Sandy were the figures of Stoney Marks and Henry Blackstone and both of them were looking down the barrels of their rifles and before they heard the reports of the guns, puffs of sand dug up at their feet. Nobody had to tell them...they jumped and ran toward the bottom at the same time and behind them they could hear the wicked whine of the bullets as they ricocheted from the sand. Neither of them realized they were clutching the toy models of the machines until they were at the bottom of Great Sandy, then suddenly tossed them into the edge of the rising tide and sped as fast as they could for the safety of the palm grove.

Their breath was coming in harsh gasps and they could see the two men thrashing through the undergrowth looking for them. Even though fear held them tightly in its grip, they didn't panic, and the men pushed by, muttering at the delay in locating a couple of kids.

Above them, the sun had almost ended its long descent and night was right behind it. The boys were stiff and tired, but too wary to move and it wasn't until they saw the light of a campfire and were able to identify the men behind it that they even tried to speak.

Josh said, "They'll be sure to find us tomorrow, Larry."

"Maybe not. Dad got our message."

"Those men know where we are. From their campfire they can cover this whole grove. One can come in looking for us while the other waits, then when they have shot us, they can look for the others. Landau Island is too little to hide anything for very long."

"Even the machines?" Larry asked.

"I don't know about those."

"But I do," Larry said.

"My friend...you are not telling me something."

"I don't think you'd like to hear what I could tell you."

"Why not?"

"Because it doesn't sound real."

Josh looked at him seriously. "But you will tell me, won't you?"

Larry grinned and nodded. Then he told him.

"It doesn't sound real at all," Josh said. His eyes looked scared and worried at the same time.

POKI GEORGE and Ben knew where the boys were. They had followed their flight and chase since it had started and now they saw Stoney and Henry starting out in the early light of dawn to close in on all those people who had kept them from their goal of riches. The guns were tight in their hands and they headed toward the clump of palms that protected Larry and Josh and in another half-hour there would be no doubt but that both boys would be within range of their rifles.

Then Poki George saw something else, and when he was sure of what was there on the horizon he stood up to his fullest and yelled, "You there!"

Below him, Stoney Marks and his partner stopped and

swung around. When they looked up and saw the old man they were almost ready to turn their guns on him, but they followed the direction of his arm, looked out to sea at the black hulled speck with the churning froth at its bow and knew it was the International Patrol ship.

All they knew now was to run.

Drop their guns and run for it.

Grab anything at hand, even if it was that crazy log raft with the chunks of board for paddles...anything to get out of there. That International Patrol ship would have them in cold irons if it caught them and there was no time to be lost at all.

As fast as Larry and Josh had made that raft move, Stoney Marks and Henry Jackson made it move faster. The International Patrol boat was close enough to see its cannon on the bow when the two men got the *Belinda* underway, but as fast as the salvage ship could move, the patrol boat was closing in.

The concerted yell from the beach was pure joy to hear, and the islanders were congratulating themselves on a victory of having rid their home of enemies.

But Larry and Josh weren't saying a thing. They were looking at the yellow bulldozer and the great scoop shovel sitting there at the end of the beach and Josh was watching his friend's face.

"You have a story to tell," He said. "Haven't you?"

Larry nodded. "Yes, pal, quite a story. Let's go back to Poki's house."

THE OLD MAN SAID, "You mean...the machines shrunk...grew smaller?"

"That's what I mean, Poki. You are living in a strange place. The area of Great Sandy has an unusual capability.

I don't know why...and maybe nobody ever will, but under certain conditions...when it storms and lighting strikes, that sandy area puts those odd forces to work and shrinks everything inside it."

"Those machines...you said they were toys..."

"We thought they were...*then*. We threw them down on the sand. When the salt water hit them and washed them off, they returned to normal."

"You aren't sure about that," Poki said softly.

"Our raft...we built it down in the pool inside Great Sandy...it was way too big to get out by itself."

"It did," Poki George told him.

"Only if it had shrunken up to a fraction of its size. Then it would float out. But then the sea touched it and it grew back again."

"It doesn't seem possible."

"A lot of things don't seem possible," Larry said. "How about your papers of ownership?"

"There's no way to explain that, my son."

"Can I try?"

"Certainly."

"One of your great fathers knew about this thing. He knew it could be good or bad, but he left it for you to decide. Once those papers were like they are now, but he left them inside Great Sandy during a storm and afterwards took a tiny speck and put it on the bottom of the model of the *El Capitan Uno*."

"Larry," Poki said befuddled, "There was no sea in here to wash them off."

"Remember Ben Westerly coming in here all wet and looking at the model?"

"Yes, he said..."

"He picked the model up," Larry interrupted. "He wet the papers without knowing it. He cleaned off whatever contamination had shrunk them."

A static charge of electricity seemed to go over the people in the room. Poki George could hardly believe what he was hearing, but he was getting the idea of what Larry was telling him.

"Wouldn't it be nice," Larry said, "If this island had the money it needed to be beautiful the way it should be, and you could have the latest radios and the best boats to carry on your business...and the kids could have their schools, and Ben his pearl raising farm."

"That would be magnificent!" Poki said.

"You can have it," Larry said.

Josh was watching his friend closely and licked his lips. "Larry...they've been without too long. Please don't promise them..."

"Don't worry, Josh."

He turned around and looked at all his new friends. "Great Sandy *was* a lagoon a long time ago. A ship called *El Capitan Uno* with a great store of gold aboard *did* anchor there."

All eyes were watching Larry when they heard another sound from overhead. Nobody had to tell them what it was or who was in it. The craft was a helicopter and Vincent and Timothy were its occupants and the boys looked at each other, pleased.

"Poki," Larry said, looking at the model on the mantlepiece, *"there's* the actual ship. That is the real *El Capitan Uno*. It is not a model. Right now it looks like one, but it was built in the shipyards of Spain as a fighting vessel of the line, filled it's captain's cabin with gold, the same little pile you see now, and when it is full size, all that treasure will belong to the people of Landau Island...and the best of luck to you!"

It had happened in front of them, they all knew suddenly, but it was hard to believe.

With a tone as soft as a breath of air, Poki George said, "Can you be sure, Larry?"

Grinning, Larry walked to the mantelpiece and took down the model of the El Capitan Uno. It felt solid in his hands, a little rough on the bottom from that old collection of barnacles and oysters.

Overhead, the helicopter was settling to the ground for a landing.

"Let's go float her and find out," he said.

A LOOK AT: THE MENACE

BY MICKEY SPILLANE AND MAX ALLAN COLLINS

BEST-SELLING AUTHOR MICKEY SPILLANE'S MOST TERRIFYING NOVEL.

In touristy Peachtree Heights, Georgia, a string of presumably accidental deaths of area physicians rouses the suspicions of Police Chief Blake Cutter. But the former big-city cop's attempts to warn Dr. Roy Ryan are viewed by his estranged wife as an attempt to muddy the waters of a custody battle over the couple's young son, Richie.

Too late to do anything more, a small, incredibly powerful creature emerges from the night to brave the walls of the doctor's compound, terrorizing the family and any and all police guarding them. The menace is suddenly real, and those physicians' deaths are anything but accidental.

And when young Richie's archeologist uncle gives the boy a grisly birthday present—an actual Aztec mummy!—the child begins to think the long-dead corpse is his friend, one who is still-breathing ...

Mickey Spillane was a best-selling mystery and crime novelist of the 20th Century, and this novel is typical of his storytelling speed and the shocking surprises only he could deliver.

AVAILABLE APRIL 2022

ABOUT THE AUTHOR

Mickey Spillane is the nation's number one mystery story writer. His Mike Hammer mysteries have been instant successes since he first published in 1947.

In July of 2006, however, Spillane, the last major mystery writer of the 20th Century, left the building. Only a handful of writers in the genre achieved such superstar status.

Spillane's position was unique—reviled by many mainstream critics, despised and envied by a number of his contemporaries in the very field he'd revitalized, the creator of Mike Hammer had an impact not just on mystery and suspense fiction but popular culture in general.

The success of the reprint editions of his startlingly violent and sexy novels jump-started the paperback original, and his redefinition of the action hero as a tough guy who mercilessly executed villains and who slept with beautiful, willing women remains influential to this day

The Day the Sea Rolled Back, his first novel for young people, was a Junior Literary Guild Selection. In *The Ship That Never Was* and *The Shrinking Island—a* third, previously unpublished book in the Josh and Larry series—Mickey Spillane offers further proof of his marvelous ability to hold readers of any age spellbound.

Made in the USA
Monee, IL
01 May 2022

95712586R00194